Leadville, Colorado is ten thousand feet up in the Rocky Mountains. A hundred and forty years ago in 1878-1880, men, women and children crossed vast frontiers to get its silver. Gold, silver, knives, guns and liquor fueled a town with few rules.

Buckskin Joe, Barney Devlin, glass plate negatives, snake oil, card cheats, fallen doves, mud, work and pioneer spirit come alive in a novel of historical fiction.

Love, technology and lead type mark the times of yesterday. Life was hard at the bottom, easy at the top. If you didn't have it you could always just take it and see what happened.

"Are you calling me a liar or telling me to shut up?"

They toiled in back breaking, dark, filthy, dangerous pain for nearly every waking hour.

Sweetwater Sally ran her hands up and down the bark of one of the pine trees growing in the theatre.

The winner of the first dog fight escaped from its cage back stage and tore the hoop jumping poodle into high pitched shreds. Next, a man recited Moliere.

"Why, The Rat Bastard Gazette is one of the finest newspapers west of the Mississippi." Inkslinger Charlie drank straight from the bottle. He carried his pistol high up on the inside of his right arm.

Cloud City Colorado In 1880 – Too Far West

A novel of historical fiction, copyright by **Roy Berger**

Published by Faux-Pas Press

January 2012

239 McEwan Avenue

Windsor, Ontario

Canada

N9B 2E3

Some of the character names and incidents are fiction, some are real.

No animals were injured in the writing of this book.

2nd Kindle edition March 21st 2012

3rd Kindle Edition July 2012

1st paper edition March 21st 2012

2nd paper edition July 2012

email- ThePrinceofCornwall@yahoo.com

Electronic Book ISBN 978-09877363-3-8

Paper ISBN 978-0-9877363-2-1

Cast of Characters

Sharon, Sister Cathy, Sister Lorie, Sister Lucy, Sullivan, Wilbur, Charlie O'Sullivan, Bad Bill, Mrs. Bindlepost, Mitch, Mr. Bill, Issac, Uncle Sylvester, Geisel, Zeke, Zeke's dog - Scampers, Henry's dog - Shep, Black Thumb Bob, Neiderguy, Dutch Honey, Molly, Mr. Hinkle Stocksworth, Mrs. Stocksworth and two boys, Rotten Joe, Sherman Platter, Joe Bloatsmen, Redge, Sister Emily, Henry, Gunter, Jim, One Eyed Jacob, Fast Eddy, Ginger Kid, Doctor Broom, Barney Devlin, Sister Helen, Father Fontaine, Butcher Knife Bill, Buckskin Joe, Lewis Kent, Sweetwater Sally, Rupert, Ross, Mr. Nelson, Brooklyn Annie, Miller Waide, Fast Gordon, Sister Susy, Cecil, Mrs. Milinda, Century Jack (rode a Pope bicycle), Brent, Deiter, Neville, Mrs. Ablemax, Loony Leo, Mrs. McTavish, Jim, Doug, Patrick, Broken Face Al, Cross Eyed Stan, Russian Betty, Albert Skofield, Dr. Wilkins, Fanny, Muldoon, Ellen, Ester, Thelma, Lesley-Ann, Three Fingers Harry, Captain Gifford, Big Jim, Texas John, Edwin Hoffer, Jill, Mother Rosy, Lionel, Jason, Earl, Bob, Steve, Jim, Donny, Long-haired Sam, Romeo, Sasha, Dave, Liz, Queen Victoria, Silver Jack, Jay, Jack, Anna, Matilda, Alvin, William, Susan B. Anthony, Baldy Steve, Apple jack, Digger Tom, Ned, Mell, One Tooth Bart, Digby, Gentlemen Joe, Ben Guggenheim, Millie.

Dedicated to

The N.D.G. Men's Club

Canadapa

City Lights

A.S.

The War of 1812

Orlo Miller

Istvan Marton

Cloud City Colorado In 1880 - Too Far West

Copyright by Roy Berger

Historical Fiction - circa 1880

75,000 words

Chapter and Notes

Chapter One

Gold, Guns, Silver Doves

Henry stared at the pile of gold coins. He knew they were related to something. It was all over the ground. Some of it lay in nuggets, some of it in veins. A lot of it had to be chipped out of the underground rock belly of the world. He had called about fifteen minutes ago. Hank was sitting to the left of him and he had anted up in the last round thus, forty dollars to Henry. The center of the table had over three hundred gold and paper dollars on it.

Gunter was sitting across from Henry. Gentleman Joe was sitting to the right of Henry with Hank facing him. Joe had opened the last round of betting with eighty dollars on a blind bluff. It now fell to him to reveal his cards or raise. He didn't think he wanted to raise anymore. Gentleman Joe placed his hand down on the table, face up for the other players to see. He had a pair of Queens and a pair of sevens and it was in fact, the worst hand at the table. They all had beards and pulled on them. He didn't look down at the table but stared past the slat door to the street outside. It was bright. The yells, squeals, shouts and frustrated animal noises were muffled by the walls. The whole world was in a hurry.

Henry looked to the other players to see if they comprehended what had happened. He had placed down a King high, straight flush. The deck of cards was well used. They sat that way for awhile. After a few minutes Henry pulled the cash, Eagles and double Eagles towards him and stood up. No one made to interfere. No one said a word. Winning hands work that way.

Henry could see the thick stair railing leading upstairs and slowly walked towards it. He had a bed up there and wanted to lie down. Henry had no idea how many games he had played or how much he had won or lost. None of them did. He pulled himself up the banister a rung at a time.

The bartender walked over. He refilled the remaining player's glasses with whisky. It took the edge off the morning. He cleared away Henry's glassware. Gunter took a sip from his shot glass and began to gather the cards together for another shuffle. He'd shuffle. Pause. Shuffle some more. There was familiarity. A cool breeze blew across the room.

One Eyed Jacob was sitting on the piano stool in front of a flat top. He was a 64 key man practicing a made up tune. It was coming together OK. He penciled in some notes. He wanted it for Friday night. It would make a nice opener. He moved some paper under a fat wax candle and stuffed a pencil back into his shirt pocket. He tapped the keys in a slow pattern, playing it back and forth. He thought, "Rose would probably like the tune."

Fast Eddy and the Ginger Kid were sitting at a table by the front window. They were sharing an apple pie and reading a story in The Rat Bastard Gazette. Doctor Broom had opened a new medical practice and was treating all and sundry. General examinations were fifty cents. Most treatments were five dollars. For five dollars he could pull a tooth or sew up a wound. For ten dollars he would pull out a bullet or set a broken limb. For infections he was always eager to recommend an amputation. He used anaesthetics and washed his hands between patients. He wanted to live scandal free. Fast Eddy was thinking about his hip. It made him walk with a limp.

The Ginger Kid had grease stained fingers. Earlier in the afternoon he had been pressing a primary gear onto the spindle shaft of Mrs. Melinda's Singer sewing machine. Ginger worked for Harry at Frank Gay's Foundry and Machine Works near the black smith's.

"Nah, nah, nah. I'll take out my own appendix, thanks. I'll do it myself," said Fast Eddy. "I don't need no anaesthesia. Anaesthesia is for polecats." He whipped out his Bowie knife and, in half a second, he whacked it down on the table top slicing some stupid fly in half. They toasted to it. Spent three bucks each on whores at one of Mattie Silk's places. No one felt bad.

They called him Century Jack because he had once rode, a Pope bicycle, a hundred miles in one day. The bike was leaning against the wall outside while Century Jack stared down a quart of beer. He'd broken all ten commandments, if you went for that stuff.

Brent was sweeping the floor. It had rained the day before and the mud had dried to dust and chunks. He moved across the room. His Derby was on a slant. He leaned the unused chairs forward to make room for his broom. He kept a wide berth around the card players, not wanting to take a chance on startling them out of their trance. Maybe he would go fishing later. Deiter would give him time.

Deiter's brother had gone to join the gold rush. He made a little pile working as a hand on mule trains to the mining camps. He loaded flour, got tips for delivering mail and kept good counsel. He sent half his earnings home to his brother who put it aside and continued to farm as normal. Sadly, Neville died.

Deiter looked to the blue sky as young men do, put his affairs in order and sold up the farm. Deiter made it to Colorado and was impressed enough to open a hotel and saloon. It was called Neville's. Like the other modern business's there he had chipped in for the boardwalk, fronting the muddy road, that turned back into a trail through the mountains.

Most of the plank frame stores had brightly painted fronts and at least one or two upstairs rooms. Some had another small house attached to it. Here the store owners usually lived.

The silver trade was prospering. There was lots to come out of the ground. Some of the silver was coming from big mines but there was still plenty of independent panning and prospecting going on in the country side. The city had everything a person needed from feed stores to restaurants, theatres, bars and hotels. Leadville was in a triangle of Durango, Pueblo and Cripple Creek. It was south of Denver, all deep enough in the woods to see the best of Ansel Adam's country. There were over thirty thousand people and hundreds of businesses servicing the traffic of drifters, grifters and pilgrims who were all seeking their fortune.

Everyone liked a street paved with gold. Some looked for silver and some looked for silver seekers. Some worked the ranches. Some had found the silver earlier. The law was fresh. The law could get lonely, an archaic ivory tower ritual. Just a few months after Leadville incorporated, on April 25th, 1878, Marshall O'Connor was murdered by bad James Bloudsworth. Mart Duggan, who was next in line, would think twice, wipe his brow and take over the next day. The Marshall got $180 a month. The Captain got $150 a month. Not bad. When needed, nineteen police at $100 a month, generally carried a rifle and a pair of pearl handled Navy Colts. Odds are they were far on the other side of town or busy screwing.

Henry lay on a dense, chicken feather, mattress. He had a ten by twelve room in Neville's. The walls were thick and there was a pot belly stove in each room. There was a water jug and bowl on the dresser. His brain was squirming.

There was a deed and several claims in his pocket. He had one for a 160 acre patch of farmland to the south of town. He'd been looking that over, thinking about who could farm it for him. It was big enough for a family. There was a fair size jug of tequila, on the floor, beside the bed. A pair of pistols was hanging on the bed post. The first thing he did when he rented the room was shove a thick leather sack of tools and equipment under the bed. Henry was pressing his temples. The dog whined. His boots were heavily scuffed. Henry had been cracking open rock samples and walking through creek beds. The open window blew a comforting breeze across him. He wanted to lay down for a week. His stomach was already yearning for some more biscuits and roast beef. Town food was way better than trail mix. Sitting at a table made him feel human, less like a cold hungry rat.

He had turned in a few bags of dust to the assayers. They took a five percent bite for exchanging it for coins. It was fair enough. Everyone loved flipping an Eagle. He wasn't so foolish as to accept paper dollars. "What God like saint would be in charge of the printing press? It would never fly. People would never accept paper money. Paper money was created out of the promise of a politician. Gold was created by God. Paper money was irrational and crazy. A two thousand year old Roman coin was still worth its weight in gold but twenty year old Confederate money was worthless." He couldn't remember who told him that, but it was a true thing.

He unwrapped himself from the sheets. He could just barely make out the tune from the piano downstairs. He sat on the edge of the bed, changed his mind, lay back down and went to sleep.

Henry woke up to the dark, scratched a penny match and held it to the wick of the kerosene lantern on the nightstand. He turned up its wick and enjoyed the comfortable stink. He sat up and washed out his mouth. He spit in the bowl and took a long leak in the chamber pot.

The music was louder and he could hear street noise. There was typical night time traffic. A buckboard wagon squeaked by on loose spokes, a pair of thick shouldered oxen pulled at its yoke. Hinkle Stockworth and family had climbed the Rocky's and were close to home. They carried seed and implements to feed the fast growing population. Their gold would be next summer's harvest of potatoes at ten cents each. It reminded Henry to go to the store.

In the morning he went to 'George Geegge's Drug Emporium and Hat Sales'. "George, you look younger than last week. I want what you are taking. How's life as town treasurer? Suit you? Got plans?" Henry leaned his hands on the counter.

"It's exciting, Henry. We're going to find the money to extend the water supply, keep the roads clean. We're going to move forward. It's a real city now." George looked over his stock. "Here you go, Henry. Try some of this. It just might be your style of choice."

George pulled a square, artfully decorated, big tin off a shelf. "Now this is just in. 'Squibbs.' Check out the label. *"Cannabis Indica, the dried flowering tops of female plants of cannabis sativas grown in the East Indies gathered while the fruit is yet fully mature."* Two dollars and fifty cents a pound, Henry."

"Sounds like they know what they are talking about. I better have two cans." He walked up and down the aisle pointing to various bottles and packages. Henry said, "That should do. What's the total?"

"What do you think of this?" George replied and pulled out a slim leather case. He put it on the counter. "Good for amputations."

Henry looked the black case over. So many sharp edged instruments recessed in a blue velvet interior. It was very impressive.

"No. I think I'm set with this." Henry tucked the merchandise into a satchel. "Thanks, George."

"Let's see you at the next town meeting, Henry." George waved. "You can argue against taxes, if you like."

Mrs. Parker looked at Henry coming out of George's store. She was pouring drinks for a few customers. "The guy who says he's a druggist will sell anything to the guy who says he's a doctor lancing a boil on the rear of the stock operator, who says there's gold in his mines." Mrs. Parker of the Silver Lies Saloon, slid a whisky shot down the counter.

"You got that right, Ann." He spit into the sawdust on the floor.

Henry walked across the street. It was freshly leveled and graded and there were a lot of wagons, horses and mules pulling loads. A stretch of the road had been covered in eight inches of slag and gravel, just recently, as an experiment. This was another benefit of an incorporated town taxing local business. Generally speaking it was great. Henry eyeballed a suspicious pot hole, filled with water, that could very well have been six feet deep. He stepped onto the boardwalk. He scraped the soles of his boots against the shoe scraper there by the door. Once upstairs, he pulled out the skeleton key Deiter gave him and opened the door to the coolness of his room.

Shep walked out of the wardrobe, at the sound of the lock turning, and sat soundlessly in front of the door. She liked the coolness too. She had a white chest, black coat, short black ears with down turned tips, a heavy body, thick coat, big paws, thick legs and a large head with a short muzzle. All her relatives were pulling sleds, carts or something made of hard work. Shep was a lucky dog.

He laughed and welcomed the greeting. Shep jumped up and put her big paws up on his chest. "Shep, we hit it. I think I'm going to like the new Leadville."

Henry put the satchel on the bed and lined the contents on the dresser top with the others. The surface was neatly arranged with brightly coloured small boxes, jars and bottles. It was a fair collection of the best and untried snake oil a man could want. There was a local patent medicine invasion of cures and remedies available for the ills of man.

There were soothing syrups and pills. Parker Davis, Eli Lilly, Squibbs Merill. New American companies produced brightening tonics. There were tinctures that induced a Moroccan fog. There was a dynamite potential for calmness, soothing and tranquility. Henry pulled the cork on *Mrs. Mill's Tonic for Lethargic Despondency*.

"Yes," Henry said. He felt both eyes pop open and the sun seemed to be cracking on the floor. "Put that away for later, wow." He pushed the small cork back in. There was a display case of twenty four blue glass bottles in the bottom of the wardrobe.

Dr. Horace's Fine Reduced Tincture of Cannabis Oil for asthmatic relief and tetanus called out to him. He poured some of the thick goop onto the tobacco in his pipe. He lit a match and held it to the oil. Henry exhaled a thick cloud of smoke, then another. He put the pipe down and walked over to the windows. It was a beautiful morning and the wind was fair. The scent of thousands of outhouses was blowing away and down the mountain. Some teamsters were coming in with a train of ten wagons. The eighties were going to be a beautiful decade.

"Lets go, Shep." The dog picked up its ears and ran a circle around Henry.

He put on his hat and strapped on a second gun belt. He felt prime. They left together. The dog went ahead, wagging its tail, down the murky stairs. They walked through a small front room of early morning drinkers and gamblers, out onto the board walk.

He wanted a newspaper, coffee and something to eat. He figured for Mrs. Ablemax's. She ran a good outfit. She had a storefront down near The Leadville Chronicle. There were a few printers in Leadville. The Leadville Weekly Herald, The Chronicle, Carbonite Hill News. Each ran a news sheet. The Rat Bastard Gazette was his favourite.

Henry walked into the Ablemax tent and sat on an upended barrel. A pair of wide, long planks ran down the center of the place with barrels, boxes and stools as seats. Shep sat by his feet, keeping her tail out of the way.

"Mr. Henry." Mrs. Abelmax came over to his table with a mug of coffee.

"Mrs. Ablemax. Do you still love your husband, Mrs. Ablemax?"

Mrs. Ablemax looked over the planks that served as a counter and smiled.

They had shown up the year before. Mr. Ablemax had been working in a mine for $10.00 a day as foreman and Mrs. Ablemax was making pies for a dollar a slice. When Mr. Ablemax had his leg crushed that first spring, the two of them thought hard and threw themselves at the restaurant business. They held hands together and sent Mr. Ward of Chicago $60.00 for just the right sort of nickel plated, wood stove and paid another $300.00 for transportation and it finally showed up.

It was a marvellous, massive, thing that could have been in a museum. The sides and legs were ornately carved and embossed. The chamber covers were blue porcelain, painted with scenes from Holland. It had two hot water tanks with brass taps, a bread oven, a pie cooler and a wide grill. Mrs. Ablemax was forty two years old. Their sign out front, loudly announced, "Beer Cheese Pie Bread."

"Oh, Henry we buy the building next week," she said.

"That's great news. We'll be the first in line won't we, Shep?" He scratched her ears. "I'm right hungry and I know Shep here would like something too."

Henry watched them prepare his order. She came back with a platter of sourdough buns, a one inch thick slab of cheese and a pair of elk short ribs for Shep.

Henry looked over the single page broad sheet. It was printed on both sides. Hayes was still President. Russia was invading the filthy Turks. Someone in San Francisco had sent away for a telephone. Dirty Joe had come back from the World Exhibition in Philadelphia. There was a letter to the editor from a woman who complained about people sleeping on the boardwalk. It was reported that in some communities it was illegal for a doctor to perform surgery while openly drunk. Bad Bill had horse-whipped Bucktoothed Charlie for calling his whore cheap and left him in the mud. Charlie came back two hours later and plunged a knife into his back during a poker game.

Bad Bill had been holding Aces over eights. The Arkansas River was still holding everyone's attention, especially after Buckskin Joe danced two thousand feet across The Great Gorge on a tight rope. The stage from Pueblo to Leadville was three dollars. The Denver and Rio Grande Railroad to San Francisco was $25.00. Laying the track by working on the railroad or cutting ties, paid three dollars a day.

Henry's belly filled up with pie. Shep licked her snout clean from a pan of butter milk. Henry paid and stood back outside on the boardwalk. He pulled out his watch and checked the time. Eleven o'clock. He snapped the lid back shut, then slipped a match out from a flat silver case. He scratched it and lit his pipe.

He stepped over Loony Leo. Shep sniffed at the stretched out arm of the muddy body. "Careful, Shep. He might be dead."

In another half hour Mrs. Ablemax would come out and beat Leo with a broom until he sort of moved on. The last two bottles of Laudanum had almost done him in. He was dehydrated, his immune system was shot, his liver was swollen. He was nutrient deficient. Loony Leo, he was in bad shape. He'd last until winter if the rains didn't get him.

Henry thought he'd go visit Three Fingers Harry. Harry had a machine shop beside Frank Gays. Frank could hammer out a new axle rod and Harry could smooth it out on his lathe and press a gear on it if needed. With a tad of blacking your Singer Treadle Sewing machine would be good.

Harry had a lathe, drill press and a milling machine. Smith did a bang up job on the big axle rods required by wagons, machines and the thousands of horseshoes required by working animals. As long as Harry didn't lose too many more fingers he had a future doing fine pieces for the boilers, lifts, hoists, pumps and other machines showing up in town to service the mines. He wished he knew more about valves and pressure. He'd have to get some books on hydraulics.

Harry was at his bench. A drill bit was stuck in its chuck. He disengaged it from the belt drive, powered by a small boiler, and began pounding it with his sledge. It loosened. He lathered in some oil and whacked it some more. The bit came loose. He saw what the problem was, a thin metal sliver had lodged in the jaw teeth.

"And luck is a hammer," shouted Henry from the entrance.

"Howdy, Henry."

"Howdy, Harry. Give me a minute." There were a few more bangs and then a clunk. Harry cursed, then said, "Good. Now, Henry I made those rods for you."

Shep stayed close to Henry's legs, scared of the machine smells and noises. Harry put a handful of rods on the counter. Each one was ten inches long, a quarter inch thick, a fine thread on one end and made of hardened steel.

Henry beamed. "That's exactly what I wanted. Fits the bill perfect."

"That's going to be some machine you're building. What's it going to do again?"

Henry rolled the rods up in a cloth and pushed a five dollar gold piece over the counter. He put them in his waistcoat pocket. "It's to spin wool into thread and wind string into braids. Did you hear Diamond Ned is in town? He's staying up at the Interlaken Hotel and looking for a game."

"Couple of swells, you mean. Abbot might be there. But you ain't going to open with no hand there less than fifty gold dollars, Henry."

"Says he takes cash too. I guess he's willing to take anything you got if you want to give it to him."

"Did you decide to stay where you are or have you given a thought to Mrs. Bindlepost's Rooming House?" Harry asked.

"Well. I still like where I am. This guy Neville runs a square house. I don't think I'll stay there for the winter but for the next month or so."

Harry looked at the traffic outside. "I can't believe all the folks showing up. I swear there's another two thousand working claims out there in the past month."

"And another two thousand show up next month, I bet." Henry laughed.

"Next week, you mean. Say. I'm picking up some crates from the stage tonight. After that I'll come over and join you for a few hands."

"I'll save a glass for you." They shook hands. Henry and Shep left the storefront and moved on.

The hills were full. Tents and storefronts were coming up all over. City lots had been doubling in price every couple of months. Strikes and washouts were moving the crowds along. But the general area wasn't played out. It was providing a steady flow of precious metals, steady enough for a lot of people to dig in and pass the word around the world.

He liked Neville's. Most people did. Deiter wasn't crazy. He simply engaged in fair trade. He had a roulette wheel and ran a few poker tables. He had a small, sit down bar and a long counter. He didn't allow faro. "I'm not Jesus," he said. He had a good assortment of bottles behind the counter. "And if you don't like any of that..." He would tell a new-comer, "I got a shotgun accurate to ten feet."

The mule trains were endless. Henry cautioned Shep, more than once, about drifting into the road. Animals and people alike were regularly crushed by those heavy wheels. It didn't help that rain turned the roads in to mud. Normally the stage coaches moved along at six to ten miles an hour. In the muck it could take days and the passengers would have to get out and push.

Harry closed up later in the afternoon and went down to the Captain's general store to wait for his delivery. Gifford's was a regular store with a yellow and green painted front and picture glass windows. Inside, he had theft proof cabinets for jewelry and up front by the cash, jars of candy. He had cans of lobster pate for fifteen dollars, flour for a dollar a pound, diamond rings for a thousand dollars, nails for a penny a piece and was a catalog outlet for Ward.

There were a half dozen men in the store. One was sitting in a half barrel chair, staring at the open front door. A romantic couple were leaning on the counter edges, looking up at all the canned goods, canvas, tent poles, champagne and dish sets. Gifford was licking a pencil and writing down a total for Texas Jack and Big Jim. They had a working claim on the south bend and were outfitting their cabin for the winter.

Gifford had two scales out on the counters for when it got busy. "That's forty ounces of your dust." He looked up.

Big Jim stood for a bit and looked down at the additions on the paper. Texas Jack gave it a nudge with his finger. Neither one could read. Jim nodded his head and they each pulled out a leather sack. They spent a little time weighing out twenty ounces each. It was a fair size load of food, a new pick, mercury and ordinary sundries. They had been working their claim for five months and were pulling out about fifty dollars a day. Five ounces a day was encouraging enough.

They had won a neighbour's claim playing cards the month before and had decided to spend the winter going down to bedrock where, maybe, the deposit was richer. They might get as far as thirty feet. They loaded up their mules. Their eyes were like raccoons. Their fingers were black. Baths and washing were not common. Men worked in the dirt, lived in the dirt and ate in the dirt. Water was something you sat your ass in as you panned out some dirt. Hot water was a memory. There were other things to worry about if you had to worry.

Texas Jack said, "If this doesn't pan out I'm going to hitch up with Tabor."

Edwin Hoffer was staring at some of the rings. "I just know that Jill would like that one." He had his eye on a diamond ring, off-set with two small rubies.

Gifford shook his head but walked over to the case. Edwin had fallen in love with Jill and was recently spending his poke on her. Jill worked over at Mother Carol's Entertainment and Sporting Lounge. Jill's eyes were so sad and she missed Edwin so much. "You're so much nicer than the others," she said.

Mother Carol was always discreet in selling the jewels back to Captain Gifford. Half for her and half for the girl, less the discount on used jewelry of course. Mother Carol had expenses. Ten percent went to Mattie Silk's.

Sometimes the girls got in trouble. Abortions were expensive and put the girls out of commission. Other times they died and that was always inconvenient as was another news item about a finding in Stillborn Alley. Paying the expense of a new girl, who probably came from New Orleans or even Europe, was more overhead. Sometimes they married a customer who'd hit it big time.

Dynamite was all the rage. If you could afford it. If no one stole it on you. A man could clear three feet of rock in a split second. Booms were familiar. Nobel was famous.

Harry was looking over some chewing tobacco when his wagon came in. He was thrilled. He pried the top off one of the boxes and pushed away the packing straw. "Just like the catalog, Captain." There was the black shine of a brand new, glossy, black, Singer Sewing machine. He had bought six of them. The Captain was going to sell the thread, cloth and compliments. He had, in fact, signed a deal with Ward to be the exclusive agent for the sewing machines within a five hundred mile area. Harry imagined how it would look in his shop window.

Lionel leaned against the counter. He bought a can of black powder, a quart of rum and some mustache wax. He was in a good mood. He had received a letter from his brother and was looking forward to reading it in his cabin later. He paid for the supplies and added a pinch for the letter. Pretty much any little thing cost a pinch. A slice of pie was a pinch. A letter was a pinch. He had two pickle jars of pinches back in his cabin.

Peter Conlay, James Dahoney and Dennis Sullivan had come west. They had traveled almost two thousand miles. They were young, strong and proud. They sat in a saloon drinking twenty five cent beers. The walls were lined with slot machines that accepted nickels. There was a table full of pickled eggs, sausages and bread, free for the taking. They were on top of the world, actually ten thousand two hundred feet up – Cloud City. They had arrived with two oxen, a wagon load of supplies and four hundred dollars. They were still short a claim and were figuring what to do. They would figure about right. They were looking for the eastern slope of Breece Hill above Evans Gulch. Old Evan, he got a piece of it back in the day but not the load. Evan lost it all in San Francisco anyway. He would tell someone, who would write someone, who would let the Boston boys in on it.

"I figure we walk in towards the source. We'll just walk towards the mountain gulches and keep our eyes out for sharp ridges. We'll look for old stream beds and do some digging. If we find something promising we'll stake it out and lay claim. Call it the Miner Boy Mining Company."

They loaded up some empty barrels and filled them with water to wash out their pans for when they were in the hills. Four hundred dollars in Boston, if carefully managed would last them almost a year - in the Colorado Silver rush, maybe two months. If they didn't hit pay dirt in six weeks they'd have to work someone else's claim for wages to get home to wherever home was. The cousins set back out to cut through town. It was late afternoon.

They were truly amazed by all they saw. They weren't country bumpkins by a long shot. They were big city boys use to big city ways. Boston was no village. The frontier journey was less than kind to weak men.

Leadville was dug out of a virgin forest. The flat floor of the valley was a sea of cabins and smokestacks and clothes lines. Tall pines, thick bush and a million flowers bursting into summer, surrounded a catastrophe of eighty two saloons, fifteen beer tents, thirty five open whore houses and dozens of opium dens, charmed by gas lit streets and gravel roads. Such thriving commerce would be recorded in the city census.

If those three could walk, ride or run through all that and still retain most of their wallet they would be past a major hurdle. It's so hard to post pone pleasure. They would continue their journey. Every saloon and beer tent held dozens of fast players, dice men and spinners waiting for their arrival. They hadn't expected any of it. They walked through. They brought with them top quality picks with hickory handles. They were glad not to pay twenty to fifty dollars for obviously inferior steel. The locals were being aggressively gouged for anything in short supply. Oysters were a dollar each on Sunday and by next Sunday they were ten cents. It really depended on the mule train, weather and choices.

The women. By 1880 there were over thirty thousand miners and about four hundred women... It was the case that many were fallen doves. There were a few who baked pies and sewed shirts. Pretty much everyone liked it that way or at least got used to it. Truth be told there was also seven churches, one school house and seven school rooms scattered around the city providing for four hundred and fifty pupils. All it took to build a church was a weak moment by a weeping, guilty, soaking rich miner and Lyman Bridge of Chicago would send up a big church kit. The Sisters sold lottery tickets to pay for a church. For five thousand dollars plus shipping they received the plans, precut wood and every nail required to build a church. Bell extra. Five thousand dollars was nothing to a man spinning the wheel on a Friday night. If he was hit on just right, it could happen. Who knows? Maybe he just killed two cowpokes for their sack and wants to make amends. Most will be broke by Sunday anyway. Fortunes changed hands every hour.

Cloud City was a great town for a man to label himself a doctor. Doctor Broom had set up shop. He had been working down in New Orleans but there had been an incident. Fortunately, he got along famously with the owner of the Rat Bastard Gazette and utilized his knowledge of paper and printing. On explaining his problem and his vast knowledge there was no problem forwarding the necessary introductory letters with attractive letterheads to his suppliers and there you have it. He was able to supply all the doctors in town with his own stock at a competitive edge and furnish patients on commission.

The doctor was easily moved. He had practiced hard in Louisiana. Between the books and his job delivering for a drug store there, he really got the knack to doctoring. He wanted to be a good doctor, not a quack, and so avoided all the medical schools. He treated the sailors, whores and scared upper class men with regularity and killed so few of them that his reputation was held high. Practicing on the city councilor's cousin was ill advised. Botching a simple abortion, it can happen. She shouldn't have been so young. What could he do? Leaving fast seemed the most prudent. Since then, he referred what he couldn't do to one of the other doctors in Leadville. If they were real cases it was better that way. Maybe they were real doctors.

Henry left Shep upstairs after dinner and sat by the bar downstairs. Harry was expected. Deiter poured out a glass of whisky.

Henry leaned back in his chair and watched some card players. There were five people betting on the wheel. "Want some company?" Fanny asked. She wasn't wearing much more than a fancy whale bone corset.

"Have a glass of tea with me until my friend comes." Henry tossed a small gold piece on the table top. He'd sat with her before. She was quiet and pretty. He was still watching the card players. He saw a card fall out of the pant leg of the fellow opposite him. Henry said nothing. He noticed that Deiter had seen the same thing and they both kept fairly still and sipped their whisky.

The players at the card table were laughing and making remarks, in general, about the state of their cards. Fanny kept puffing on her cigar, oblivious to anything. If Henry got bored he might take her upstairs. The cards were being dealt for another round. Henry started to smile. He noticed the cheat was reaching for and not finding his prize card. He thought he could smell the sweat. He looked at Fanny's pushed up boobs.

Deiter caught it first. The cheat's shoulders moved in a particular way and he folded. The other four players were surprised by the development after such aggressive betting. One made to look at the floor and shouted, "Hey." At this point he yanked open the cheat's jacket and shirt, revealing a complicated long arm mechanical gripper that pushed cards into various sleeves and trouser legs.

The cheat immediately pulled out a 44 caliber Colt pistol with the barrel completely removed, short like a Derringer. He bolted backwards, knocking the chair over. Dieter went for the shotgun behind the bar. The cheat aimed the gun at the man opposite him and pulled the trigger. There was a familiar click. Maybe his rounds were wet or his hammer bent. He looked a little surprised and then his face relaxed. No one at the table waited. The cheater took about twelve shots to the chest and head.

"Throw him out. I run a square house," shouted Deiter.

The body was dragged out back and left in the alley.

The boys at the table split the contents of his poke and added his watch to the pot. "It was only fair. He did have bad luck though tonight didn't he?" They all laughed.

"His boots fit me."

"This pistol is no good."

"My vote says he was stupid."

Brent poured a scoop of sawdust on the blood.

Harry walked in from the street, through the fresh gun smoke, up to Deiter. "I never thought this was a boring town," said Harry.

Deiter put a bottle on the table and notched it without asking. Henry crooked his thumb at Fanny and pushed a glass to Harry.

"You tired of me, Henry? How about your friend?"

Harry looked her over, "Honey Dove. I wouldn't insult you with less than a thousand dollars and I'm just short a thousand dollars."

Fanny laughed and moved on, cackling with the other girls in the back.

There was a stink of kerosene all through the place. Autumn was coming and the street was growing dark. The gas light street lamps were just being installed.

Neville's was as busy as ever.

"I was talking to Jacob, who handles accounts, up at the mill. He was talking about putting in some electricity. He said he could put electricity right here in the hotel. We already got the telegraph," said Deiter.

Harry nodded. "I've heard of that electricity. They got it in New York. Edison's burning down houses and killing elephants with it regular."

"Costs a lot to rent the equipment," said Henry.

"I heard it turns your hair grey and scares horses."

"Oh yeah?" Deiter was open to any information about electricity. He had heard of electric fans and rug cleaners.

Dennis, James and Peter had gone on to prospect. They kept moving up and around the mountain, finally abandoned the wagon due to the thickness of the forest, and dragged their supplies by ox.

"Here. We go towards Breece Hill."

"The eastern slope?"

"Yeah, above Evans Gulch. That's gotta be it," he pointed.

James knelt by a creek. It was clean and he filled his canteen. They crossed the creek. James filled his mouth with water and spit it out onto a rock outcropping. The splash of water made the fool's gold there shine a bright yellow.

James chuckled to himself. He bent a little closer and took his knife to pry at the iron pyrite between the sedimentary layers of rock. He thought to himself, for an alarming minute, "Pyrite sparkles. This is flat." He wedged his knife in and pried some of the stuff out.

"Ah. Would you look at this. I guess they call it fool's gold for a reason cause I'm a real fool. You fellows want to share the joke on me?" James held up a muddy rock.

Dennis and Peter retraced their steps. They dug into it with their knives. Dennis went to their kit and came back with a glass bottle of nitric acid. They did a few other tests. They started digging. They had hit an exposed vein. It was slanted down about thirty degrees and was four feet wide and three to six inches thick. They had to decide on which plots to stake their claims on. They dug like crazy knowing it couldn't last. If there was anything easy on top, they were looking for it. The vein yielded an easy sixty ounces of gold for every foot dug. They kept looking over their backs.

"Making camp here."

"We can't leave this. Anything we dig up is ours."

"Unless someone else already has a claim to it."

"Couldn't be. We'll put some stakes out in the morning, fifty by a hundred and fifty feet each. It could really be something."

"With what we take out of the ground tomorrow, we could lay claim and hire someone else to do the digging. Maybe sell shares." They had a sleepless night and took turns at watch. They were in the middle of cougar, bob cat and Ute Indian territory. Even with a cold camp, there was also the possibility of a bushwhacker. The next day they dug down, sifted through and washed out five feet. They put up about five hundred pounds of what they figured to be eighty percent pure gold. At about three hundred and fifty dollars a pound it was their fortune. It would be discussed in a string of mining news articles in the papers.

"We need more tools and we've got to lay proper claim to it. Someone should stay and the other two cash in and register claims. Three days in. A half day laying claim. A half day gathering supplies. Three days back."

"This is a great spot for a rocker. The water is right there. I bet we can buy one ready made for three hundred dollars. Save some time. Could be we get enough out of here before the snow sticks."

So that was the plan. Dennis stayed and wished they had brought a dog.

Peter and James carried two hundred pounds back. A.M. McLeod, the assayer, had no problem accepting delivery of their high grade dust and samples. He noticed it had a particular sheen of green to it. The bank offered an extra five percent if they accepted Federal notes.

They were Easterners and knew the value of Federal Gold notes. It saved a lot of worry too. They could easily split up the cash which they promptly did. Peter found a fellow who was clearing out and still had a rocker up for sale. He took five hundred in notes for it. The cousins picked up a kettle, nails and a few other items. Several friends of the assayers felt enlightened and made a trip to the claims office.

The two cousins returned and were delighted to find Dennis alive and all things well. He'd started to cut some timber to shore up the diggings. Their claims were in hand. They were overjoyed. In short order they got the rocker assembled, in place and started to wash the dust out.

Two days later fifteen other miners had also shown up and started digging and staking claims all around and adjacent to theirs. Then more men showed up. The creek was filled with placers and panners, shovels and picks. In two weeks there were five hundred men digging and washing the ground away.

In another two months the cousin's claim appeared to be thinning out. The water would get colder. The nights would get longer. Men were knocking down trees for shoring and cabins. The brothers looked at one another.

A three inch by two inch by three quarter inch ingot of the stuff weighed a hundred ounces. A cubic foot weighs a ton. Their poor mules deserved medals. It was all they could haul.

The cousins sold their equipment on the spot. They kept back only their personal possessions, Remingtons, Colts and gold. They walked out of the woods during the morning. Everyone there seemed to be getting some kind of colour out of the ground and so there was no dangerous jealously at their leaving. Clearly, they were walking out heavy and armed to the teeth. Some get to. The timing was right. They expected some funny business along the way. There was traffic coming both ways now. A strong path was being made. They couldn't hide how heavy they were. Coming into Leadville was going to start a panic but there was no way out of it. Panic was their big time pal. Banks and merchants had more to brag about.

"Near a ton. Did you hear it? Three cousins were watering their mules and one fell into a ditch of pure gold."

"I heard they just scooped it out with their bare hands like it was butter."

It was real. Dennis, Peter and James dragged the sacks into the assayers while James walked back and forth holding a cocked shotgun.

It was that familiar green tinge again. Muldoon hadn't heard yet but felt strongly that the tip and grubstakes he laid out for his front men would pay off. He couldn't believe it though. Fifteen hundred pounds. Course it took up less space than a box of whisky. He looked across the counter at them.

They stank. Their faces were bleeding from branch scratches and deer fly bites. They hadn't changed their clothes for a week. They spit tobacco juice on his floor. Their filthy hands were holding rifles. There was a crowd in the room. Men were already leaving and packing their mules for the three day climb up to Evan's Gulch. The June 17th, 1879 issue of The Rat Bastard Gazette would print, "...and in regards to the famous cousins, after their easy riches on this side of the summer solstice, with the coming winter, the boys decided to sell their Miner Boy shares for seventy five thousand dollars." They dragged in another five hundred pounds each, loading up mules. They had almost a ton of gold.

Two days later they were sitting in the Interlaken Hotel. They had many thousands of dollars in the bank. They carried ten thousand dollars each on their persons. They were sleeping in ten dollar a night rooms. They leaned back in chairs up against the hotel wall. The porch offered a magnificent view of the mountains and the crystal clear lake.

"I'll put a paddle wheel boat in their someday," said the owner.

Their suits were new and clean. They had been taking soda water baths in the hot springs while drinking ice cold beer. The sun was high in the sky and they each had a cigar burning.

"Eleanor Riley will have to marry me now. Maybe she likes that dullard Ranton Hoffer some but I guess I'll be it now," said Dennis.

The two older cousins looked at him. "How do you figure that creek will be next month?"

"Tonight there will be an argument over a shovel full of dirt and someone will get a knife in the belly. More than one will lose a week's pay dirt to crooked cards or dice."

"For the price of a fifty foot city plot here I can buy a farm and a wife back east."

"It's all filthy work here. It's all hard. If we go back we can do what we want and live pretty easy," said James.

"If we stay here we'll never have enough."

"I had a real fine room in Boston for fifty cents a day. Beer for a nickel with lunch, thank you. Everybody is so crazy out here."

"We could be in Kansas in a week and back home the week after that. I don't want to get snowed in. We get snowed in, we get bored. We'll be broke by spring."

"That's it."

They decided on a fine meal at the Interlaken Hotel for the next day and then to get out.

The Ginger Kid looked up from his vise. "What do you think, Frank? Is it crazy?"

Mr. Frank Gay wasn't sure. It was busy. There was always work to do. Now the Ginger Kid wanted to pack it in and move on to Durango. He wanted to be boss and call his own shots.

"Frank, the mines are hauling gold out like a Midas shit-house. It looks to me that I could be successful."

Harry didn't want to lose him all the way. Mechanics and most skilled labour were hard to come by right now. Everyone wanted to pick apple size nuggets off the ground and pan out fifty dollars a swish. Five dollars a day, working for him, didn't seem like enough for most. The Kid had saved up a thousand dollars from card games and mule selling. He always seemed to have a different mule or ox in his small stable. He had a good head on his shoulders, he could read a blue print, he could shape metal.

"How about if I were to stake you part way, Kid? You got the smarts and I know you can do it. I don't know how I'll be able to keep up with all the work I have now, if you go, but I'll solve that. We go in together and if something comes up I'll pitch in."

The Ginger Kid thought something like this might come up. "We could talk about that, Mr. Gay. My first thought though is I don't want to give up more than twenty five percent. There is room to talk though. It's not like I have to do it today. Durango is growing straight up and my share is just lying there to be picked up."

"I can't stand in your way. I'm glad to hear there is room to talk though."

Fast Eddy leaned into the Friday night din at Deiter's saloon. "None of that warm piss then, Deiter. Give me a glacial cold one."

Deiter slid a massive mug into Fast Eddy's paw. Eddy turned around with his glass and continued to explain to Gunter that the only way to really find water was with a willow rod. He put his pipe down on the bar and made divining motions.

"Watch this." said Deiter motioning to Henry at the end of the counter. He continued serving up beers and yelling at the girls. Two of them were upstairs. Three were working the tables, talking to the men.

"KABANG!"

Two women screamed. Deiter and Henry were laughing hysterically and then so was the rest of the bar. Deiter had snuck a blasting cap into Fast Eddy's pipe. When he held the match to it and took a draw, the cap had blown the pipe to bits and singed Eddy's eyebrows. It was a huge laugh. Two people spit up. It was funny because he didn't lose an eye or have his nose blown off. Even then... Eddy had seen it happen to others and realized he had asked for it by leaving his pipe untended. Deiter was bent over, laughing and slid another mug down the counter. Dynamite was just coming into widespread use and the humour and frivolity of blasting caps were still being explored.

Brent lay by the creek. It was his day off. He had made his own fishing rod but had used store bought hooks. He didn't use a reel and in fact jigged for the fish. The creek was rushing. He sat near the bend where a shallow had been created over time. This shallow was sometimes good for gathering speckled trout. He saw some shadows down there. He could see the smoke and hear the pounding of the huge hammers and wheels that were crushing stone. Gold veins were being pried and separated from their quartz resting place. Brent moved the line. He had been using a hook baited with a piece of beef that had a lock of deer fur tied to it. Brent wasn't sure of his reasoning but he idly ran the line back and forth across the surface of the shallow. It was a sunny day. He looked at the sharp edged, ice capped, mountains. He took a handful of grass and ripped it from the ground. It smelt good. A little three inch something snagged his line.

"Whoop," he shouted. He gave it a few playful tugs to pretend it was a whale on the other end. He pulled it up and out. It flopped and bent. He looked close and saw that the hook had gone clean through its cheek. He pulled it off and threw the fish into the woods.

He reached into his pouch and selected another lure. It was a rolled up piece of cheese and bread with a small bird feather stuck in it.

Sometimes the wind shifted and he'd wrinkle his nose from the smell of so much household waste. There was no central garbage pit or depot. You burnt it, ate it or dumped it, whichever it was, into the alley.

Drinking water was not yet a problem. Some of the ladies, who had massed together to build a church, were aware that there had been diphtheria and cholera problems in other communities and some of the big modern cities too. The water table was being stressed but more so from mercury, acid and a wide variety of caustic sodas along with the cyanide salts used to distill and separate the precious metals from their volcanic memory.

The church lady meeting was in progress. Ester could see that all those town women were filthy whores. Both she and Thelma and Lesley-Ann all agreed on that. They couldn't find any places in the bible where the Lord actually cast out filthy whores but they were certain it was wrong.

Thelma had a wise cracking brother who had asked, "Are you sure now that they aren't filthy sluts? Which do you think the Lord prefers – sluts or whores, my dear sister?" Thelma's brother had surprised them anyway by wanting to engage in theological matters but now they could see that he just wanted to set up an argument.

Thelma replied, "I think you are even being sarcastic. It's wicked to be sarcastic, Rupert. The baby Jesus cries when you are sarcastic."

"Will a whore enter heaven before a rich man? Maybe you should start a platform to bring in heathen, non-Christian whores." Rupert left the drawing room for his father's study. He planned to steal some decent Port.

The stuff called wine, in the general stores, was often moldy and off. Some dirty miner might enjoy it out of desperation if he didn't want to pay for the California or European barrels. "Yes. Get rid of all the whores. Then it will just be you three, grandmother and thirty thousand enthusiastic men. I'll sleep in the barn," he shouted. "Your infidelity to God makes you all whores," he laughed and twisted the cork out.

The women looked at one another. Annunciation church lady discussions always came down to this. Not always so vocally. Rubert was so crude. There were four hundred women in Leadville. Three hundred were plain whores. The remaining hundred were business women doing laundry, sewing shirts and providing other retail services. There were even a few women out in the fields, helping their husbands, and a cloister of nuns supplementing their charity.

"Sister Susy and the other nuns have been using some sinful money to build God's house."

"They raised most of it. It would be really something if we could bring in the balance."

One Eyed Jacob and Rose lived with their baby in one of the rooms above Cecil's Printing. Their room was like most others. It came with a Franklin stove. Everything else they furnished themselves. They had a bed, wardrobe, table, two chairs and several framed prints. Just lately they had a crib. If company came by they sat on the bed.

Rose had a candle burning by the window. It bit into the frost starting to form. The baby had cried for awhile but was sleeping.

Rose loved Jacob as if she had loved him forever. Her father worked up at the big mill and Jacob met her while tutoring her sister in piano lessons.

Mr. Nelson was quite angry at this. He didn't raise his daughter to marry some drunken piano player from a whorehouse. He didn't raise his daughter to squeeze out some bastard in a ditch by the side of the road. Mr. Nelson fired three perfectly good men. They were coughing anyway. Stupid deaf bastards.

Mrs. Nelson felt compelled to explore the issue further. She found, in fact, that One Eyed Jacob, although not temperate, drank far less than most. Most drank at least a dozen ounces of whisky a day. Some of his tunes were actually quite creative. True, his voice wasn't perfect but he said, he played piano and he was often playing at The Anthenaeum. He said, "Yes Ma'am and no ma'am," to her. As a gift to Rose's mother he had presented her with two oranges.

He gave Rose's father two Cuban cigars. He'd gotten the cigars from a ship's Captain who had recently set up store in Leadville. The Captain had been piloting a three masted barque to port in San Francisco. His New England master had gone bankrupt on a venture in Cuba which was lost to rebellion and was without ability to pay.

On reading the two month old letter, Captain Gifford loaded the ship's contents onto the wharf and rented three wagons. Before leaving he sold the ship to a real estate agent who was in need of cut planks to build some houses. Along the way he had taken on some crates of good Cuban stogies. First he considered Telluride but then smelt the boom of Leadville. Leadville it was. This way, Mr. Nelson ended up with some decent cigars.

All the women in the house were yelling at him. Nelson had put his foot down but both his wife and two daughters were ganging up on him. His supper was served cold and they 'Harrumphed.' at him all the time. In the morning they wouldn't even talk to him. Rose was always running off to cry and wail whenever he looked at her. Then his wife would soothe Rose. Then his youngest daughter would just glare at him and say, "I would poison myself with a silver goblet and throw myself off a cliff, under the moonlight, if you separated me from my lover."

"You. You're thirteen years old and you better not have a lover!" Nelson shouted. Then the thirteen year old called him a beast and ran crying from the room. Everyone hated him.

Finally Mr. Nelson asked around. He discovered that Jacob wasn't an opium addict. He had lost his eye while fighting against that scoundrel, Lincoln. He, in fact, could play a waltz. He regularly played at several of the theatres and opera houses during both artistic Roman plays and lively dog fights on stage. Jacob had hoped to marry Rose and raise a family because he loved her.

Nelson rubbed his brow. The teacher at the school who roomed with the Episcopalian Minster said that Mr. Jacob understood musical notation and gave lessons. Mr. Nelson didn't stand a chance.

Lionel had a cabin about a half hour's walk from his claim. He had a partner on it. They took turns in twelve hour shifts. Someone could walk away to go do their business in the woods and expect to come back OK. But leave your claim for any length of time and people would be sticking their shovels in fast. Lionel and his partner were filling bags with the diggings and dragging them into each other's cabin. Over the winter they would have more to sift through and wash. It would make up for time not by the river.

Lionel's cabin was like most. The rough cut timber were partially dressed logs, caulked with clay and grass. It was one room with one door and one window. There was a bed, a large pot belly stove and a table and two chairs. The floor was planked and there was a rough wood counter. The walls held a pair of snowshoes, two rifles and a mounted deer head. A few wooden crates held canned goods, jars and sacks. There was a picture of his mother on one wall. The other had some small framed photos. There was a broom in the corner. The other corner had a Waring Earth Commode. Against one wall was a carved walnut cabinet containing a four place matched Wedgwood dish set complete with tea cups. A cabinet drawer held an eight piece silver service cutlery set in an ornate, wooden box.

There were sacks of dirt and tailings all around the cabin. One by one he would bring them in and wash the dirt out in heated water.

In some ways it was more comfortable. He wondered how much his partner was stealing. He glanced over at the wood stove and wondered if he had enough wood for the winter. No one likes chopping frozen wood. If it was a normal winter he had enough. Lionel decided to chop a few more cords, just to be sure. With the heat question resolved, he considered food. Last winter, getting meat was no problem but with the twenty fold surge in population, the game was thinning out so hunters had to look for it.

Sweetwater Sally wanted just the right thing. She walked up and down Captain Gifford's general store. She could feel the eyes on her. The men were talking about their business. She had slept with all of them more than once. They were men. She liked men. She felt for them. They were so ruled by their senses. But then again so was she. She couldn't help herself. They did need her. They were all needed. She came in last fall with Dutch Honey, anticipating the rewards of silver doves.

She paid five dollars for the two oranges and took them to Miller Waide. He was coughing and laying down in his cabin. Laying down in a cabin was serious. He wasn't a drinker and was use to working. Sally knocked on the door and announced herself. She walked in. Miller was lying on a cot. At least it was off the ground. There was blood on his shoulder from when he spit. She peeled the oranges for him. There was kindling for a small fire and she got a pot of coffee going.

Miller brightened up and told her he loved her so much.

They got out some of his letters from back home. Sally made a little show of slipping a flask of rum out from underneath her garters and gave their coffee a little taste. They laughed about that. He hadn't seen oranges except once before and wondered what the peels were good for. She split one under his nose and the spray tickled him until he sneezed. He enjoyed the scent. Sally pulled the chair closer and they talked about where his mother was born and how he was only sixteen at Bulls Run. By midnight they were talked out. She gave Miller a good spoon full of Laudanum and slipped out.

"Where were you? You know Fast Gordon looks for you on a Friday night."

"I was with Miller."

"Fast Gordon took up with Millie and gave her fifty dollars in gold."

Sally fingered the three silver pieces Miller had given her. Back in Brooklyn fifty dollars was unheard of. Back home even the uptown girls didn't get more than two dollars. Fifty cents had always been good enough back there.

Miller wouldn't see the winter. He made $2.50 a day in the mines working a half hour on, half hour off. Where he worked it was 110 degrees. Most of that half hour was spent in the ice room. He thought maybe he picked up a cold there. But the coughing persisted and the silica crystals were ripping his lungs to shreds.

Henry sat on the edge of his bed. It always felt good to play cards. Even when he lost he enjoyed the game. Tonight he and Harry had cleaned out Tom the Liar. The guy couldn't tell a story true if you were watching him live it. Sometimes Tom got the cards but not tonight. They touched him for fifty dollars. No one wanted his marker.

"That's it for here," said Harry

"You don't want to come up for a drink?" said Henry.

"Not that wild stuff you drink. I got chased home by giant, flying, purple snakes last time I tried to keep up with you."

Henry chuckled at Harry's remark and went to his room alone. He drew out the sack of rods. It was a fine art to balance Mrs. Mills Tonic with Dr. Ricks mendicant. Opening a drawer he took out the axle rods and threaded on some matching nuts. There was a roll of thin wire on a spool under the bed. He forced a pair of spools onto the thick, stepped, center shoulder of each rod and began winding the wire on to the spool. He turned each one evenly, counting the windings. As the evening progressed he fit several metal sheets into slotted panels and added some magnetic bars to its walls. He looked at it for a bit and made a few pencil marks on the floor of the box. He took a compass and measured the width of the windings. He needed more parts. "Should work once," he thought. Henry took the thing apart and slipped it back into its box under the bed.

Shep lay on the bed cover watching him.

Henry washed his face from a bowl there and considered some tincture.

The Provisional Sisters of Freedom kept a clean house. It was two stories, had a wrap around porch and cost $3,500.00, prefabricated in Chicago. They had no truck with liquor and were responsible for the building of two churches and one hospital. They ran lotteries. The lotteries were regular and straight up. Fifty cents could win as much as seventy five dollars. The ladies there were concerned with spiritual freedom.

Shotgun Susy spent her time amongst Henry's claims, the hospital and a room she kept at the Sister's house. Henry had some rich claims. He staked her fair and only took half the gold. It was wise enough. He got half for sitting on his bum and with the other half there was enough for her and some for wages for when she took a break. The Sisters appreciated the dust in their way. Some said it was crazy for a nun to work a claim. More that one dead man went out to prove something about that to her. There must have been something about her dented bowler hat and thick rawhide jacket that inspired them. Boot Hill was as full of heroes, idiots and cowards as ever.

Susy hooked up with Henry early. She was being laughed at in a general store one day, prompting Henry to stake her on a bet. Henry already had several rich claims. The claims kept him in style. He wasn't losing all his gold, not as far as he could figure anyway. Some was paper, some was coin but most of it was paper.

His routine was to turn the gold into the bank and then wire the money to New York where he was buying gold backed rail road bonds at six percent interest. There was a lot of interest in building rail roads and there was a lot more track to come. If you were right there, if you were feeling the country right and watching how people bought, spent and lived, you could know when was the right time to get in or out. Henry liked the bonds. Henry liked the bucket shops where mining shares were exchanged. He had big and small chunks of a dozen mines. Lots of people did. Some men were making a thousand dollars a day just for getting up in the morning and they had equal company to keep and to come.

Electricity was the key. The telegraph changed everything. No one seemed to be catching on yet or they were doing the same thing. Henry was moving his fortune back east. Some men made a fortune betting the right way on a cougar fighting a bear, in a ring fight, or a bear fighting a bull.

It was a great time to be a gambler. It was the best time to be a gambler. It was a great time to be a crook or a cheat. It was a great time to sit in a saloon, make a deal with the saloon keeper and set up some cards and chips. All deals were final on the card table unless you were playing the Mexicans for three card Monte. Then who knew? People were taking chests of coin out on the stages everyday. It was happening all around. Fortunes were being made.

Cecil had made his choices early. Some men walked the range with a Remington Rifle and fired lead into the hearts of their enemies. Other men, like Cecil, walked heavy with a Remington typewriter and fired lead into the memory of man.

He started off with a hundred dollar typewriter from Remington and Co. and charged a dollar a letter to send missives, back home, for the men. He saw quickly that the community was going to grow and had a hunger for information. Eventually, he had a single arm press set up in the tent. Then he was installed in a wooden storefront and his paper didn't go all wrinkly when it rained.

Down on the farm Hinkle Stocksworth was putting up his third wall. He had purchased a hundred and sixty acre plot of agricultural land from Henry and been assured that there wasn't a speck of gold on it anywhere. It had been criss-crossed and prospected more than a thousand times. He was assured it was worthless dirt. His wife was turning the earth over with a good iron plough. She was walking steady behind the ox and the two boys, aged five and seven, were tossing rocks out of the furrow. Flocks of birds followed them looking for tasty bits. There would be no crop this year. They had got in late. They just didn't realize the dimensions of the Rocky's and their calculations and money were a few months late. Fortunately, several acres had already been clear cut providing fuel for the locals. The stumps were still there though and had to be pulled or blowed out.

They were worried it might happen but had allowed for it. It wouldn't be a rich winter but it wouldn't be dire. They would probably have a roof over their heads in another couple of weeks. But it did mean there was no extra to buy cows or a place to keep them. They would pen a few turkeys. They had seed potatoes and Hinkle and Stella had dug a large root cellar and lined it with branches to protect their stock.

Flour was sometimes a dollar a pound and that wasn't what either one had expected. Hinkle would fair well for game but they would have a meat rich diet. The wood, branches, brush, logs and animal skins provided some excellent beds and they had two. One for them and one for the boys. They used skins for windows but just plugged them up in the winter. Kerosene was three fifty a gallon. It was burned with caution. They decided to save money on an iron stove and built a large fireplace. Hinkle had some plans and installed a grate and damper.

Since wood was not a problem they had some wonderful evenings staring at the fire and listening to the high pitched tone of Hinkle's banjo. The banjo was something he picked up from the days of his colourful past. Stella teased him about the dances they used to go to. The boys wrestled. There would be no vegetables for soup that winter except for those guilty heated discussions when a seed potato would be added to the diet. Those were very expensive meals.

They were both book read and had a thick family bible.

The tent would be turned into a table cloth, mattress cover, drapes, five pairs of pants, a coverall and two shirts. In the long nights they would cleave onto each other in a biblical way. Come spring she would push that plough and lift buckets of water and be heavy with child. There were not that many sod busters out that way yet.

If they didn't eat their future. If they could get out that first crop. If it rained just right. If it didn't rot. If Christ was a cowboy, those potatoes would put them over the top. They would be potato royalty and the boys would have fine shoes and they could buy a buy a milk cow if they wanted. She looked at him with big eyes and wondered, where they could go if she bought a real print dress. He guessed, while they were at the store getting her a dress, they may as well buy a log splitter and a sewing machine too. The loving was good that night. The boys giggled.

Brent had it pretty easy. He shared a room with Rotten Joe and Sherman Platter. It was warm all winter. Among the three of them they had enough wood and whisky. Joe and Sherman both worked in the mines and Brent found he was required at Neville's. The three of them had enough. They joked about mine roofs falling on someone's head. They talked about the Knights of Labour. "There might be a meeting at Carbonite Hill." The owners would try to increase the day by an hour but not pay for it. Sometimes the National Guard had occasionally been called in to settle the discussions. "They'd shot rail road workers before." Plenty slept with their boots on.

In New York, Joe Rainmaker had been trying to get a handle on this latest share offering. There was a new issue of the Hannibal Express Railroad being offered at one hundred dollars a share. His company was active as one of the underwriters. There had already been a large accumulative purchase, nearly eight percent by some Colorado miner, who was purchasing in trust, from some unlikely town named Leadville.

Warren sat by the hoist. The hoist was about twenty feet across and fifteen feet round. A one inch thick steel cable was wrapped around a spool lowering a cage, ten miners at a time, about a quarter mile down. The hoist was driven by a large boiler giving energy to a gear system that translated the energy into forward and reverse. It was all the stuff that made a locomotive race down a track. Warren looked after it. He greased it and watched out for stress cracks. He had a maintenance book to go by and was often servicing a valve or replacing a gasket. He was compensating for one of the great arms being out of service. A new one was being cast but it wouldn't arrive for another two months.

The boiler was sparkling. The belt was vibrating up and down a little too much and he increased the tension. The lift was coming up now for shift change. He kept his eye on the cable wrap to avoid any doubling up. The cable was old but not too old and should probably last another three months. A new one was on order.

He wasn't sure what difference electricity would make. He guessed the boiler would be replaced but maybe that's what would drive the electric motor. He wasn't sure. There was a click as the cage came to its surface exit.

The miners left the cage. They were black with dust. They carried chunks of ice in their hands. They walked down the hill to their shared tents and rooms. At three fifty a day they would find some beer and whisky to fit a Friday night budget. With luck, there would be a good shooting at a card came and a whopper of a story from some carpet bagger. Pick Axe Clyde might roll the dice for drinks on the counter, get lucky and have two dollars to give to some nice woman. First, he would have a fifty cent steak to build up some energy for it. Clyde wiped the dirt out of his eyes and joined some of the other boys at the chop house. The sign said Beef Steaks and that's what they got. They laughed and then went home to get their pistols for a night on the town. There were nickel crap games to be had. There was action in the tents. Penny and nickel slot machines were showing up in every barber shop. Some might even get their beards cut off, maybe.

Chapter Two - Shotgun Susy and the Provisional Sisters of Freedom

Shotgun Susy wrapped her horse's rein to the post by the watering trough. She scraped off her boots against an iron edge and walked into the house. It was her house as much as it was the house of the other Sisters. It was obvious to anyone with half a Catholic conscience that they would be needed on a gold rush frontier. Between one sort of divine intervention and another, the Sisters had founded the construction and habitation of a large style mansion and hospital for indigents and others. It had rooms for wayward waifs, attention for beaten women and salvation through freedom.

Sister Susy placed her brace of shotguns on a rack by the door. "Sister Emily. It's good to see you."

"Oh. Sister Susy, with you there is abundance, faith and bliss." Sister Emily held her hands across her chest.

"I saw your posters for the new building lottery. Twenty five cents a ticket seems reasonable," Susy said as she sat at the table in the large kitchen. A pot of steeped, black tea was on the stove. Emily poured her a cup.

"Well it may take a few Holy lotteries. I expect there will be orphans soon enough and we should prepare for them. Poor things."

There was a ring at the door. Another Sister went to answer it, noticed Susy and waved. A man was standing on the porch.

"Sister Helen. Is Sister Susy in?" He directed his chin at her horse.

"Oh. Father Fontaine. Come in. Let me check. Please have a seat."

Sister Helen walked into the kitchen. "That bastard is here. He wants to see you," she whispered to Susy.

Sister Susy rose and walked to the sitting room. She hadn't freshened up yet and still had the glow of the trail about her. Her brown leather vest clashed with her black habit. "Father. To what do we owe the pleasure of your visit? What news of Rome?"

"Well. To be blunt. When we last talked, it was of giving your remittance to Rome. The tithing is ten percent and that demands an accounting of your revenue. We did discuss this. I wondered how you had managed towards that end? When I saw you ride into town I thought it would be favorable to approach you."

Susy put a sack down on the table in front of them. She opened it to reveal butter yellow sand. "I worked for that."

She reached for a goblet of wine placed in front of her. "To tell you the truth, Rome can go work for it too. Perhaps if Pope Joan was sitting on the throne I would feel different but your patriarchal, incestuous clan, of boy slurping, deviants are on their own. Shot of Irish, Father?"

"The consecration of your house will be held up. Your so called Sisters are self proclaimed. They are rogue, practically heretical." Fontaine was getting red in the face.

"They remain Provisional Sisters and this is the house of freedom from pain and want and ignorance. Freedom from the anti-Christ and his Masonic agents of carpet baggers." She crossed herself. "May Mary give us mercy." She took a swallow of wine and tore off a small chunk of bread.

There was a commotion outside. A man was yelling. "Sharon. I know you're in there. You come out and go back to our home!"

Sharon was in a second floor bedroom. She was curled up on the bed. Her eyes were blackened and bruised. Her arms red with welts. Sister Cathy, Sister Debbie and Sister Lorie sat on the edge of her bed.

"Sharon. You get out here. Now don't make me more mad. I forgive you." They heard through the open window.

The priest looked to Susy, "Don't you think you are interfering with their sacred marriage? A man and wife should work out their differences together. Perhaps she was disobedient to her husband. That might account for her beating." The priest offered.

"Sharon. You stupid bitch. You couldn't organize a blow job in a whorehouse. Now you get out here or I'm coming in."

Susy stood up. Several other nuns came down the stairs. A few kids stood behind them. Susy picked up a shotgun from the rack and opened the door. She stepped outside and immediately fired a round into the sky then held the instrument across her chest. The man was weaving slightly. He stood in the middle of the yard. "You witch," he said on seeing Sister Susy. He brought his arm back to unravel a whip. The black leather uncoiled behind him against a bright blue sky.

As he brought his hand forward, Susy shot at him point blank. The large lead shot broke several of his ribs, tore through his heart and burst his eyes. He died in about two seconds. She crossed herself. There were many witnesses. All could see it was a fair fight or duel of circumstance. He was asking for it.

Sharon sobbed.

"I can't believe you broke the fifth commandment. How could you?" The Priest's face drained white.

"That's Old Testament. Old Testament says, 'Thou shall not murder.' New Testament says, 'Thou shall not kill.' T'wasn't murder. I'm an old testament gal." She broke the shotgun in two, shook out the empty shells and refilled the chambers from her belt. "He wasn't a good Catholic, Father. He choose suicide. Can't be buried here."

The Leadville Weekly Herald headline would be, "Crazy With A Whip" and The Mining District Republican masthead said, "Shotgun Susy Saves Sisters". The accounts were so favourable that the Sheriff didn't bother to investigate the killing.

"This is too much for me, Sister. I fear for your souls. I'm afraid for you. Your road is not right." Fontaine put on his hat.

"I'm always glad for your concern, Father. If the Pope comes to Leadville he'll have a busy day."

The father left and Sister Susy shut the door behind him. Two nuns and three orphans loaded the corpse onto a buckboard.

Sister Lucy said, "I'll draw out a hot bath for you. You've been gone for ten days. Maybe you haven't seen much hot water. Maybe you haven't smelt much rose soap either." She smiled and set about getting a bathing tub ready in Sister Susy's room.

Sister Lucy had put her book reading skills to work. Using an 1879 copy of *Modern Physics for The Student* she had a small water tower constructed on the property. It had a double shell allowing for the burning of a few candles which prevented it's freezing during the cold winters.

The bottom of the water tank had a two foot layer of charcoal acting as a filter. They noticed a taste difference right away.

Several of the local smelters had been approached by nosy matrons about the refiners habit of pouring mercury and tailing by-products into the water table. The smelter owners responded by saying, they were pouring the mercury onto their own grounds, their own property. There were eight refiners. The Great Gold and Silver Amalgamated Miners Company purchased a life time subscription to the Rat Bastard Gazette. In return the Gazette pointed out that Mrs. Oliver, who was leading the petition, use to be a fallen dove in Crazy Carols Sporting Lounge. The argument wouldn't resurface for another ten years. No one would ever do anything so stupid as to admit mercury to waste disposal or ground water sites again. At any rate, Sister Susy's bath was drawn with sparkling water. Fresh cut flowers stood in a narrow vase on her dresser. Sky blue curtains were drawn against her windows.

"Please, someone look after Blaze and brush him down. I need to clean up, get right with JC and his dad." A small crowd parted, allowing her to walk up the staircase.

It was tough enough on the good and the strong on the frontier. But stupid, angry, men had a way of being culled from the herd. They didn't really last that long. She'd certainly killed him but there was no way out of it. Disrespect for the Lord's house and work couldn't be tolerated. She sank into the soapy water and hummed to herself.

Eight and ten year old boys, Jim and Doug, grunted as they took the saddle bags off Blaze. They complained and lifted eight, twenty pound leather bags of gold dust and dragged them into the sitting room. They enjoyed grooming horses and looked forward to taking Blaze to his stall in the barn. They dreamed of fighting dragons and playing ball.

The Ginger Kid looked at the Herald's headline. He wiped foam off his lips and said, "People either aim to be polite or aim for yur heart. Why would you want to get into it? I got nothing to tempt anyone by. A horse, saddle and jerky."

"Christ, I don't know. If I'd of pulled a gun every time I wanted to I'd have used it, I guess, about three times in my life. Probably still be in jail for the first time. Pride, humiliation. It was a high enough ante. It would have been right to do it though. Hard to cure stupid. They all deserved to get killed and some of their friends too. Most people don't think that's a big deal. Not around here. But I'm going to be so mad if there ain't no heaven. I ought to be able to squeeze through them gates. There was a lot of people that needed killing. Considering what they did to others, after me, maybe it's a worse thing I did to not kill them. I hate philosophy. People only came up with it to rationalize a loss."

"There ain't no God. When you're done you're done," said Butcher Joe.

"You don't believe that."

"Yeah, I do."

"Well then. Why haven't you killed? I've known you a long time, far as I know you never killed anyone. Sorry I guess that's a question that I shouldn't even ask," said Butcher.

"I don't know why you don't, I don't know why you don't rush out there, right now, and let a bunch of guys have it. The guy that owns the gold stamping mill for instance. Do you think his larder would have less food in it if he paid his workers ten cents more? Shoot him. That's the one that needs it."

The Ginger Kid asked, "What about those card games? How many times you seen a man killed cheating? You really think that's reasonable? Do the wrong thing with a piece of paper and you're in the ground?"

"In the first place. Every time I seen that, the cheat reached for his own pistol first. Second, they'd of hung him even if he didn't reach for his gun. When someone sits at a card table they're bringing their stakes with 'em. That pile is equal to years of work and risk. He figures he's taking another reasonable risk built on that. If he gets cheated out of it, which is actually theft, he loses years of his life, years of his effort. All of his judgments and choices come to naught then. It's all a dead waste. So yeah. Shoot the bugger. He knew what he was doing. How many lives did he wreck and get away with? Anyway I still don't understand why you don't pull the trigger? You wear one," Joe asked.

Ginger said, "No. I never killed anyone, except in war. I look like I could get my licks in. I practice a lot. People know that. They complain to the Sheriff. Words out. I practice a lot. Cost me five bucks for disturbing the peace once. A bargain."

"I wear it. It's like a hat around here. I ain't beggin for it. I ain't trying to set myself up. Just trying to stay straight and friendly or move on. There's lots of space. But then again. In the diggins there is no space and you can't move on. There's no where to go. That nun had no where to go. You only got as much space as your claim says. One shovel full beyond that well...that's part of the price of gold too isn't it? Gold and guns. Gold has been around for awhile. People get the fever when they actually get their hands on it. When you feel the weight of a bar slowly growing warm in your hands. It gets in your eyes pretty quick. It's hard to not want more. No one ever asks where it came from. It's the same everywhere. You can't invent it out of nothing. It's no false promise. It's got the same value everywhere. Talk about it in the bible, even. Well that's some pedigree. They didn't talk about no Confederate paper money in the bible and look at what that's worth." Joe raised an eyebrow.

"I like gold too. I wouldn't kill for it." Ginger said.

"No. but you might risk getting killed for it." Butcher Joe insisted

"Yes I suppose there is a fine difference..." Ginger admitted.

"Yeah. Twenty eight dollars an ounce difference. Some coach boy in New York is busting his balls shoveling manure out of a stable. He picks up a newspaper, tells the boss to piss off and goes west. Now he's dreaming about a shovel full with a month's pay in every scoop instead of horse manure. Another dozen show up here every day just like him. One lucky one will find it. One lucky one will walk two thousand miles back home. The rest will adapt or die."

"I don't know what it is about gold."

"I don't know either really but for four thousand years there's always been someone willing to buy it."

"It does make us smile." Joe said.

Sister Susy asked Sister Emily. "How close are you to the required amount?"

"We have three thousand gold dollars. The Annunciation Church Guild has five hundred. Leyman Brothers in Chicago can provide a complete kit, no bell, for thirty five hundred. Six hundred for transportation. More lotteries?"

"Prepare the order. I'll get the balance tonight from Madame Silks and The Purple Rose. Whores and nuns, we both need to reap the rewards of sin," Susy said.

"Have rosary, will travel," Sister Emily laughed.

Charlie O'Sullivan was amazed at all he saw. The further west he went, the more he liked it. Selling his New York livery stable and going to Colorado was the dream of a life time. He and his horse were on an incline. He watched as the wind blew across the peaks of snow capped mountains. The wind blew from west to east, gathering long chains of puffed, stark-white clouds against the sky. The smell of the pine was deep. Purple and white flowers grew in splashes. He followed the trail. It was well worn. Behind his horse he'd tethered an ox carrying a load of camping and mining supplies. His plan was to prospect for a promising claim. He'd work it for a month and if he wasn't meant to be a gold miner he'd open a general store. He would find his fortune there. He had two thousand gold dollars in his money belt and would assess the situation when he got to Leadville. His wife would be pleased and would make the journey up, in comfort, after he established his store. His son to be, a great man. He hoped she would see the blooms.

Charlie pulled on the reins and looked puzzled when he noticed a man's head appear from behind a rock outcropping. He thought it might have been a grizzly bear. Charlie fell from his horse, dead before he hit the ground.

Bad Bill pulled the body off the trail. He ran after Charlie's horse and tethered it by a creek. He felt the body and quickly pulled off the money belt. Bad Bill's eyes widened. It was the dream of a life time. Two thousand dollars plus whatever else he found. Probably lots more good stuff in the provisions.

Better to plant the body soon. He used the high grade pick and shovel that Charlie had brought with him and dug a deep grave in two hours. Bill buried the body with its identifiable saddle and started cross country to an abandoned miner's shack. It was made of log and nestled near a deep scar in the mountain side that proved out to be nothing. Bill was looking forward to a drink of whisky. He rode his own horse and pulled his ox along. It was a nice day.

Bad Bill wasn't known in Leadville. That is, it might be the case that some folks in Colorado had been aware of Ward William Mitchel alias Bad Bill, alias Wild Ward...the reward of $500.00 was posted in Arizona regarding his excess passions. But Colorado had no extradition with Arizona so the gallows in Tombstone could wait. Since he'd committed no crimes in Colorado he was safe and a man of substance. He put the horse and ox in a small corral after tossing their loads into the cabin. He found no branding marks on either and resolved to do so himself. He didn't want to be confused with being a horse or cattle thief. That was a hanging offense anywhere. He found a few hundred more dollars, in paper notes, while he drank straight from a bottle of whisky. He found many letters and a handful of books which he tossed in the fireplace without looking at the contents. He laughed while enlarging his provisions in the shack. He'd be able to winter in the town but would leave this place stocked as a back up. He could really size things up and take advantage of opportunity. Reaping what others sowed was working out fine.

Six months dealing cards in Carson City taught him all about how the big outfits worked. They didn't like competition much but out here, if he got his digs in early, he could do well. All his dreams handed to him on a platter. He smiled and planned a trip to town and wondered what he would do. Have his own tough guys. He liked tough guys. They made sense. "It made sense to prey on people, it made no sense to be prey. God made it so easy, he must approve." Yeah, he'd have some tough guys.

Henry put the used book down on the side stand. "Such a book. Jules Verne's, *From The Earth To The Moon* was terrific. It was a ripping, yarn that started with a beginning and moved right to the end. "Really, a surprise that no one had thought of it before." He would write him a letter. No, he would have one typed by the printer and send him a letter. Really show Mr. Verne that he was a modern man. What would he say? Should he write in French or English? Well he would say something. A book like that really deserved comment. He would address it to his publisher in Paris.

Henry swung his feet out of bed, careful not to disturb the dog. It was curled up, muzzle between its paws. It opened one eye for half a moment to see Henry reaching for a tincture of oil for asthma. The dog moved its head slightly to the side. One ear twitched when it heard a match being struck. Henry looked at his pocket watch. It was just as well he didn't write the book. The whole thing would have taken place in Carol's Sporting House.

He raised the glass and lit the wick. He turned it up. There were plenty of lights outside. There was still noise but a lot of the piss and vinegar crowd had left for Bonanza Creek. The dunes were solid yellow dust. You only had to pick it up off the ground. The old timers knew it would be better to show up with liquor, candles and tobacco for sale, than most other things. It would turn into a huge moment of history. The depression was over.

Henry exhaled a cloud of white smoke. He had mixed some of the opium with some of the cannabis oil and mixed it in his pipe with a pinch of tobacco. He pulled a chair up to the window. He turned the wick in the lamp down. He drew a gun and sat. He puffed on the pipe, holding his gun in the other hand. He watched as people moved back and forth. Henry wanted to be ready. A large purple snake could easily fly through the open window. Maybe Martians would land. He hated Martians. He took another puff of the peppermint smoke and burst out laughing. He got a lazy smile on his face and he didn't know who any of the people were that went about their late evening business.

Henry considered what he didn't know for awhile and when he didn't know it. He noticed there was a pipe on the night stand. He reached out and found the bowl warm. He lit it. He thought about who ever might have left the pipe and felt a halo encircle his head. He thought he was wearing a warm golden hat. The dog was bored and fell asleep. He reached for a bottle of sarsaparilla.

He couldn't feel his body. He was glad for his dog. Henry realized, at this point, it would take him a half hour to find his gun. The dog people would be his only defense. J.P. Morgan would do crap for him. "Oh, don't go there. Don't start getting all paranoid. Just keep looking out the window," he thought. He took aim at a stage driver. He put the gun down and re-light the pipe. He looked at his watch. The short hand had just passed the four. The longer hand was on the same number four. It didn't really make a lot of sense. He looked up at the night sky. Most of the stars were moving around. He didn't see any dragons up close. He knew men were working underground, even then, pulling ore out. They would sweat and spit.

He opened his tin of tobacco. He needed more tobacco. "Oh, yeah. That's right." There was a reason for the box under the bed. He'd have to deal with the banks, back east, soon. Right. He'd have to set that all up. He wouldn't be making any waves pulling up stakes now. It wouldn't change anything. Once he got to St. Louis, it was a fast trip to New York. He'd be expected. A few telegrams would set up his reception. He would later receive a telegram back. For a tip, three dollars and fifty cents a telegram, he would get the information first. Everything was going to work out. If he could make it to the bed he would get some sleep. He slid off his chair and crawled the three feet to bed. The dog was stubborn about moving from the pillow. The mattress was too high. He managed to drag a pillow down to the floor. He had dreams about sleeping out on the open range. The dog knew it would work out that way.

The bushwhackers were improving their aim. Shotgun Susy listened to the woman who was with her. She'd only made a casual reference in a quip.

"You just brought it all back. The neighbour's wife got murdered and my husband was taken away. They hung him a month later. Even though he had been with me the whole time. I tell you it was four years of hell. I had to move and feed the kids and feed the dog and feed the baby. It was really terrible. After four years of living like a church mouse I went straight to Madam Elley. I'd talked with her before. She let me know I could make plenty of coin at her house but I never wanted to. The stares and sneers and the hardship on the kids was already bad. I told her, as far as I could tell, I was being run out of Dodge and I said, I'd do it but not in Carson or Dodge. She said the next rush was in Leadville. The kids wouldn't be made to be ashamed of such a highly valued mother." The woman looked along her rifle barrel and smiled at Susy. "Well, she said, I ought to be sure and she offered me the weekend at her parlour to see if I really could." She smiled. "I paid the stage coach fare and left town with three hundred dollars on Monday afternoon. They were glad to see me and I've gold in my purse." She fired off another shot at the claim jumpers. It tore off a branch and made a hat duck behind a rock.

Susy could feel her emotions. The joy of marriage with its solidarity and union ripped apart overnight by outrage, humiliation, ridicule and poverty.

"I guess whores and nuns make good company," she said to Susy.

They each poked their rifles out of the see-hole and took a shot at a frustrated claim jumper.

"I grabbed her and threw her against the wall. She cussed me out. She knew I was already having a bad day. I couldn't allow my daughter to talk that way to me. It looked bad I guess. She weighs in at two hundred pounds. She called me a bitch then, so I grabbed her by the hair and dragged her to the table. Meanwhile my fella is watching all of this in silence."

The two groups continued shooting at each other until a man screamed at midnight.

The bachelor farmer looked the woman over. With a shrug of his shoulders and a tilt to his head he thought he was putting out sort of an egotistical challenge. "While you're here why don't you think about staying a little longer? There's a stage at least every few days this time of year."

Matilda hadn't expected that. His remark didn't require an immediate response. Jay and Christine were outside doing something with the kids. They needn't know if she turned him down or not. She smiled at him. "That coffee would sure be fine."

"Have you had the place long? The logs look fresh cut," she said.

"I bought it off Silver Jack. He came out here about five years ago as a mule skinner. He was a foreman who came in from San Francisco. Well he made his agricultural claim a hundred acre patch along the trail."

Eric continued, "Silver Jack was a gambler. By the time he finished the cabin and got a cow shed half built he hit it big in town. He held out a pair of Queens against a high card and a pair of tens. He picked up an eighth interest in a mine said to be worth two hundred and fifty bucks and another nine hundred in cash. He was in a real mood then and kept that hotel room for a week and had himself a pretty good time. By the end of the week, wasn't it true that his no where mine hit it. A three foot vein of gold. It was forty feet down, five feet wide and another hundred feet going on a slant. He sold his shares out for thirty thousand the next day. Jack's a big man in Denver now. Goes to the opera. I built on the second room and put in a root cellar. I got some cider, Jay!" He yelled out the door.

He heard Jay say to his wife. "Well we ain't going now. Let's have a pass of Eric's jug while we're here."

Eric's dog barked at the rooster that had wandered into the cabin. "Guess I run a loose ship here," he laughed.

Jay walked in.

Eric pointed. "Texas chili on the stove and those biscuits were fresh yesterday."

He saw Jay, Christine and the kids about every two or three months. They each stopped in or "hellowed" the other, on trips to town. It was another fifteen miles to Leadville and his was a cut in the other direction. Same with Jay's place. It was another three miles down the valley. This time Christine brought her cousin, Matilda.

Matilda stood and examined a shelf above the sink, beside the indoor hand pump. "That's a lovely tea pot. It's so funny to see store bought things this far west and so deep into the country.

"We got it all here, Matilda. It's modern times. Store bought and factory made are only as far as a Ward catalog and a Wells Fargo wagon."

"Christine said, canning was going to be as good as gold. And that if I was busy all summer I could make a living selling preserves all winter. I know my numbers and can keep track of expenses," she said.

"You like books?"

"Pa! Quick. It's a coyote!"

There was a boom. "Don't touch it!"

Matilda, Eric and Christine rushed outside with the barking dog. They joined Jay and the kids. In front of the cow shed an adult coyote was lying in the dust. Its blood was matting its fur. Jay had shot it square in the midsection. He held the rifle at his side.

"You did good there." Eric said.

"Broad daylight and not scared." He nudged its jaw with the tip of his boot. Some foam was visible.

"Bury it or burn it, you figure?"

"Both. Dig a pit. Burn it. Then bury. We don't need an outbreak here. It got into some of the raccoons this spring. Get away," he shouted at the dog.

"Right now, I guess."

Eric went to the cabin and retrieved a shovel from the farm implements he kept there.

"Let's leave the men to this dirty work and see about a meal." Christine took Matilda's arm and they turned.

The kids yelled, "We want to watch."

"Nope. Not on this. It's bad stuff. Rabid. Can't take a risk there, honeys. You kids got to go in with us. Let's go."

They kicked dust and turned.

"Git." Jay threw a clod of earth at the puzzled dog.

Eric slid the coyote up on the shovel head and carried it about fifty feet away. He returned to scoop up the bloodied earth. He poured kerosene on it, once it lay in the pit, and set it afire. The fur started and they tossed on some dried bush and thicker branches.

Matilda brought out mugs of cold cider.

It got going good and they added some thicker branches until the thing was reduced to white ash. Once the pit was filled in they walked away and hoped it was behind them. He knew, so far, that he liked the sound of a woman's voice in his cabin. Eric pushed back his sweaty, smoked hair and felt his beard.

Chapter Three – The Beginning

If Leadville had a memory it would recall Alvinus Wood and William Stevens.

There was nothing wrong with it. The silver years, they were tender. They were raw and barely learned by the experiences of the forty-niners, during the California rush, and later the load at Pike's Peak. It's enough that it stood out as a gold rush town but its second boom was in the late seventies. Its first was in 1860 to 1865 when the gold drew the population from a few dozen pan handlers on a creek to ten thousand and then back down to a ghostly few, once the gold was scratched out.

Ten years later, by 1877, there were a few hundred miners going through their chores. Black, crushed sand and rock plugged-up sluices were all that was left. Sharp, jagged and crushed black crap, grew in piles. Calcium carbonate lay as filth and clutter and waste from every gold mine, pan, placer and sluice. Pushed out by black junk, the crowds left.

Alvin and William had worked together before and were trying their heads and hands. William looked at the chunk of rock on the table and picked it up. Alvin accumulated more foam on his mustache.

Wind blew through the cabin door. Alvin leaned back on his chair with a poker smile on his face.

"Heavy enough. It clogs everyone's sluices. You know a place that doesn't have the problem? It keeps falling back into the dig. Awful stuff. The mud road is black with it." William said.

"You still have too much cash? Would you like an opportunity to be called a fool by every pan handler in town? Your mother will cry and your father will yell at you." Alvin said.

"What then?"

Alvin said, "You come and it'll be a big surprise."

William went along. They rode for awhile and came to Alvin's cabin. There was a small forge out back and a rebuilt blast furnace, once used by the last blacksmith to leave town.

William watched as Alvin loaded up a vessel with the black crap and placed it in the furnace. He took a few swallows of whisky and waited. Alvin explained that he was thinking of filtering the stuff through sulphuric acid. Within an hour, Alvin poured off one ingot over the top and another from the bottom by pulling a plug. There was a large grey one and a large white one. He used a pair of tongs and dropped them into water. It boiled and hissed. He picked them up with leather gloves and dropped them on the table. They hit with loud thunks and shook the jug of whisky.

"No." William said. He reached forward and gingerly felt the heat radiating off the bars and picked one up.

"See, it's silver bearing lead carbonate. There's a lot of sulphides too but like I said, that can be acid washed. I had some samples assayed," Alvin raised an eyebrow, "Back east."

William looked out the window. It was a field of black mounds as far as the eye could see. No one wanted the stuff. No one wanted it because it was crap. Tons of crap.

They were both nervous. Abandoned mines lay everywhere.

They rode around. Quietly, they noted which gold mines were played out and abandoned or barely working. The harder job was seeking out existing owners. Right away, each knew of several shares and claims that were up for sale. They hired wagons and men to haul away the tailings that they bought. The previous owners laughed, knowing that the gold wasn't worth the effort. Fifteen or twenty grams a ton was just so much garbage. There were a few rumours that the friends were so desperate for money they were gambling on some wild scheme involving the rapid milling of crushed rock but it looked to be failing. This went on all summer and all winter. Halfway through the winter, the secret was finally figured out. Those two weren't crazy. They'd just paid out pennies for dollars. Everyone knew then, by the winter of 1877. A few hundred knew. All that were there certainly knew what to look for and where and how to establish a claim. The word was out but the word doesn't get very far in 300 inches of snowfall in the highest mountains packed with Ute Indians and two hundred mile and hour winds.

That fall, Susan B. Anthony, fresh from her appearance in Wagon Wheel Gap and Lake City, rolled into town. Posters had been circulated by the Women's Medical Association. Votes for women, was the topic. The Colorado Women's Medical Association continued putting up posters.

Baldie Steve and Apple Jack crowded into the saloon. "Suffrage. We suffer with them all right!"

"You'd suffer if you didn't have five dollars to pay for it," shouted a whore from one of the dozens of women at the back.

Men laughed.

Susan looked the audience over. A hundred had crowded into the saloon. Every other man was smoking a pipe or spitting into a spittoon. They wore large knives, large beards and large guns. Some wore filth. Some wore suits with bow ties. They shouted encouragement at her while she talked. She was surprised but these mud swishing mountain men were agreeing and clapping as she spoke.

"Why, Miss Anthony we like women and anyone that can make it up here deserves as much say as anyone else."

"God said women should be a help mate not a leader," said a preacher.

"Now, do you mean all women or just white women?" Black Charlie asked.

"Slavery is wrong. All men should live free and equal. Women should be allowed to own property," she said. "It's not right that a man can immigrate here and buy land but I and my sisters who have been here longer may not. It's an outrage."

The men could understand that.

Limpy Joe said, "Mines would fill up with slaves. There would be no work left. The mountains would fill up with chinks and niggers working for nothing."

"It's an extension of the liberty our grandfathers fought for a hundred years ago." Her dress was heavy and swayed around her ankles. Her boots laced up to the knee. She started to cough and waved her hands. She was overpowered by the heavy smoke in the room.

Billy Nye shouted into the crowd, "The previous rule of closed bar is relaxed if people will put out their pipes." Everyone loved her more then.

The October 2, 1877 issue of The Rat Bastard Gazette would quote Billy saying, "Just because I gave her a place to talk doesn't mean I'm a communist. I'm not a communist."

Digger Tom looked at Mr. Dill from the Leadville Weekly Herald. "Far as I'm concerned women don't have a sense of shame or guilt. Put that in your four page paper."

"We just finished fighting a civil war and massacring a thousand Indians and stealing the gold fields from the Ute. Who could feel guilt or shame?" Mr. Dill said.

After the lecture, Susan Anthony found herself surprisingly refreshed by breaking habit and drinking Columbian wine. She tried to answer the questions put to her. Several gave her donations and tips of places to see in Denver, her next destination. She was staying at the Grand Hotel and would leave in the morning.

There was a spare seat on her stage in the morning and a cursing match to see who would ride shotgun. She turned down several offers towards more drinks and one offer of marriage. She was invited to the following spring's frog jumping contest and graciously accepted. The men were in a bright and positive mood. Life was coming to them with every nugget they found. After Susan left the winter snows would start.

By dawn they would be back to digging holes and swishing their pans.

Once realizing what Alvinus and William had been up to, the rest of the local population hadn't spent the time getting angry – they were grabbing their shovels and pans.

There were hundreds of them living among the trees and streams that fall and winter of 1878. No one else was going to stand a chance until the 1879 spring. Some would snow shoe in early to make their claims. They would come by the thousands.

Over the year five thousand new souls had arrived, then another snow, then by 1880 over thirty five thousand would show up. They came from Pennsylvania, Nova Scotia, Alabama, California, Ireland, Europe, Australia and the rest of the world.

After two years of filth, hardship, pain and sometimes terrible risk William looked at Alvin. "We'll meet again. Perhaps in New York."

Alvin shook his hand as he put a foot up to the stage. "Good by old friend."

William sat down on the seat, felt the bulge of his wallet and dreamed what he would do with the money. Lots of men worked hard for two or three dollars a day. He offered his bottle to the man beside him and then took a swallow.

It wasn't bad to be driven, to have narrow sighted goals. All who would be king and would cater to the king would have to climb to the top of the mountain. They threw themselves at it in a continuous fashion, arresting the attention of a fascinated world, intrigued by the telegraphic speed of news. The difference between news and rumour did not matter because the purpose was the quest. The solution is the question vain, desired and only with risk. A path of clarity and sharpness in loneliness and solitude. It's trying. It's failing. It's victory life.

Just about everyone drank a quart of liquor a day. Just about everyone had a gun or Derringer of some kind. The long stretches of intense cold made people short of temper. Gunshots rang all night long. Wagons were always moving. The railroad would arrive soon. People were laughing and cursing and yelling along Harrison Avenue all night. Specially on a Saturday night. A miner would walk out with a fifteen or twenty dollar pay for his six days of labour. Depending on his arrangement, he's paying four to seven dollars a week at a boarding house. A tent could do for the short summer. A tent in the winter was a likely tomb not to be found until Spring. Leadville swallowed all the local trees into its sawmills. Men walked up gulches and creeks stopping to pan and dig. If it looked good enough they would knock together a small log cabin and play it out. Every week another miner hit it, pulling out forty to sixty percent pure ore with every shovel full. Some fool kicked over a twelve pound gold nugget in a creek bed. Bells rang and jingled on sleigh horses. Deep ruts of slush and mud sucked at boots. The wind never stopped blowing.

Mr. Phelps owned the Leadville Weekly Herald and had Mr. Dill as managing editor. "Well, Tabor is elected by no surprise," he said.

"It's going to be a new year like no other," said Dill.

Phelps shoved some paper under the door. "Here's the lead, 'Happy New Year 1878. The Little Wagon Shop, owned by Gilbert, was host to the incorporation of Leadville this January 14th, 1878...

"Our town of three hundred living in a sea of seventy three houses, shanties and tents is now a city.' If you can find it under the snow, that is."

Mr. Dill gathered together some type and poured more liquor into his cup.

The call to the west was wild. Mack wanted to be like his brother Bob. He grew his hair and quit his job. He was planting potatoes, turning the soil and tossing stone out of his way. He had five sacks that he stored and fretted over all winter. He kept going to the root cellar and turning them over, searching out any early rot. They all had well established roots poking out of their eyes. He cut them into quarters and halfs.

It was a short growing season. He mainly sweat that summer. The log cabin needed more mud and grass between the cracks. His acreage included some woods and bush. Sometimes on a Saturday night he sat up late, drinking whisky and strumming on his guitar. Here he would sell his potatoes and corn. There was an eager market and it would grow. The corn he could sell for the livestock. Then something else would take his fancy.

He thumbed an open G string and then fooled around pressing the D string on different frets. He did that for awhile and then decided to draw on a plug of tobacco he had in his pipe. St. Louis had been no where for him.

Mack had got caught up in the greed of the city and had lost most of what he built up. He had few friends there like Patrick and Eddy. Basic supplies and food stuffs provided a more dependable rate of return than chasing the golden dragon. He wasn't interested in the gambling outfits. Everyone was talking about Cloud City and he pulled in with his ox, plough and future, in over stuffed bags and trunks. He needed a change of life. Fewer cards, guns and women.

Next spring he would buy some plank wood at Tisdales' Sawmill in Iowa Gulch. The cabin was made out of logs that had been notched together. The roof was split log. Even though it was small, at ten by fifteen feet, there was a center post supporting the roof. By February, over two hundred inches of snow would collect. People would dig tunnels in the snow. Some log cabins would cave in under the weight and crush the occupants to trap and smother their faces.

He picked up his guitar and set down the jar of whisky. The soil was moist. There was plenty of rock and tree roots too but he had it all down.

Telegraph lines and phones would be in soon, was the talk. That would beat the mail if you had forty cents for six words. He started making plans for the next day. He wanted to enclose the current shed for the ox. It was exposed on three sides and he didn't want the animal in the cabin this winter.

He could hear insects humming.

Sometimes the wind was strong enough and he could hear it whistle through and move the tall boughs. He didn't feel like doing anymore. It was warm enough to sit outside and build a cheery fire. He heard coyotes yipping. He slid off his boots and dug his feet into the ground. He had about a hundred days to plant, grow and harvest to market. That's what he had and all he thought about. He didn't have anything left in his poke beyond this year's needs. If the harvest failed to work out, his back up plan was to sell the ox and find a very fortunate hand of faro. But he drew back on his pipe and thought about the half bushel of corn seed yet to sow. If he had so much as an acre of corn and an acre of potato, well at least he and the ox could eat.

He need not have worried beyond a half sip of liquor. There were cabins and storefronts. There were two story plank houses. There were brick buildings. Mack would soon have demand as tens of thousands would throw themselves on the door step of the mountain. Usually they had enough to last them for a few weeks of prospecting. Thousands were on the way in the race to stake out a claim. The first days of spring would allow for a trickle of the toughest, who had fought through winter passes and frightening storms to be first in. First new man anyway. A man stood a chance then. He could keep any claim he could sit on and register. If he sat on it long enough and worked it hard enough he could take a pinch of dust and buy some potatoes for his dinner. If not, then he could rob the occasional stage.

Mack was drunk, pleasantly so. He guessed it would all be OKAY. He'd done what he could and planned to continue. He'd run low on kerosene. He kept a small box of coins underneath a flagstone in the fireplace. He'd lie down inside soon. The nights were still crisp. His bunk was full of straw, boughs, flowers and leaves. The Remington stood by his bunk.

In the morning he swished out the coffee pot and tossed in some fresh grounds. He poured water into a mix and made up some griddle cakes. He boiled water for porridge. There were two rabbits hanging off the cabin edge, draining and curing. Mainly today would be a ploughing and stone throwing day. He'd sow more in the afternoon. After three months there was enough stone to build a wall, a foundation and another wall. Everything moved in the breeze. Corn ran tall. Potato plants were two and three feet high with thick stalks and spread all over. He pulled one out and dug out the tubers. There were a dozen the size of his fist.

Boston hadn't really offered him much more in security. Mack's boss was the same as most. He could be dismissed in a moment. He wasn't really paid more than he needed to live. He was only able to slowly make a purse by not going out with the lads after work. He didn't go chasing the neighborhood women or the sisters of his fellows.

He was no saint. Still a man of earth and human, he disciplined himself to a fifty cent girl every two months.

He unpacked crates and nailed crates shut. Because he could read, he occasionally filled out a manifest. Mainly he packed and unpacked crates. The goods would cross the Atlantic, get dealt with by the warehouse swabbies and then to the Mississippi and points west. His father had been a farmer until the potato blight in Ireland finally forced a move. A move made possible by thrift. As he swung his pry bar he thought of pushing a plough. "I suppose', he thought, " that pushing an ox or plough horse out of the muck is as difficult as ripping open crates all day."

Mack's summer day in Boston was twelve hours long. The heat melted his skin. The filth and dust mixed with the sweat between his skin and clothes. His hair was filled with the bodies of crushed flies. At night he fell onto his cot and passed out. On Sundays he'd refer to his note book. He'd been making lists and plotting out actions to take. One day, the triple crossing of money, location and inspiration would intersect. He'd made drawings of different ways of setting out the land. Somewhere west. Somewhere on the frontier. Somewhere he had more control. The teamsters needed sober drivers in St. Louis. The cattle yards there also needed men. That was far west. In the end it could just as well have been Denver but he had good maps of Lake County, Colorado. There would always be some kind of mining going on or armies that needed provisions and he was a farmer not a gambler and a farmer tired of unloading wagons.

The Leadville saloons and drinking boxes were so desirable. They drew in strangers. A sign on the wall made Mell laugh. It said, "Poor pianists will be shot."

Mell didn't last long. He'd never played the piano before. He sat down to play. He played for two minutes without improving. It was actually pretty awful but he was sipping his whisky and glad to be in town.

One Tooth Bart shot Mell from the poker table. "Now that was really bad!" He laughed. Everyone roared with him. He poured more Columbian tonic water into his Red Panther Whisky.

Mell had just come into Leadville that afternoon. He had said, "Hi. I'm Mell." before he sat down to play. That was all anyone knew. It was a good laugh though. In a day or two Mell's body would be found in Tiger Alley. "Bad for business," said a Silver Dove, "Can't have it."

Park City was in Stray Horse Gulch just outside of Leadville. A lot of miners lived there in one room cabins. They were small so as to have maximum strength come snowfall. A small space meant less fuel for the stove or fireplace. They worked the mines, taking a wagon back and forth. The wages were still 20 to 30 dollars a week, in the first year of the boom, plus whatever a man panned out on his own. A man could get ahead if he wasn't maimed or killed too bad. It was hard to live past thirty in any gold field.

In the beginning there was a shortage of common labor. In the first year a common miner could get thirty dollars a week plus shares. The land had grown trees on top of a sheet of gold and silver, five to ten feet thick, for a hundred miles in any direction.

Known and unknown mining shares would often change hands for two hundred and fifty dollars for a sixth. Every newspaper had a half page devoted to mines being bought, sold, discovered and assayed.

California and Colorado voted against slavery, not due to moral ambiguity, but cash. There wasn't a doubt in the mind of the average working man that the big mine owners would bring coolies over by the thousands to work like slaves for a third of the wage or less. These outfits. These corporations with stock certificates bolder and more ornate than a birth certificate for a human were soul less. The mines were without heart, compassion or soul. Men would be used up and spent and there were more to come.

Digby O'Day was having a good year. He'd spent the summer in a tent while hacking a cabin out of the woods. He'd saved two hundred dollars of wages and panned out jars and cans full of silver and gold. His fingers and hands were raw and thick like candles. His skin was red from smacking into rock. His chest and arms were solid iron from shoveling and lifting ore onto cars. Ore. It wasn't ore it was rock. Rock and stone is heavy. All day he picked up arm loads and handfuls of sharp rock, freshly blasted or pried from the mine wall.

Sometimes there was three grams of gold to the ton. Other times eight hundred ounces per ton. He followed veins of metallic glitter on a trail to middle earth. Ten feet down, forty feet down, even a hundred feet down.

He was free from rent. He was free to come and go as he pleased. He could sell his cabin up and take the stage coach out any time. Twenty five dollars to San Francisco, eight dollars to Denver. A few proper Derringers to be sensible and then do a jig. Knowing that and knowing that he would be well received anywhere with a few hundred thousand dollars in his pocket, he persevered. It was glorious and exciting at the best of times. And there was always the chance he would trip over a nugget of gold as big as a mule's kick at any moment.

Brick buildings were going up all over Harrison Avenue. Not only Tabor's money but lots of others were pulling it in. Once you hit it rich who cared if it took ten or even thirty thousand to build a two story bar? The opening of Tabor's opera house was a grand event in November 1879. Thousands of gallons of liquor were being consumed. Absinthe retained popularity. Liquor warehouses sprang up. Jacob Schloss moved from 34 State Street to 116 West Second Street to expand. Most of the gambling was run by one outfit or another.

The hearts and minds of women were drawn to the boom. Here there were men. If a woman was a little bit sought after back east, she was worshiped here. If she was the most common whore in San Francisco she was a paid princess in Leadville. The nuns would make no less head way. Their gold mine was sin and the fruits of sin. Sin was always good business for the sinners as saints, tithed with their actions.

The noise, music and cacophony were awesome any night. Corners were thick with men laughing, drinking and telling wild stories. They plotted, planned and made new partners and shot old partners. Some were hungry for news and would hang out at the hotels, drinking in the newspapers and overhearing conversations.

The man standing beside Pennsylvania Phil, at the bar, had an oyster in his mug of beer. "One dollar an oyster in five cent beer. He must have made out all right." His hands were clean and soft. His Stetson heavily weathered and of the finest quality. His pistols had buffalo bone grips. His boots were sharp and tight. He'd had a fresh shave and smelt of soap.

Shane looked over the miner. He was short and strong. He had a dime store pistol hanging off his belt. His boots were thick soled and caked in dirt. He had four fingers wrapped around a glass. "The fifth finger is under a rock somewhere in a Pennsylvania coal mine," Phil said to the cowboy.

Cowboy Shane replied. "Hell of a price to pay, to dig for some rich bastards. I use to farm. Me and my brothers lost that in the depression. Been punching around on cattle drives mainly. Sometimes I work the rail road and ride shotgun...got an invite to Palmer's gang." He swallowed the oyster and dropped in a shot glass of whisky.

"Pianist is good here," said Pennsylvania Phil but come by my camp and I've got better accommodations."

They rode out of town.

"Nice place. I guess you got California Gulch to yourself," said Shane.

"Well I quit the claim. All that gold is gone now. But one of the Slaters he'd knocked together this place and it was still standing. Everyone was leaving then or planning on it," said Phil He pulled a clay jug up from beneath the table. It dropped there with a thunk.

His visitor took a pull back on the jug. He just took a taste at first. Then he raised his eyebrows and swallowed a mouthful, "That is good fine whisky, Phil. My!"

"Boy, that which preserves us still maintains a fix on the homeland. That is the best Irish whisky that rolled off the boat."

"I love whisky."

"I love whisky."

The table was split log and level. Its surface was stained and dirty but worn smooth. There were candle wax puddles, burnt rings, tobacco spit stains and black crud between the cracks. Phil said, "There's a raccoon or wood chuck living under the floor. That's what that smell is."

"Yeah I can tell. I was gonna say, you got one of the expensive shacks with a wooden floor." Shane drew a pouch of tobacco from his pants pocket and began stuffing it into a short pipe he took from his shirt.

Phil stood up and went to a set of crates. They were stacked one on top of the other as shelves. He brought back a small box that had once contained cigars. He flipped the lid open revealing a large black and brown slab of gummy spice.

"Here," he said breaking off a chunk. He tossed it towards his buddy. "Put that in your pipe and smoke it." He smiled.

"What is it?"

"I got it off this teamster. He'd been hired on in Carson City with the provision that he not drink. So he found this stuff to replace his need for something to relax with. This chunk, he said, came off a clipper in San Francisco that had loaded up on cotton from Egypt, tea from China and spice from Morocco. It's called hashish and it's much loved."

The cabin began to fill with the aroma of the hash and tobacco and the pine walls, still damp with sap in places, and the smell of the raccoon or whatever it was that lived under the floor.

Chapter Four – More Reasons

"**That's** right go. Go, you bastard and forget about your responsibilities here. Forget about what you have going for you here. Go suck a cock on the other side of the rainbow and impress your friends. They just can't wait. What's Wilbur going to do next? I thought you were going to grow up? Leave all that child stuff behind. Piss off then. Get out. You don't want to make a commitment to me, so get out."

Wilbur packed. She and her son stood there, staring at him. "A strong man..." He thought. "A strong man would leave her in a heart beat." The line had become a mantra to him.

Blue skies, mountains, a destiny with gold or a filthy city hovel with the daily shrieking shrew. The humiliation, sadness, anger, disappointment and hurt in the air made every moment a long drawn out black thing. He half expected it. He wanted to be on the open plain, looking forward.

"You're an immature bastard. Your ideas are in the sky. All you do is drink. Your intentionality is all wrong. I give you credit for going to work every day. I'm surprised about that but you drink when you come home."

"You don't do anything around here and when you do it's no good, just some fast thing you've thrown together. You only do half a job. You don't think. Your friends just live through you cause they don't have to feed the baby. Why don't you run off with Sally, then? I see you talking to her all the time? Or did you already ask her and she said no? Is that it? Or are you just lazy? You've always been lazy," she said again.

Somewhere in a valley there would be a creek, he thought. He stuffed his shaving kit into his gunny sack. Yep, he'd lean into the creek for a drink of icy mountain water and see the glint of yellow.

"Where will you go?" She asked.

"Train to St. Louis first. See from there."

"They will be sold out." She stared at him.

"I already have my ticket," Wilbur said.

She shrieked, "You planned it. You planned to leave. You knew in advance. How long ago did you do that?"

"Two days ago," he lied.

"Two days!" You bastard. Get out of here. It's not just your dreams that are wrong. It's your whole loose and unstructured behaviour. You don't think. You take no responsibility. You don't want to make a commitment. All you do is react. You haven't any integrity and you're a cheap skate."

"Who are you? I'll always be asking who was that masked man? What's it like to be you? What are you really doing? What are you planning? You take. You're a spectacle. You move boxes for a living."

A vulture screamed at a hot shadow. It shrieked from atop an ancient cactus. A scorpion crawled around its base.

"Even my dreams are wrong?"

She nodded her head. Lips pursed. Eyes narrow. "And the sex is ...pifft."

The vulture made a dismissive sound, waving an open claw. Its beak sniffed the air.

He tilted his head and raised his eyebrows. "Christ," he thought. He looked at the bed and wished he was asleep. His head was swinging low, worn out, like a pack animal. He glanced at the door and then back to the legs of the kitchen table. "Christ," he thought. "Why do you do this in front of the boy?"

Then he would fill his canteen with fresh water from the creek and fill his saddle bags with yellow dust. He had to hide his smile when he turned around to face her. If he showed happiness she always pounced on him. He looked, hoping there were no kitchen knives anywhere. He stepped over to the kitchen table. "Here," he said, "I'm not an animal." He put a leather pouch with fifty dollars in it on the table.

"There's fifty dollars there. That should see you for a few months. We don't laugh," he continued. "I need to laugh every day. I need to have smiles and compassion and soothing talk. I'm willing to go out and bust my nuts all day to put something together. I don't know why you can't just listen to what I have to say for an hour or two after work. You could look at me with fondness in your eyes and pretend to listen with a bit of amazement and laugh even if you think my jokes aren't that funny. You can fake it once and a while can't you? Maybe some cheerful banter and anecdotes about your day, that don't involve criticizing me or undermining me? You're not very obedient at all. You're not nice. I don't think you want strong men around you. I think you like men weak or to destroy them, probably both. Demoralize them daily, like an emotional vampire. So yes, if I can't pan for the gold of home sweet home here, I'll pan for the gold out West. I stand a better chance crossing a mountain on a broken leg, being chased by Indians then I ever will in gaining your approval. There's nowhere here for me. Not with no laughs and only arguing about all the things wrong with me. It's too hot in the kitchen. There never was any room at the table for me," he looked at the pouch, the clutter, the table and the room. He turned, shook his head and walked out.

Wilbur didn't know what happened after that.

Leaving a bad wife is like the house is on fire. You grab what's some of yours.

"You're shitting on us. You're a bully."

"I'm sick of this."

"Why are you taking that?"

He was in a daze. He didn't know what to think. He woke up empty. The room was sterile and empty. The noise outside rough and loud.

Philip, another man, in a different place, got out on a different bandwagon of fallen hearts.

"It would be a holy and beautiful thing," Philip looked into her eyes. He could see her eyes were watering. He knew enough about women to know it was a good sign. "All those things we wanted and dreams we had. We could have them together. We'd never have to stop. I have enough for both of us. When we got there we would have enough to last two years. You know how much I have."

"Not him," she thought, "It can't be him.

He was like a brother to her. Just as dependable and undependable as a brother could be. They'd shared a lot for many years. One day he looked at her as a woman. She parted her hair different. Then it was too late.

He had been compiling the pros and cons of making a major move. There, in Kansas he'd achieved more than most. He'd worked himself up to a commission position in a good general store.

He was thrifty. He took risks but he saved. He had twelve hundred dollars in the bank and it was percolating into a fantasy. Every paper and newcomer had a story to retell about the silver strikes in Colorado. He could go and he wanted to go. The reality of getting instantly rich was like looking in the mirror. It was so obvious. He was going to hit it. She had to come with him. He couldn't leave her behind. Not to these Kansas City wolves. Two loves. The love bug bit him twice at about the same time.

"We could have the wedding here," Phillip said.

"Look. I got you this ring," he put the little box with the ring, on the table. Every woman wanted a ring and this would convince her.

Her skin turned red. The tears rolled down her face. She kept shaking her head and walked out of the room, waving a hand behind her.

He wondered if she understood him. He thought, perhaps she didn't understand what he meant. It didn't make any sense that she had replied, "Not you. Anyone but you." But she had left the room. She should be here so they could discuss it. He left and returned to his own room.

She no longer answered her door or responded to his letters.

For the next three weeks he completed his list and then quit his job. He would leave nothing unresolved. Nothing in the east was unknown to him. That left the west.

A wagon train loaded down with fresh cut European families, live stock, mechanical breakdowns, dicey maps, changing climates, odd trails and occasional hostilities didn't move much faster than walking speed. So it wasn't an unusual thing for a man to walk from one side of the country to another. He might have been bound with a wagon train, by himself or with a partner. A good horse could easily cost two to three hundred dollars without saddle and gear. So if you still wanted to see the elephant and you only had fifty bucks, you walked. The frontier grocery store was crawling with life all along the way. A prudent man carried rifle, compass and canteen before proceeding into the desert.

Phil's heart was busted, grieving, sore. It bled through his eyes. It was nailed to his internal cross. He never got to kiss her lips. By rail, stage and buck board he brought his shattered heart, strong back and purse to Cloud City.

"We're off to The Stuttering Parrot after this," Al dug his shovel in. A load of coal had spilled and they were refilling bags.

The Ginger Kid held the mouth of a sack open, "I can't believe this is what I do for a living."

"Grab a shovel while you're waiting, Kid. You guys are working too slow. I need these barrels transferred," the foreman shouted from a loading dock.

"I'm here for the money," Al laughed.

They loaded the last sack and started rolling barrels over and up a ramp to a waiting buck board. One of the waiting horses lifted its tail and ejected a generous flop. Flies appeared from nowhere. The foreman noticed and yelled for some twelve year old kid to bring a shovel and the bucket. "Quit talking and get to work," he yelled at the two men. He shoved a cigar back into his mouth.

Since it was Saturday they finished early at five o'clock. A dozen men and three boys lined up at the paymaster's wicket. The men received eight dollars a week. The boys got four. Some grumbled. Some smiled. All folded the money and put it into their pockets.

Al and Ginger walked in the remaining sunshine along the busy road. "Cold beer was a great invention, Kid. You ever tried one?" He laughed.

They stood up against the crowded counter and wiped foam off their beards. Al reached into a bowl of pickled eggs.

"I think about five guys quit this week. That foreman is such a prick."

"I'd be glad to kick him in the teeth and show him how to seduce his wife properly."

"There's a willing line up of volunteers at that door," said Ginger. He took another swallow and smoothed back his red hair. "I don't know if I want to go back on Monday. I don't know if that's a guarantee, really...with the job no good and home..."

He shook his head. "Apparently I ain't making a good impression there. If either one was working – but it's neither really. I'll just go. That's it then."

"You're done thinking about it?"

"Yep. I'm gone. I'll be leaving town by Monday. Maybe sooner. I'm gone."

"I think we should have another beer. New York, Montreal, New Orleans or California. Where shall you go?"

"The silver streets of Colorado. Every week we hear or read something about the silver strikes. I'm working for slave wages here. Yeah. Why not a silver rush?" His face lifted and he lost several wrinkles."

"How will you go?"

The Ginger Kid said, "Fast. Faster with more beer I suspect."

Every store front in Leadville was new and brightly painted. Red, blue and yellow store fronts, often with gold lettered signs, proclaimed their business. The city was a rainbow of hope.

Bad Bill rode into town and took a room. It was at Mrs. Bindlepost's house. A two story wood plank home with five bedrooms. She was a widow of forty three. Her husband was crushed to death when the roof gave way in a mine. She kept two rooms for her self and offered room and board for three. She was a surrogate mother to three men at a time.

Seven dollars a week was what she charged and there was no drinking or smoking in the house. She made them breakfast at four thirty in the morning, packed them a lunch and provided a supper at seven in the evening. On Sundays she made only the evening meal. One room and border was seventeen, the other twenty two and Bill twenty seven. She had a good reputation as a provider and she provided well for herself.

Breakfast was all the porridge you wanted, a large hunk of bread, baked beans and all the thin black coffee you wanted. She packed them a lunch of bread, a chunk of salted bacon and what ever fruit or nuts in season. On Fridays they got salted cod. For Saturday's lunch she made a rice pudding with raisin. The Saturday night supper was usually a substantial affair including a joint of mutton, beef or ham with a mountain of vegetables. She knew they were going to go out and pollute themselves and felt they stood a better chance on a full stomach. She needed to go to church on Sundays and so provided no breakfast. She knew they would all be unavailable due to hangovers, romancing whores and starting fights until supper anyway. Naturally, the rent was due on Saturday before they all went about their evening rituals. She never crossed the line. In a town like this, she couldn't be seen as a provider of sex nor one of temptation so she retained her modesty.

Her suppers were famously, handsomely and wisely, heavy as lead. A man with a bulging stomach will think less about bulging trousers.

Mitch sat down next to the new border, Mr. Bill. The last house Mitch was in, provided a bowl and spoon and you better be fast with your reach. At the Mrs. he had a plate, knife and fork. There was a spoon tonight so that meant either a soup or stew.

A central platter contained the pieces of three rabbits with a separate gravy boat of jugged rabbit blood. There were two, still warm, loaves of bread. There was a thick pea soup with bacon fat and a baked apple and rice pudding. They ate until it was all gone. She heard each of them belch and look a little stiff eyed. They all had black coffee.

She left for her rooms and heard them go to bed around eight. She cleaned up then. She pumped up some water from the cistern. Having an indoor pump made all the difference. Her parents would have been amazed. In New York they had to buy drinking water from a horse and cart. Even then it could be bad. She set a large pot on the stove to warm up some water and another with cool water for a rinse. She tossed some kindling into the stove to hasten the heat. A large bowl sat on the counter. It held enough dough to make four loaves of bread. It was waiting to be punched down for a second rise. She brushed her hair back across her forehead and dealt with the dishes. She brought in some wood for the morning cooking, wiped the dishes dry, hung the pots and punched down the bread. By ten o'clock everything was as it should be.

She glanced out the window. The chicken coup was quiet. She sat at the table and poured out two fingers of whisky. She added some hot water, a dab of butter and a tea spoon of sugar. A hurricane lamp lit the kitchen. She turned the wick down and sipped her drink. She would sleep a deep sleep for six hours and have the bread loaves in the oven by the time the first heavy boots hit the floor. The men had mugs of coffee as they sat at the table. By the time their first cup was downed the table was set with a hot breakfast. On Mondays they tended to eat in silence.

Leadville men were hairy. Their beards were full, their hair was long. They wiped their mouths with their shirt sleeves, bandannas and handkerchiefs. They burped in admiration of good meals. One by one they left taking a wax paper wrapped bundle for lunch. They met their wagons for the ride to the mines.

The mines were a lot of fun. Some guy, who guessed he knew how, would erect reinforcing timbers as they went along. The days were twelve hours long and there were six of them in a week. In the early days miners with experience and real knowledge were highly desired and cut themselves great deals. They would smash rock and move rock and dig gravel and smash more rock in dim light. They would squint with unprotected eyes as their picks kicked up slivers and shards of razor sharp particles.

They would sweat and grunt for half an hour and then shuffle to the ice room. An internal chamber filled with ice blocks, hauled down from the nearby mountains, would give them relief from the 135 to 150 degree temperatures. Then they would trudge back with ice shards in their pants and hats, back to their tools and squint and smash for another half hour and hope nothing bad would happen. It was a really good idea to get out before you started spitting blood. Everyone kept their ear out for share prices. The wages were high. They were high enough for professional miners to migrate from Ireland and Pennsylvania. A clear headed man could pay room and board and be able to send fifteen dollars a week back home or provide a nest egg for as much of his family as possible for the trip over. If a man stayed away from spinning wheels, one armed bandits, footpads, knives, liquor and bullet holes, choices opened up.

They toiled in back-breaking, dark, filthy, dangerous pain for nearly every waking hour. It was difficult to not be drawn to the light of gay hilarity and sudden success. Saving has always proved to be the most boring thing in the world. It's way more fun to spend.

"Flour is a dollar pound this week," she thought. She would have to put her prices up. As it was, she was adding oatmeal and grains. There was a shortage of everything with the influx of men. Demand far exceeded supply. A barrel of nails took up as much space as a barrel of flour. Oysters just went down, from a dollar a piece to five cents, as speculators flooded the market.

She would have to have a successful garden this year with many preserves and relishes to get through. She started to calculate the cost and the possibility of selling the excess. On Tuesdays she went to tea with some other ladies. Tomorrow's discussion was to revolve around mining shares, raising money for a new church and a pie contest. Some of the nuns promised to come. They were busy with doings in the hospital and so their presence would be exciting. They were learning to be tolerant of Papists. "Those heathen Episcopalians are planning on putting up a church to Saint George," she thought. Everyone was getting ahead. Legends were being made by laundresses charging a pinch of silver for a clean shirt. A thumb of silver for a piece of pie. She must visit one of the bucket shops for investment advice on railroad bonds.

Getting to Leadville was the thing, be it horse, wagon or walking in with the breeze. The railroad would get there by July 1880 to welcome a summer of transportation. In fact, all kinds of lines had been drawn on rail road maps. Hundreds of men were cutting ties in camps. Naturally, competing camps shot at each other.

There were still enough empty pockets and graft to go around before a steam whistle would be blown. The railroad was creating nations and empires, pumping energetic blood back and forth. You took a risk or took nothing.

Railroad men, mechanics, Chinese, stockholders, cows, dime-novel western writers and train robbers, all depended on those tracks.

The best of industrial civilization was being built and afforded by the fortune of metal mines. Hydraulics, engineering, physics and dynamite would come together to form a prestigious institution of learning. The mines would last for over a hundred years. The self made and self motivated and self dependent man had not yet discovered teenagers, possibly because middle age was fifteen and old age thirty. The frontiers were full of men who just didn't give a damn except to get a piece of whatever there was to have.

To live, for Geisel, meant to record the lives of others. His wagon, all of wood and converted over from a sundries articles and hardware wagon, rolled in to Park City, June, 1879. It was two more miles to Leadville. The wagon was full of glass plates. He had bottles, jars, cans and packets full of precious liquids and powders. From his uncle Sylvester in Boston he had learned the fine art of daguerreotypes but when he explored the fine world of glass negatives with their vastly superior images, he saw the future upside down through a wooden box. He fixed images, washing the fix back and forth, inhaling familiar fumes.

The cabin revealed itself. The stiffly standing men stood unsmiling, looking back at his camera, surprised by the magnesium flash. They crowded around the thin little man. He showed them images. They were amazed. He was a little scared of them but was careful to not put on any airs. He wondered if he could charge five dollars a photo and looked forward to town.

The inside of his wagon carried a dozen wooden boxes with glass plates held in slots about an eighth of an inch apart so they wouldn't touch to scratch or shatter. Photos of the new west was his dream. The point at which man and nature were separated by their will, force against force. Would one lose? Would they merge? Are all relationships symbiotic? Would free will be cut into the mountains? Everything changes. Only change is permanent – that and a photo. He was finally going to live.

He hated the mundane pictures he made for lockets and family mantle places. He and his uncle argued but in the end he didn't want the family business. He wanted adventure. He wanted people to see what he saw. He wanted to bring the photos back to Boston. He wanted his uncle to be proud. He was inspired by pictures of the terrible civil war. He would be the bystander. The undeclared participant. The follower. The wheels went round and round. He'd grease the axles again tonight. His wagon was his home. It was his everything. It was his life. The contents, his soul and future. No one had seen this before. He'd seen Carleton Watkins landscapes from the 1860's and they pulled him. Timothy O'Sullivan's wet plates were proof of grim awe and borrowed reality, in a way, that astonished Geisel when he'd seen them. Matthew Brady's pictures of the civil war inspired hundreds to the medium.

He brought the wagon to the apparent edge of the park. The road was a hard packed muddy trail about twenty feet wide. The area itself was thick with three and four hundred foot pines. Their trunks, great. The moving green canopy, awesome and grand.

Outside of an ice age and occasional fire, the trees had never witnessed destruction before. Thin creeks ran here and there. Geisel saw a man step out of his cabin as he turned his horses off the road. "Hey. It be alright if I water and rest here for a few days?" The cabin like most of the others was smooth wooden plank. Circular saw blades had found there way into the jungle.

The man gave a nod. "Free country."

Geisel loosened the straps and buckles and tethered the horses near a creek. He'd only walked twenty feet in with the beasts when he was in a jungle. No one had stepped here before. The fauna was ancient. The humus sprang back under his feet. He went back to the wagon to prepare some feed. He looked over the wheels. "I've got a few loose bands and spokes here. Think there is a decent Smith in town?" He noticed the man still standing there sipping out of a tin cup.

The horses had found some blue berries and were licking the branches dry. A dog came hobbling out to stand beside Zeke, the man with the tin cup. The dog was blind in one eye and missing a leg. Scampers loved his master and never left the property.

"I seen photographs before. What are you going to take pictures of?"

"Modern times, sir. My name is Geisel." He walked over with his hand out. "I'm making photographs of right here and right now. Looks like you've been dug in for awhile."

"Yep. Came in last year with a partner. We hit the digs right away. Our claim is down stream by a small falls."

He set up camp and began to unload. He wanted to take some pictures of the outlying area. The center of the road was what he had in mind. Explaining a view or moment in time was so easy now with the fabulous wet plate picture. Unthinkable really, just fifty years ago. *The Silver Sunbeam* by John Towler was his bible. Published in 1864 it had been the supplement to his current skills and absent uncle's advice.

He felt like an instant picture. He opened the rear wagon steps and flipped them down. He looked along the shelves and built in cabinets and trunks. He pulled out the twenty gallon water barrels and set up a table. Inside, he set up several trays and found the right jars and packets. He un-boxed the scales. He gathered some wood and kindling to start a fire and then brought the water jugs to where the horses were tethered. Once there he filled the jugs and brought them back by horse. In his continuing pursuit he set the water to heat in a kettle. He filled a tray with Mawsons Original Colloidal Solution and added enough warm water to turn it to a syrup. He set up the camera, arranged the tripod and attached the hood. Each glass plate rested in a slotted wooden case specially lined with felt in a wooden box in a trunk lined with cotton.

The cabinets were filled with labeled small boxes and bottles. Other cases contained a scale, magnifying glass, funnels, Bunsen burner, flasks, thermometers and two large field cameras.

There were protective awnings about the wagon. His bunk doubled as a lab work table top to hold the trays intended to wash and prepare the glass plates. He was getting use to it. His set up took less than two hours to prepare. It was late afternoon and he could take a test plate or two. He hadn't inspected his outfit for a week and was anxious that it should be intact. In over fifteen hundred miles of travel he'd only broken a single test tube. He had bottles of ether, packets of iodide of lithium, bromide of lithium, nitrates of silver. He had small boxes and tins of iron sulphate and lead nitrate, formic acid and potassium cyanide. He would inhale pyrogallic acid, nitric acid and collodion. The alcohol and ether mix sometimes made him feel woozy.

He set the camera up a few feet away and focused it on Zeke's cabin, showing the road in its background. He tossed the black hood over his head, sighted the picture and arranged the lens. Done, he slipped the lens cap back into place.

Outside, the colloidal syrup just needed a stir. He tipped two plates in the bath and then held them out allowing the thick film to drain off. At that point he took them through the double door into the dark wagon and plunged them into a silver nitrate bath. His red kerosene lamp showed the glass foggy, so he treated it with a pinch of potassium cyanide. Pleased, he washed his hands in a jug of water and transferred the dripping wet glass to a portable sealed wooden frame. This he carried to the camera and slid into place. Flipping a latch he pulled the frame away leaving the glass plate in place. Drips fell from the camera to the grass below.

"Ready. Hold on!"

He removed the lens cap allowing the image of light to strike the plate. Checking his pocket watch he replaced the lens cap after twenty seconds. He ducked back under the camera hood, sneezed from the fumes and sealed the glass plate back into its light impervious frame and went to the wagon. He submersed the plate into an iron sulphate and vinegar wash. Within another fifteen minutes he washed the plate again and brought it outside to show Zeke.

"Amazing, a totally independent instant picture."

"Wait. I'll make a copy," he placed a prepared sheet of paper, treated with egg white against the glass and pressed it together, leaving it face up towards the sun. The rays of the sun would eventually burn the image onto the card stock. There was a dark blur in the corner, being as the dog needed to pee before posterity.

Geisel un-tethered the horses and hitched them back to the wagon to continue into California Gulch. He heard the sweetest violin music he'd heard in a long time. The landscape changed abruptly. The trees were mostly gone. It was a sea of one room log cabins. The violin player's cabin was a fortress. Twelve logs high with the bark still on. Twelve feet long. Five more logs ran across to compose the base for a roof that was gently sloping with a hole cut out for a Franklin stove.

There was a single door. The roof was plank. There were no windows. It took fifty four interlocking logs. The logs were the thickness of telegraph poles. These structures would survive the weight and drifts of Rocky Mountain winters.

A half dozen men watched his approach. The wagon jostled back and forth as its wheels ran in and out of ruts and bumps. The men were lying on the ground, leaning against the walls and sitting on boxes. Long rifles, shovels and picks were nearby. The man playing the violin had a grand smile. His mustache and beard were painstakingly groomed and trimmed. Several men were wearing buckskin jackets covered in fringes and hanging to their knees like robes. A young man brought out a frying pan full of biscuits and passed them around. Beaver, fox and otter pelts were tacked and stretched across the exterior log walls. It looked so typical and normal.

He brought the wagon to a stop, nodded to them and got off.

"The name is Geisel, sir. I take photograph pictures and I'd like to take yours."

"Five dollars," the man said.

Geisel thought it was a question, "No. I'd do it for free, even give you a copy."

"For you to have the immeasurable delight of preserving my image and taking the thunder of my soul I would demand five gold dollars or perceive injury," Buckskin Joe said.

Geisel opened his eyes.

The speaker wore his gun high on his right hip. If he hung his arms straight down the handles touched his elbow. He had fifty cartridges on his gun belt. His pant legs were tucked into his boots. He wore a necklace of purple stones. A wide, foot long knife blade hung under his jacket to his knee. He had wide cheek bones and long hair to just below his shoulders. His hair was parted in the middle.

Butcher Knife Bill laughed at Geisel. He first met his violin playing partner, Buckskin Joe in 1862 when they were on opposite sides, shooting at one another during the civil war. Bill wore a Bowler hat in contrast to Joe's wide brimmed Stetson. Bill wore a bow tie with a white shirt with a grey vest and a matching two button jacket. Both had well waxed mustache tips. They looked more like Boston business men then prospectors. Almost dandified in dress. These men had a way of standing and sitting that beamed a commanding owner ship of all the space they could see. Here, present and alive they had climbed to the highest point in the world over the bodies of a hundred hard fought animals and men to plunge their hands into the earth for gold and planned to explore further jungles competing with others of their kind. They were normal for their time.

Geisel wanted to do more than just take pictures. He wanted to write about each picture and compose a book about it. It would be a photo essay. Everyone back east was fascinated by the west. It would be a best seller. He wondered about the costs though. If he could sell enough by subscription, perhaps he could convince someone to underwrite it.

"Is he gonna try and take something that isn't his?" asked Butcher Knife Bill.

"Says he's gonna just take our photo, worth five dollars and run."

"Didn't we just hang some turkey and clothes line thieves like that?"

"No. The town council voted to hang them if they didn't leave town in four hours. Said if they ever came back it was the noose. They left in one hour. Now, is taking a turkey the same thing as taking a man's image?"

Geisel could see they all had the wrong idea. They weren't the simple backwoods buffoons that he thought he'd first encountered. He decided to show them some photos he'd printed and reached in to his breast pocket.

Their eyes burned on to his hand and he was careful to pull it out slow and he distributed some prints.

Men were living and moving all over the mountains. Patrick had staked out an acre. He'd followed a stream, saw a few Utes and was shoveling. A few days went by and he started felling trees for a cabin. He slept under a lean to of boughs. During the night Broken Face Al and Cross eyed Stan stabbed the prospector/homesteader in the chest. They took everything he had, buried his body, noted his stakes and filed a claim at the mining office in town. It turned out to be a good mine. They sold it for twenty thousand dollars the next week.

"It wasn't tent city anymore. Yeah, of course that is we were down to just two hundred or so by seventy-six. The elephant dream was somewhere else so sure, there were lots of empty cabins at one point. Then the news got out about the silver extractions. That first spring and summer there were plenty of tents." The Ginger kid dealt some cards around.

There was a boom in the construction of log cabins. They had to be built well. Buckskin Joe's place had solid beam cross members. It might have been possible for hundred mile an hour plus winds to rip a plank off the roof but the roof itself wouldn't cave in under the weight of snow.

Butcher Knife Joe had been snowshoeing for the better part of an hour. He hadn't seen Jim and Donny for a week. Just as a hello he had brought some coffee and a quart of whisky. Jim and Donny had come all the way from Cork Ireland and had set up in the fall.

They established their claim against a ravine wall by an outcropping with a stretch going into the trees. Their shack was built into the overhang into the mountain wall. Butcher Joe was coming to the bend in the trail that led to a dip that brought him to the face they were digging into.

The dip wasn't there. From where he stood he saw only a flat white plain even with his current footing. There was no valley, no smokestack. He imagined about where the cabin was and estimated it to be under forty feet of snow. He stood there for awhile and let out a sigh. The logs and timbers of the cabin were spread and crushed. The roof had started to splinter. They heard each other pray in the dark as the walls slowly pushed in.

Joe would go back to town and tell the others. A group would come the next day and dig out the frozen bodies.

Chapter Five - Gentleman Joe

It had been a good night. In fact it was one of the reasons he came up. Gentleman Joe left San Francisco and took the stage to Leadville. He slipped a watch out of his vest. It was midnight. They'd agreed on final hands by then. He'd taken on all comers. The cards went his way all night. He carried six hundred dollars in folding money and another thousand in gold.

"Final shot of panther juice, Ben?"

"That's fine, Joe." They bumped shoulders.

Ben Guggenheim had agreed to walk with Joe back to the Grand Hotel. There was still plenty of traffic out front. One of the small time miners had been upset over losing two hundred dollars and almost accused Joe of cheating. Joe didn't need to cheat. He knew the odds by heart. He had a bigger stake on the table. And every time the miner got a face card his left eyebrow would go up. If he got a pair he reached for his pipe. If he had nothing, he'd check his cards three times.

Ben listened as Joe gave him the tells.

"Amazing," said Ben, "but true."

Joe parted with Ben, hid the money in his room and left for Tiger Alley off sixth. He quickly opened the door of a building and slipped inside. There were doors on either side of a hallway. He selected one towards the end marked with the number eight.

A woman opened the door at his knock and let him in. There were two rooms with a high ceiling. The floors were covered in rich, thick, Persian carpets. Gold brocade and burgundy ropes trimmed the dark blue walls. There were long couches and chairs with lion paw feet. Framed colourful prints tilted forward from the walls. Velvet curtains covered the window. There were five other people there. On the coffee table, beside the couch, was a hookah. On the other end of the hose was a fresh faced daughter of the Silver Mountain set. Her eye lids were at half mast and minty, white, smoke drifted from her nostrils. Gentleman Joe had his own but had purchased an additional black ball of gum and paid a small entrance fee after entering. He sat on a Victorian easy chair, sinking into its rich ornate cushions. He pinched three grams, about fifty cents worth of opium and dropped it into the hookah. He kept thinking about his last couple of hands and then visualized a seven of hearts. He fell into the heart. He felt its redness. He tasted the seven of diamonds next. A magic carpet slowly transported him about the room. His eyes and brain ebbed back and forth. His skin sung and vibrated into ecstasy. He spasmed. Occasionally a wave would grab him and pull him up and he would smile. The woman lying on the couch was laughing. After three hours he stood up. The hostess showed him to a wash basin.

"Yes. Thank you, Millie," he whispered.

He poured some water into the bowl and washed his face and hands. He leaned against the wall for a moment and then felt OK to go back to The Grand.

Gentleman Joe walked along the boardwalk. There were clumps of three and four men here and there. The sky was dark and the air crisp. No one bothered him. A few people noticed him. Some knew him. Some didn't. Either way, anyone who wore two pistols with eyes like that probably didn't want to be bothered. Joe would go back to his room and sleep until six in the evening. He would rise. He would take a great supper from the hotel's legendary kitchen. He would gamble until midnight. It had been the same in San Francisco.

Gentleman Joe had been on the pipe for about a year. He found it a refreshing reward for the manic highs and lows of the card game. It was how he made a living. His roll was slowly growing. He looked forward to bigger games. There were a half dozen banks in town. He choose Tabor's. The safe was massive. Hired guns watched it. The bank was safe. It was a prize of course but it would have meant wading through a town full of thousands of guns. Most were a fair shot. The best way, everyone knew, was to rob a stage coach with its rich customers trying to take their wealth out.

Anyone who didn't trust banks, which was most after so many memories of bank failures, had to carry their gold and cash out. That meant the stage or wagon or horse until the railroad came in 1880. Then that could get robbed too.

Quietly slipping out of town was an art. Joining a wagon train or group either way, made the most sense.

Ned walked up the outside stairs. Black Thumb Bob and Neiderguy might be in. He knocked on the door. It rattled. He was "Hallowed," and pushed it in. It was a big one room apartment with a Franklin stove. The boys were sprawled out. Bottles, corks, caps, blackened spoons, funnels and a makeshift spittoon cluttered the place. There were grins on both their faces. Neiderguy held up an empty palm and made cricket noises. He thought he was chirping out a greeting sound. Neiderguy had his own flask of whisky and poured some into a cup. He added some burnt coffee from a pot on the stove. Neiderguy continued chirping. Black Thumb Bob said, "Have you heard from Molly?"

Ned made a sign of the cross and took a swig from a narrow small bottle with a torn label on it. He stroked his beard and pulled. "The Mollys are coming. The Mollys are coming. The Mollys are here." He pointed at the slat wood floor. "Right here," he hissed.

They heard some gunshots outside. It wasn't so close they cared. Ned felt his eyeballs glow red. The shots, pills and smoke were starting to sink in. He liked the Mollys and they him. His grandfather had been a pirate and so he'd learned the value of silence. A mob of Mollys could seethe and boil like a cauldron of snakes, thirsting for freedom from want and heat and the lynch. The thought of tying a rope tight around the neck of his foreman was inspiring.

He noticed a cloud of cannabis smoke pouring in his direction. The room was filled with top quality fog. The fog immersed him. In one chair, sat a cricket wearing a Bowler hat. In the other, by the table, a small moose was fiddling with the mendicants. The sound of a piano came drifting in. There was an accordion too. The window vibrated with colour. A woman flew by the window all in white. Ned picked up another bottle of pills and rattled them back and forth.

The cricket got upset as it was scared of garter snakes. "Bitter foul gum of noise and racks of haste and sharpness fill the void of spastic vibrating youth.! Live on your knees proud beholders of ancient destiny. Live on your knees for freedom," it said.

The cricket fell into the mattress. It chirped and drank some whisky. Ned got on his hands and knees and crawled to the window. He glanced out. The city was black with silver. The pockets of men bulged with gold. Now there were several women flying back and forth in front of the window. One held up a sign, "Buggy ride to Ireland, fifty cents." He knew he had fifty cents. He dug in the pocket of his vest and pulled out a large ball of vegetable gum. It was black. There was another knock at the door. No one knew what to do. It opened. Dutch Honey walked in laughing. She drew up a chair, pulled the hem of her skirt above her ankles and took off her hat. "It'll be work to catch up to you boys," she laughed. They smiled.

"...don't exhale until it's time to inhale," someone said.

Leonhard Summer was riding in on his horse, Maggie. A dark haired stallion from Mississippi. He was still ten miles from Oro City.

He saw the backside of a man walking along the trail. He was carrying a bag on a stick.

"Halloo. What's up, stranger?" he shouted ahead as he approached.

"Names, Jack," the man stopped, "I've been on the road since Kansas City, on my way to Leadville," he doffed his hat.

"Sorry you couldn't get a stage," Leonhard said, "I can ride you in the last few miles."

"Oh that's a kind offer but I'll tell you, guess what? Old rail road Neil, he bet me three hundred and fifty dollars that I couldn't walk to Leadville from Kansas City in just ten days. Allen is gonna just howl when he finds out. You can be part of my proof. Ha."

Leonhard admired the man's desire and ability to keep a bet honest and continued on his way. He gave some thought as to where to camp. The next morning he started his campfire and got up to make some coffee and biscuits. The sun slowly curved on a high line.

He heard a moan and saw some movement off to the right in a clump of brush and rock. The horse caught it first, twitching an ear. Sam pulled his pistol right away, hunkered low in the saddle and came close.

It was a man. He was scarcely breathing. He was naked and in great pain, lying at the base of a tree. "Ug. Ah. Oh." The man said. His mouth opened to gasp for air, showing a pink hole, in contrast to the surface of the rest of his body. His skin was thick with black tar and matted feathers. His rolling and dragging had collected additional twigs, weeds and grass. He'd given up rubbing the crap off his skin. His ribs hurt from where he'd been kicked. His breathing was increasing. Sam looked closer. The man was near death. The beatings, the exposure and the toxic oil leeching into his skin were driving him into a coma. He'd been vomiting for several hours. He barely noticed the sun and his hands clutched at the grass, grinding dirt under his finger nails.

"What a wretch," thought Sam. He walked away and got back on his horse. Tarred and feathered, the man would die soon. There was no where to take him, certainly not from where he just came from. So that left death. He'd of shot him if he asked. He didn't. He left him to his fate. He rode in silence and looked forward to a mug of beer.

Jacob's mine employed eight men. They worked for shares and five dollars a day. After three weeks they were pulling out five thousand ounces of gold a day and another six thousand of silver. They were wealthy and filthy. On Sundays they wore bowler hats and visited the parlors. Most of the original mines had sold their shares up in a couple of months leaving their positions to men with regular wages as they now had something and preferred to live to spend it.

Ben Guggenheim had spent the afternoon with Taylor and Beech. They were a couple of commission salesmen who'd given him the tour of a pair of mines. Their walls had breeched an underground stream and both mines flooded. Once the deed had been registered, Taylor and Beech spent the afternoon laughing and talking about how smart they were.

"A.Y.? Minnie?" Gentleman Joe said.

Joe had heard of the mines, "Last I hear, Ben they were played out six months ago. I read about it in the Carbonite Weekly. Nice numbers for the first fifty feet then nothing, then water. I can hear them laughing from here."

"I'll drain the mines and plug the holes. Their laughter will ripen to hysterics I suppose. Who will build museums to my ineptitude?"

The Carbonite Weekly and the Leadville Herald often combined their literary talent with out of town journalists to produce vast empty barrels of liquor. They laughed and pointed and slapped the table. They welcomed Gazetteers from other states and across the ocean. They told their tales in rapid fire succession.

Charles Dow said, "For the first time in twenty years the US is able to pay off its debts in silver. This is very exciting. A great influx of change, mountains high, bring investment and employees of real foreign Kings, Dukes and Potentates. I came in last year from Providence, Rhode Island and am paying the first two rounds."

After a year of watching men shoot and scream, as caged bears and bulls fought one another on a bet, he was writing his final dispatch from Leadville. The Providence Rhode Island Journal had faithfully printed his articles. The gold strikes, silver strikes and stock exchanges, he noted, had everything to do with ending the depression. Now he would take his notes and follow the money back east to New York. His uncle would arrange several formal dinners. In New York he would meet and tell hair raising whoppers to another promising young man, Edward Jones.

He filled Jones' glass and said, "Hi. I'm Dow."

Fields full of precious metals were sprinkled with hyacinth and mules ear. Blue wind flowers and daises would compete with high pressure hoses intent on washing them into sluices. The men of the world. Adventurers, trappers, traders, cooks and crooks lusted for gold. The infinite supply of the stuff overwhelmed all other desires. Desire drew gold. Mountains of silver cracked heads, spun wagon wheels, consumed boat loads of provisions while motivating men to shoot, squander, spend and fight in the business of free gold. It was a story that pulled at every newspaper and magazine in the world. Between the Zulus fighting the British and the lawless empire of wealth in Colorado, Leadville, both were flooded by journalists from every part of the globe.

Confidence men, pick pockets and schemers of malfeasance were alerted to the heavy purse. The black hearted, smooth talking, sand ticks of the American desert were blown up hill to Leadville. They were glib, friendly and talkative. They were secretive, quiet and worked in pairs and groups. They worked as lone timber wolves and wild eagles, quick to dart on familiar prey.

Vultures ripped at the carrion's flesh. His surface was no good but since he had stopped screaming, the flim-flam man had proved to be a delightful taste treat. "He got his intentionality wrong," said one of the vultures. It ripped at some soft rotten meat.

No longer was he charging rent on rooms he didn't own. Now he would live freely strewn about the woods. New comers were coming in at such a rate, that he'd rented out a room for himself and then fraudulently accepted rent in advance, posing as the landlord, from eight different people in one afternoon. His plan to take the stage to Denver had been embarrassed by two hood-winked customers who saw him get on. His hands were occupied by carpet bags as his eyes followed two hammer locked Colts. The gun owners looked angry and mean.

Peter Koper said, "He's got the kind of face you wouldn't get tired of kicking." They'd already been fueled by liquor and would later spread the news to other disappointed tenants which would directly lead to his rib kicking stomp out and tar baby suit. His long career from east to west stopped about then. His snake oil plans for Denver were unrealized.

Koper was kicking the back of his head, wishing he had his fifteen dollars rent money back. Housing couldn't be built fast enough and competition for space was fierce.

Lewis Kent observed the scuffle and dragging of the man by the stage. He was delighted that the city should live up to its reputation with no delay. He had telegrammed ahead, selecting a fine room at The Grand Hotel.

Sweetwater Sally shuffled up to the apothecary counter. Her skin was yellow. She was missing a tooth. The hem of her skirt was dirty and frayed. She looked guilty and upset. She pushed her hair up while waiting. She smiled when she slid a five cent piece across the counter.

"Three grains," the druggist said. "It's hardly worth weighing."

"Please," her eyes were sunken in pits like shallow graves.

He walked over to his balance and with a scalpel neatly sliced off .19 grams of opium. A fifth of a gram. Hardly even one pull on the hose. A grain was .064 grams. She was a long way from her joyful dollar a day habit. He stuck the black gum smear onto a piece of paper, folded it and gave it to her. She leapt on it with both dirty hands and pulled it to her. She turned and headed to an alley. She sat down inside a wheeless wagon, pulled out her pipe and carefully lit her match. She drew the smoke down and knew she would be good until noon. The edge would be off until then.

The Martian canals were still in the news. Prospectors wondered about placer mining in a gulch on Mars. "It's pretty obvious their engineering skills are strong." He wondered what they used for dredging equipment. "Maybe there is a Martian Tom Sawyer on a raft up there somewhere. What if Jules Verne met Mark Twain?"

Dr. Adam Baulm couldn't stop promoting, "We'll get there in giant cannon balls or hot air balloons. There will be hundreds of flights a day."

"You could sell shares in an outfit like that," they all laughed.

"Say, we could fire the giant cannon balls from the balloons."

"Now that is sensible. I look forward to the assays."

Otter Dave was tired from putting up a fence but had to earn fifty cents if he wanted to see Lovilla. Big Stinky worked at a livery stable. Coffin Trader put an incense stick in a beer bottle. Drum Pixie was making some fudge. Mr. Twinkle swept the shavings off the floor of his shop. Lovilla wanted another dozen pillows for her bed. White Bull put a deer head beside the door. Mouser Man threw a stick for his dog. Undertaker cleaned his pistols one at a time. Railroad Bill was getting twenty dollars a week kick-back for coal. Pop Gun Tony had a shotgun behind his back in an arrow holder. Au Contraire pulled a rose coloured garter up her thigh.

Silver Moose won a pinch of dust throwing a hatchet. Lumber Jack Dave bought a bowie knife. Loony Leo's hands shook as he twisted the cork out of a bottle of Mrs. Winslow's Soothing Syrup. Rainmaker stared out the window at a dog drinking from a puddle. Longshot Ed put a nickel in the slot machine. Juicy Lucy put six mugs of beer on a tray. Silver Hand Bart had a straight. Hen Eggs Sally put six bread loaves in the oven. Frenchy kept his dog on a chain.

Like any good detective, Lance the Pinkerton man, had found a reason to respond to his client's wish. He'd found a trace and followed the sign to Denver and then maybe beyond that.

She was nearby. She'd taken a position running a small grocery. Her enthusiasm saturated the air. Her memory was profound. Her daughter, Raven filled with grace and a mind twice as sharp as a barber's razor. Her husband had been shot out of a tree by a communist neighbour mistaking him for a giant owl. It was that journal notice that had found Mr. Lancer's attention.

"Wacky Owl Leaves Lady In Lurch In Leadville."

Mr. Lance finished eating his toast and looked at the masthead. The Rat Bastard Gazette had published the article. Working for Pinkertons kept him abreast of as much news as he could handle. This edition was from three weeks earlier and came from Leadville. He wouldn't send his client a guess so he packed for the trip.

"We'll miss you in San Francisco, Lance. Better bring a double fist full of iron. You're walking right into it. You after Jesse James? He's up there."

"No. I'm looking for love."

"What?"

"Love, magic, chocolate, family, unicorns and the whole dam thing." He adjusted his shoulder holster and stuffed a Derringer into his hat. "Affair of the heart." He checked the barrel of his Colt.

"Look up Frank Smith while you're there. Collect a glass of whisky for me."

Lance smiled, "That part of an old war story?"

"Yeah, we dug a few ditches. He looked over Pinkerton's but in the end, well Smith's the detective up there, works straight for the Mayor."

"What are you looking for in Leadville, Lance?"

Lance said, "Some guy's heart. He lost it. Lost his pride, lost his family, lost his daughter, lost his mind, lost respect. Nothing left for him to do but want."

Brown Eyed Cecil's heart had felt better days. She was leaving for he didn't know where. She was taking her daughter and going somewhere, maybe Canada.

They spent a week of love and were pulled apart by previously set in forces of madness. It took ten years for him to recover any balance at all.

A Pinkerton's man found a rumour of her in Timmons at some gold camp. Then a trace near Fort Kingston on a reserve near Carrying Place. Then nothing for a year. So he answered the query, " Did he wish the investigation to continue?"

It was a trial. A burning in his eyes. Cecil's chest ached. He wrote another cheque. He had a faded photo. Tomorrow he would think of other things while he ate another slice of the world. He'd lost everything he owned, in the world, six times. At this point, in the swing of his pendulum, he'd gotten back on top seven times and so was of good mood and clear headed. He put on a freshly ironed suit.

Dutch Honey was inhaling on a hookah hose, bubbling smoke. She stopped, took a sip of wine and continued bubbling. She slouched in the over stuffed chair by a window. She carried three Derringers. One was biting into her hip. Out of habit she left it there. Gradually the minor pain went away. The tonic kept her perky though. She lit a candle in the middle of the table. Even though it was still daylight out, it cast a cheery glow.

She put her feet up on a stool not caring if her chums saw her ankles or not. Her hair was full and thick. Her lips were a deep red. Her eyes had the well trained look of innocence.

She knew the promise of tomorrow. Life was fun like a successful adventure. She pushed back her hair and watched people walk into the bookstore across the street.

A customer was ranting at the bookstore clerk, "French? Why? Do you have some new filth by Zola in? Thomas Hardy makes me puke. *Return of the Native* or *Tom Sawyer*? Mark Twain, now that's real story telling. Still I don't know how we'll replace George Sands."

Mishka needed to slap the customer with a chair. Mishka had been clerking at John Leininger's bookstore for three months while John rolled up his sleeves and went prospecting with a mule and a bible. He was astonished that the store existed at all. But tough people are not stupid people. They devoured newspapers from last month. They purchased tickets in advance for plays and operas. Tabor had built an opera house. They were capable of building a civilization.

Last week, Mishka stabbed a French Count in the face when the count said, "Henry James is an impudent buffoon who doesn't know his place. Only an American would hold a trollop like Daisy for public witness." This forced Mishka's hand.

The Count found himself waking up on top of a dead cat in the alley. His cheek was gashed. His suit was covered in mud and garbage bits. Mishka was a loyal subscriber to *The Atlantic Monthly*. "The pillars of society sent him running, like a cat on fire, for his Swinburne. I had no choice," Mishka said.

They all laughed.

"Let's see. One and a half bushels of Dwarf Bean seeds, ten quarts of corn seed, two pounds of cucumber seed, two bushels of peas, eight bushels of potatoes and four pounds of squash and one Planet Junior Combined drill, wheel hoe, cultivator and plough. Yes, sir. I'll sign right here."

"They paid the freight and everything," said Captain Gifford.

"I gotta admit Vick's is the best. They got my money." Mr. Flowers started loading his wagon.

"I've got fifteen acres cleared so this will be the first planting. Hand me that bushel."

They filled the wagon with boxes and bags, including a splendid assortment of flower seeds. He looked forward to putting in the seed. The land was wet and ready.

His dog barked as they pushed up the gate on the wagon.

"That truck should keep." Mr. Flowers tossed the dog a baked pig's ear.

"Yep, now just fight the traffic out." He offered a clay jug to his pal. "Next year we'll be drinking my own special liquor. Real Alabama corn shine. You won't mind it." He thought about making a still. It was a most wonderful day.

At the foot of Mount Elbert, about 23 miles away, the three cousins drank well and admired Glacier Lake.

"We want some fine meals, real meals. This will be our last night. The best you've got." The cousins had slick haircuts and lounged at the Interlaken Hotel.

"Yeah, what you give Tabor and his buddies for supper when they've hit it." He paid their lunch bill.

The matri'd was use to this. They had the clothes and the money. They had no idea of their wants. "We have the finest beef steak," he suggested.

"No. No," said Dennis. "We are stinking rich decadent capitalists. We don't want to be charged five dollars for a fifty cent steak we want a two hundred dollar meal, maybe even a three hundred dollar meal with desert. I heard you had a real chef back there."

"He is the best. He came from New York and he is the best," he defended then continued, "Very well. Of course. If you would care to consult our special menu for dignified persons you may please place the order and it will be ready for dinner, sirs."

"A two hundred dollar meal?"

"Oh I assure you sirs. It will be at least that." He offered them each a menu of four pages on stiff paper. It was tucked into a leather holder and separated by velvet markers of blue and red.

The boys sat, extending their lunch. They had been ordering pots of coffee and making notations and discussing the courses. After an hour and a half they had decided on their orders. They were informed that they may dine for eight o'clock.

The chef laughed and swore. "That is nothing. That is what I do. Ba. Not even a challenge. Where is that stupid pot washer? My pantry is in order. Get out of my way. I don't even want your help. Get out. Go change some table cloths."

The matrid'd left.

"It has to be fabulous. It must be fresh," thought the chef. He studied the order. Some spinal marrow of veal, sweet breads and a woodcock pie. A dish of blackbirds a la degrange, a striped bass with hollandaise. He expected the Pigeons a la valenciennes. Vegetables, sauces and Deserts of course...' "You. Prepare my timers. You, fill that pot with fresh bones. Make my ovens hot.'"

The fall menu reflected the local game but the preparations reflected the genius and dedication of the chef. He had spent three years as the number three chef at Delmonico's. Here anywhere west of Ohio he was a culinary god. No one could meet his measure. He had few peers in Haute Cuisine. He named his own salary and taking control of the kitchen wasn't even a question. Cleanliness and perfection determined by scrubbing, thermometers and timers were implicit in his scientific method which included paying attention to altitude.

"If you bite the hand that feeds you and you burn the bridges behind you, there is nowhere left to go but forward," Otter Dave winced and squinted. "There will be blood in the streets. That's how it'll be decided with your Knights of Labour or Mollys. When the rivers run red, when the creeks are full of corpses that's when you need friends more than you need flags. Me. I seen all that last decade. Across a plain, men running up a hill. The shooting and stabbing through a fog of blinding gunsmoke...it could happen here. They take too much. I can appreciate destiny and destiny to rule but doing so with such a squeezing iron fist, searching for the bottom, will only find rage. I don't know how much it's a matter of being right or wrong or just where one is placed. If you want to play at the table you have to play with the cards you're given, which is just a function of where you sit. The rest is all posture and back up cash."

"Agreed, but how much rage? Your Fenian cousins got crushed. The Grange movement crushed. Why should it be different now? I don't think the numbers are there. There are so many independents and the big miners all have their own militias like Tabor's Light Calvary. We'd be fighting each other."

Otter Dave said, "Well in the end I think Leadville has brought too much attention to itself. Law and order will come. It'll be just like back east, fences and all. There's enough treasure here to command the attention of armies. Which army dominates is what's of the greatest interest to me. I can't join an army for the protecting of these massive capitalist interests. Not on this scale."

"Tabor's larder would be no less full if he doubled the wages of each of his men tomorrow. His freedom to exploit must be countered by our freedom to strike and prevent anyone from taking our place. See how long this freedom town lasts."

Henry careful wound the gold thread around the blue veined stone. It would be linked with another in a series. To anyone looking it appeared to be an intricate necklace. He held some cobalt pebbles into the recesses of a dimpled piece of quartz about the size of two fists and shaped like a tetrahedron. He held the pebbles in place and hummed to himself as he snugged up the silver wire he was using and counted the windings. The piece of quartz had a hole neatly drilled down its center point of gravity leaving it perfectly balanced. Using electrolysis he'd gold plated a few of the rods that Harry had made for him. He slipped one of these in to the quartz and spun it. The gold center post encountered some friction so he smoothed it down until he was satisfied with its free movement. He had enough mercury to fill the tray, that would be its bed. That would come later. He pressed the necklace like thing into its clay form holder. It was still incomplete. The clay would insulate the floor from catching fire by resisting the heat.

Adam Baulm decided to visit the job printer, Inkslinger Charlie with his idea.

The printer was looking over a file of illustrated sheets. "You mean you actually want to sell these?"

Adam said, "Sure. It's a great idea. Who knows what's there?"

"How do you even know you can live there?

"Someone does. Someone in His image. The canals prove that. Giovanni gives us scientific proof of that. That was last year's headline around the world, 1877, Giovanni Schiaparelli observes canals on Mars. Canals, man. Canals. Newton's laws will determine weight, speed and trajectory. We have the technology we never had before. These are modern times. Never seen anything like it." Dr. Adam Baulm reached for a cigar.

Inkslinger Charlie looked at the drawing. He had a perfectly new Washington Press and could easily make the plates and pull off the certificates. "Cannon Ball Express – One Share," it would read. He took a rag and wiped a trail of ink off the side of the press.

Adam Baulm spit a cigar's tip onto the floor. "Imagine sitting in the comfort of a large deck chair while you casually coast to Mars. The outer walls would be coated with Indian rubber so the impact of landing would be slight. I've already thought about separate cannon balls for general live stock and construction materials. It would take awhile but soon they would be able to fire back cannon balls of their own, filled with Martian gold and silver. If we build them to the right specifications they could be reusable. There's money to be saved, right there."

"Ah. You've thought of that too," Charlie eyeballed the stock promoter. "I can print these up. I'll need a deposit and have them ready in five days. I've some jobs ahead of you."

"Hand bills for stores mainly and some for The Coliseum. I always leave a window open for them. They can have some pretty good dog fights and Mozart Clarinet quintets and such." He pulled out a sheet of blank paper. It was thick with rag content and well watermarked. "This would be a handsome certificate."

"Yes. Perfect."

The printer thought, if he already hadn't seen the telephone, the telegraph, air balloons and electricity he'd of pegged him for a crazy carpet bagger.

All the deciduous trees had lost most of their leaves, leaving the prouder coniferous varieties to prosper evergreen.

"The rabbits were fatter and slower," the chef thought as he stirred the jugged rabbit's blood. The quail tongues he'd already instructed to be diced with a third cup of walnuts. The forest had been a fine provider of porcupine bellies and some slow witted otters had provided the tails necessary as a consume dash to the onion soup garnished with a Parmesan cheese, worth more than its weight in gold. His bread pans. He'd insisted that the hotel provide bread pans made from Russian cast iron. "Anything else was obviously foolish," he thought as he observed the potato broth cooling in preparation for the bread dough.

He selected a calf's head from the cooler, put it back and took another of his preference. He was upset that the turtle meat was still in the field or rather up the creek.

Oliver had been earning money providing for the local menu and was in the process of returning with some fine specimens and some, hidden away, crayfish as well.

Buckskin Joe was eyeballing, what looked like, a growing manifestation of quartz. He was pulling a laden mule through some thick brush. It was all thick but sometimes it was thicker. The sweat was beading on his forehead and rolling down over his eyebrows to sting. This would be his last claim before winter. He would make his way south back to Leadville and formally register his claims.

The first step in getting gold is to keep it. That's one of those two thousand year old rules. Once the locations were duly noted his claim was first. Maybe some fancy claim jumper with a lawyer on the cuff would also lay a claim across his to complicate things but he was usually top side in these events. He might eventually take Tabor up on protecting his mines...if he got bored.

The mule trudged along heavy with samples for the assayer's office. Backed by a decent assayer certificate he might just sell a claim or two. It was always easier to sell than dig. The town had grown, even in the last three months, since he came in by stage. The road was crowded with all kinds of wagons in the rush before snow fell too thick. Goods could still come in by sleigh but it was less and not dependable. Merchants were placing larger orders. Some found themselves getting into the transportation business, having bought multiple delivery wagons and hired full time drivers.

Joe tied reins to the hitching post in front of the assayer's office. He took two heavy satchels off the mule and laid them down with a thud on the counter.

"I'll tell you what," the assayer said, "I'll have your results in three days." He pointed to a shelf of numbered canvas sacks.

Joe made sure his ore samples were labeled, took his receipts and made his way to the claims office. From there he had every intention of having some fun.

The Dead Dog Saloon wisely sold Dead Dog whisky to anyone that could stand up.

Some drunk said, "I saw a girl. A woman."

The drunk's pal said, "Go get her. I got three goats out back. Here's a bag. Forget Lincoln for a moment."

"No. I mean I like her." He slurred his words.

"Marry her. Then bring her back." He looked at his glass.

Joe ordered a bottle and sat down. The bar room was half full. Most of the tables had patrons. There was still plenty of standing room left at the counter. Quite a few faces had turned his way. His clothes were pure bright, amber, buckskin. From head to toe his soft tanned deer skin pants, jacket and shirt were bordered by a stream of foot long fringes at all the seams. He'd made it himself.

"You look like an injun." A man leaned with his back to the bar, "Or at least an injun lover. That what you are?"

Joe ignored the man and pulled a deck of cards out of his vest pocket and set it on the table. He swallowed half a shot of liquor and made to cut the cards.

"Your squaw let you drink liquor?" He laughed hard and nudged the man beside him.

Joe turned and looked. He pushed his long shoulder length hair out of the way and wondered if he would turn a good profit on his claims.

"Jesus," said Billy Two-Rivers, two tables away, "I think that's Buckskin Joe. "I was in Minneapolis and saw him walk a tightrope over St. Anthony Falls. Could be him, he was a short fella."

Joe stood up and turned to face the two men. He noticed their hands weren't that far from their gun belts. Joe looked them over, stuck out his tongue and smiled. He did a standing somersault, spinning feet over head in the air. While still air born he threw a knife with each hand into the right hand cuffs of each of the two men, firmly tacking their arms to the wooden bar. On landing, he then produced a large Colt in each hand from his two side holsters. He took a step forward and pushed the barrels into their surprised faces and past their teeth. "If I knew you any better I'd kill you both," he said.

"Yep, that's Buckskin Joe alright. Yep. I saw him walk a tightrope four stories up, pushing a wheelbarrow and then starting a nice little campfire in it to cook dinner. Wonder if he brought his orchestra with him." Billy drew on his pipe.

His drinking companion had a sour look on his face. He gestured with his chin. "These Canadians. Joe there, Canadian. Remember that Bat Masterson guy? Canadian. That Louis guy, what's his name, in Minneapolis? Red River Canadian. There's way too many Canadians here. They're Mayors and Sheriffs all over the place." He spit on the floor.

Buckskin Joe holstered his guns and retrieved his knives, giving each of the scared men a healthy smile. He turned his back on them with a grin and slowly walked back to his table. He sat down and returned his knives to their sheaths. The two men moved real slow and backed away, out the door, into the cold wind. Buckskin Joe nodded to the hooting and applause from his fellow drinkers.

"I bet you don't lose much at cards," said Gentleman Joe. He spoke up from a table close by. "The Rat Bastard Gazette said you walked a tightrope two thousand feet over the Grand Gorge on the Arkansas. I like a man that doesn't blink."

"Blink? I think it's within the realm of possibility that I did that one blindfolded, probably celebrating my third daughter, Flotina. Come then. Join me in cards. Teach me greater loss. We will discuss risk, company and the odds," Joe smiled, "Yes. A little risk, a chance." He knocked the deck he was holding. "Cards though. Cards are all about chance. Shooting a card in two when placed on someone's head, that's pure math and Newton's physics. I can do that all day long so long as the cartridge load ain't fixed."

"You sound American. You on the Union side?" Gentleman Joe asked.

"I suppose. Near the end of the civil war I remembered I was Canadian, born in Magog, Quebec. If you ask the priests anyway. Any man naturally forgets what the war is about after he puts his foot into one mud and maggot filled corpse too many. That's a fetid stink I can tell you. Unnerves your soul to a chill. Fighting grass hoppers in Kansas made more sense. Most lately, all the talk is Leadville and I toured with a theatre company and sold enough claims this summer to encourage my heart and fortify my family," He dealt out cards, "My wife and daughters are on the way."

Upstairs, Russian Betty was holding her breath. "I was hoping you would say that. It's important to keep Jesus in mind. We'll use this." She held up a translucent, white gown with blue trim to her shoulders. A long black rosary hung from her neck. "I have a crucifix right here." She held one up for him to see. "I need to get dressed and changed but you better take those clothes off right now." She pointed to the floor. "Throw them there."

"Tip in advance," he thought. Whores were one of his favourite inventions. There just wasn't anything you could say bad about them. "Honest women," he'd said more than once. "It's real nice what they do."

Goggles Jake shouted across the bar counter, "If they would just serve pie and coffee too."

They laughed.

"Hmmm," he thought, "How about playing to a man's other desires? What would that be like? There'd be one in every city. Call it Homes."

"Oh yeah. And how would that go?"

"You'd walk in and be greeted. There would be a selection process. Maybe a real modern one with their portraits on the wall or photographs of the women in an album. Then you'd go sit out in the kitchen. This place would have a lot of kitchens in it. So you'd sit down and your part time sweetie would enter. She'd make a big fuss all over her customer and brew him up a cup of coffee on the spot. There would be fresh pies and she would draw him out. That's half of it right there. Draw him out. Let him talk about his day. They she would just laugh and shake her head at his jokes and be just, so amazed and in awe of all sorts of things he talked about. Mean while she'd actually be preparing him a hot meal and just say the most agreeable things. Just like that. For a whole hour. You see, you'd fill up on a good meal and feel good that you were OK and a good guy. A real confidence builder. Big boost in moral. I can see it drawing a good membership. Maybe a good tip would lead to a gratifying mount, it would stand to reason. The main thing though is that pretend fantasy hour of the meal and a refreshing, agreeable wife. That's gotta be worth two or even three dollars. A day's pay and the guy walks out on a cloud and digs sixteen tons."

"If a woman smiles at you and doesn't yell she's the most beautiful woman in the world. When they yell at you they all look alike. When their face gets all twisted and squished and their eyes get all narrow...I just get scared of them. They aren't scared of me, I'm scared of them. Asking me every six hours if I still love her, starting massive fights before important occasions. Belittling me in front of people because she knows I don't argue in front of company. Do you think a whore does that? Sure I'd like a friend, a lover and confident...but not at any price."

Big Dan noticed Buckskin cutting the deck with Gentleman Joe and inquired if there was a chair open. It turned out there was, so he took a chair and pulled a pile of paper cash out of his jacket billfold and placed it on the table. "Is it table stakes, friends?"

Chapter Six - Big Dan

Big Dan introduced himself, "I just got off the stage from Denver today. Seed salesman. I'm lining up some spring time customers who want to grow the finest produce." He took a pinch of snuff and put the small snuff box on the table. He sneezed and separated out a small pile of cash and gold eagles. "Big Dan from Ohio," he said, "I go back to Denver in a few weeks. I enjoy five card stud a fair bit. My wife, her father's a preacher, my wife, she don't like my habits though."

Buckskin Joe was talking about a Wild West show he was going to buy and a circus where he use to perform a high wire act. As he was fanning the cards in his hand, he noticed that his ace of hearts had a tiny nick at the top of the card about half way across the top. He discarded and took two cards. The Jack of diamonds had a tiny nick a quarter of the way across the top.

The seed salesman lost most of the hands but kept winning big pots when he did win. Big Dan shuffled the deck. He did so a half dozen times so everyone could see. He was telling a joke about a bashful sheep farmer while gradually moving the nicked ace into place.

Dan flipped the cards out to the other players. He planned on giving Gentleman Joe a pair of aces down and did so. Buckskin received the bullets too and Goggles Jake got two pair, King high. Dan gave himself a straight flush of clubs, Queen high. He was smooth. There wasn't the slightest hesitation. He guessed he must have practiced this particular move for three thousand hours. For another thousand hours he sat in front of a mirror and riffled a deck, moving a card from the middle to the top. His shot glass was also reflecting the colour of the bottom card of the deck whenever he dealt. He practiced until he was perfect and then practiced more.

Gentleman Joe called for a fresh deck.

Dan agreed and called for a round. On his next turn, as dealer, Dan replaced the fresh deck with a better deck, one he kept just special. He'd practiced replacing decks for two thousand hours in front of a hundred hotel room mirrors. Everyone got the cards he wanted to give. There was no risk in losing unless he wanted to lose. "A duck, a moose and a rabbi walk into a saloon…" He started.

The salesman was discussing the Pittsburgh mine when he saw he had a flush. Buckskin Joe caught the change in his inflexion. The whole thing felt staged.

Dan knew all the odds for every hand but cheating was a hundred percent sure win. He called with ten dollars and palmed a twenty dollar eagle, out of the pot, on the way back. Practicing made him absolutely perfect. He was looking forward to a lot of games.

He could tell that Gentleman Joe was an expert player. He liked professionals. They gambled big money. Dan didn't gamble. That was the big advantage of cheating. It took out the risk and doubt. He'd win the second last hand, give the final one to Buckskin. Goggles Jake, the stock and shares broker had already said, "Cards ain't my game but gold shares sure are. You want to meet my pal, Adam Baulm." He came to lose anyway. Pros didn't often encounter cheats. Who would dare cheat a pro? The absolute proof of his expertise was that he wasn't dead. No one cut off his fingers. On the Mississippi river boats, he often let himself be talked into games. "Beginners luck," they all said. He'd lose some pretty close hands and namely the last couple of pots. But the hands that counted, the lion pots, he took those. It was money, so he took it.

"I couldn't find my pants." A miner at the bar said.

One whore said to another. "If he loses it all to a pretty face, he deserves it."

"Money is life," said the bartender.

"I think she wants it," a young miner looked over a dancing girl.

"Ask her if she wants to try something different. Penetrate her from behind and grip her with both hands. Then tell her she's the worse piece of ass you ever had and then hold on for dear life. That's the rodeo."

Everyone laughed.

Dan remembered his master, Evans, advice. "Leave some on the table if you plan on coming back, otherwise take every penny, mount their wives and grab some silverware on your way out the back window." He played out the last hand, leaving a quarter of the table to be split among Buckskin, Goggles and Gentleman Joe. His own hand was full of crap but he wanted to be caught out bluffing in a high-low hand. It made everyone feel good. Dan bought another round of drinks and left with smiles all around. The stock promoter soon followed.

The remaining two players chatted about the game. Joe thought maybe a few cards were nicked.

Dan checked in at The Grand. He tossed off his hat and pulled at his boots. He opened his trunk and took out a half bottle of whisky. He'd hoped to work the town for a month and then get gone fast. Maybe two weeks if it looked like the heavy snows were coming to close the pass. New Orleans might enjoy his company after that. All those river bottom captains and sailors could benefit his purse with his advantage style playing.

He picked a pair of dice out of a cup. Sailors liked dice games. He tossed them. They came up four and three. They always came up four and three. The other pair of di came up double fours. They cost him a hundred and fifty dollars a pair. They were perfect, made by a Parisian craftsman he'd met in the sewers somewhere.

The secret was in the swap. One brought them into play at the critical moment and then just as quickly brought the regular dice back. After winning of course. Maybe three straight passes with sevens then double boxcars. Then crap out. Burn the game. Get out.

"It must be so difficult to be a man," Russian Betty said.

He eyed her as she tightened the lid on a jar of pickled eggs. Her skirt twirled around her ankles. She stepped over and poured him out a full mug of coffee. Her cleavage awed him. He looked deep between her breasts and caught the scent of her perfume. She leaned into him to pour out coffee and set down a plate of hot buttered bread and molasses.

Gentleman Joe said good night and left his game at the bar. He turned to a darkened still rowdy street. It was a good time to visit his favourite dragon den. There was a chill in the air but men continued to fill the boardwalks as they blew from saloon to saloon in and out of the many cat houses. Almost all of them looked in rough shape with full beards and worn clothes. No one wasn't armed. If a fist full of iron was too much for a weak, stock clerk the Derringer made him equal to any, at least for one shot. It was dark but kerosene and gas light came from the doors and windows where the action was more intense and loud with music, bands and yelling. He walked down the middle of the street with a gun in his hand and the hammer cocked.

He was then to find the right entrance with the right door. He fell under a white cloud. His eyes and skin pulsed in ecstasy.

He needed to fall back and rode a velvet cushion. He rode a wave of red cushions. They were clouds in an air stream. His skin pulsated. His eyes smiled. He shivered. It was close to dawn when he left. He propped himself up for a moment leaning against the door jamb. He made his exit. It was early violet blue. He could only hear the quietest slithering as men moved around and behind beams, corners and each other. He walked down the road as before, only with both hands full of pistols. He noticed men slumped in doorways, leaning on barrels and coming out of alleys. He had three blocks to go before the bright entrance of The Grand.

Gaiten stared after him. He shifted his position in a recessed doorway. He slipped a butcher knife out from his rope belt. He ran the rusty edge against his dirty fingers. He noticed Gentleman Joe swinging his pistols back and forth with his gait. Gaiten pressed back in the doorway and looked down the boardwalk for some other pedestrian. It wouldn't do to bring a knife to a gun fight.

Gentleman Joe would have a bath right in his suite. It was fifteen dollars a day in a town where a miner made three. Thousands kept coming. No one could keep up. He passed four men laughing in conversation on the boardwalk. Two of them were holding bottles. They fell silent as Joe walked down the center of the road. At the last alley, before he reached the hotel, he heard a yell and a thump and the ruckus of trash being kicked around and disturbed.

He heard a woman shout, "Don't. Please."

A man yelled, "Make her love it."

There was laughter else where in the dark. He looked up at the moon. The air smelt so crisp, filled with the fine dust of broken leaves and pine needles. He stretched his muscles and arched his back a bit.

He didn't expect five of them. They were standing above some broken doll of a woman, half splayed out and cowering against the outside back wall of a saloon. He kept marching towards them wishing he was going the other way. He already regretted giving a damn. The smell of night waste was strong and he knew he would have to launder the stink off his suit. The odds were lousy.

"Twenty five cents and you can have a piece of her yourself, Mister."

The others laughed, looking at him with mean smiles and gut grunts. The woman's knee moved. Her dress was crumpled half way up her calves. Joe stood about ten feet away.

Their faces were clear enough. He could see their skin was filthy. He came closer and held out five double eagles. Joe dropped them on the ground. "One for each of you. I'll buy her out right."

They looked at each other, surprised. The greediest one, he tilted his head and said, "That coin came out pretty easy and I think you got a lot more of it."

Joe thought about a smart remark but immediately stabbed a dagger into the man's face, right through his eye and into his brain.

He pushed a pistol into the next man's face. "Run now or fight forever," Joe said.

They ran, leaving their dead crony behind. Joe knelt down and looked over the ragged woman. Her nose was bloody and her lip was puffed up. She was smeared with mud. "Are you cut up?"

"No. Are they gone?" She stared at her feet.

"Yes. Except for that dead one there. I think we should leave." He put a hand lightly on her arm.

"Where? This is nice. It's perfect and fits me so well. I don't have better."

"Here, we'll go to my room then. Those footpads will be back in a few moments if only to rob their friend's corpse."

Sweetwater Sally leaned on him. They walked to the rear entrance of The Grand. There was a bell hop and a doorman. He gave them a silver dollar each and winked as he walked the empty stair case to his room. He couldn't account for the smell.

The doorman looked at the bell hop and shook his head. "If it wasn't just five in the morning."

The Bell hop wondered if his sexual deviance would be so extreme when he got that old. She clearly stank of piss and her blood was fresh. "If that was what he wanted he picked the right town for it. Her face was raw like a rare steak."

He ran hot water for a bath. "You need this. You can take this bath."

She nodded. Not questioning. Not caring. They were the same. All the same. She sat in the bath, smelling lye soap.

He ordered some dinners. He was known to tip well.

She washed her face and looked at the blood that stained her breasts, her purple eyes.

He turned up the gas light and slid one of the windows open. The morning traffic had already started. More wagons and mules kept coming. He looked at the grey cold sky.

She came out wearing the robe he'd left there for her. She looked at him blankly.

The table was set. A pair of steaks steamed when he removed the cover. She fell to a full course meal. They both ate. He watched her take in the food. Her body grabbed, chopped, sliced, lifted and swallowed like an automatic clock. It ate beef, potatoes and greens with no self will. It swallowed a quart of milk. It tore apart buns. Sally's hands pushed tender bits of gravy soaked bread past her puffed lips. Joe had already sat back, not finishing his own meal. She looked up wide eyed and burped. They both laughed. He didn't even ask. He took out his pipe and placed a small ball of black gum in it and blew the smoke out the window. He passed it to her.

"I'll do?" She asked.

"You're a gift," he said.

They slept. She first. Then he lay down beside her. He put his arm around her and they both slept.

Dr. Adam Baulm spread some papers flat on a table. "See now I understand these principles of the natural forces." He was drawing a circle with a compass on some note paper. "There will be windows here and the door here."

"Wireless transmission of magnetic fields. It's the coming thing." He drew in a port to let in fresh air. "Much better than a cannon shot."

"They'll need these seat belts at the end when it rolls to a stop. I've thought of everything. Course it's how the stock certificate looks too. I'll need a board of directors so people understand this is no sham – this is capitalism at its best, financing adventure, glory and sacred gain."

"A man on Mars and all the way from Leadville." The Rat Bastard reporter wrote in his notebook.

"Man. A colony. The Cannonball Express Company will found and subsidize all colonists in return, of course, for a fair percentage. Wood and lead sheet would make a perfect shell of containment." Aiming would be easy. Current astronomical values were highly accurate. He would reveal a working model. A prototype would impress potential stockholders. It would hold six people, he thought.

It was difficult to tell if crime was on a rampage or if the city was exploding straight up. Leadville wasn't cowering and quivering in fear. It did make more sense than shooting a rocket out of a cannon. The Rat Bastard Gazette had another scoop.

Sister Susy reflected on shooting Sharon's husband. He looked ridiculous laying there. One arm was twisted behind his neck, his face turned into the dirt and his legs were splayed wide open. He looked like a fool. Death often looked stupid and foolish. She turned restlessly and prayed for forgiveness. Henry would have learned of the shooting. People were laughing about it all over town. It drew the wrong kind of attention to the Sisters' works. Liberty without security was a tough one.

Donny Sullivan said, "Do you think if we got paid a dollar a day more, that the mine owners would suffer one less slice of cake? Do you think their wives would stand straighter with one less strand of pearls? Why let them draw breath in the morning?"

He looked around the fresh planked drinking box. They were nervous, listening to him. Sullivan had called the meeting. The night before the 'Anti-Catholic Vigilance Committee' had beaten two of his friends by dragging them out of their shacks and setting on them with boots.

"Tabor and his pals encourage that behaviour. The mine owners and their boot lickers want us running and scared," a man said.

Another man said, "They change the working hours every week. Yesterday we had to work an eleven hour shift with no advance warning and for the same pay. 'Get out. Clear off if you don't like it.' Riding my back. But I still don't want to get run out of town."

"We have to deal with that vigilante group. Get their names. You're all Captains here. Talk to your people." Sullivan spit on the ground and cleared his throat.

Sullivan's shack was burned down the next night. He wasn't seen again. The miners continued to work. Catholic wives and daughters were harassed. Men beaten next to death.

Shea and O'Henry explained their new grieves to Sister Lucy who was looking after one of their friends. He had his jaw broken and received a concussion.

Sister Lucy expressed her sadness at the men's losing battle while explaining it to Sister Susy. The next morning Sister Susy sent a telegram to Pittsburgh Pennsylvania.

The boy in uniform ran down the Pennsylvania street. He banged at Mickey O'Donnley's door and received a two cent tip. Mickey stood there opening the envelope.

"In great need. Money wired on request. Sister Molly."

He knew who it was. She was so far away. But they were cousins and she wouldn't use the word Molly lightly.

His blood was hot. The Pennsylvania strikes were street clashes of iron bars, loose pistols and wooden planks. "Alright. I go and bring my posse with me."

The boom town would draw him in. He would meet his brothers first then mail a letter to Ireland and telegram Sister Susy back for travel funds. She would be relieved. An army of Molly Maguires was on the way. Even if it was just five of them – they knew what to do. "Bring discipline to the undisciplined. Create a mob. Turn a mob to order. Push around the rich. That was the trick." He shouted, Leadville would be his greatest achievement.

They had a friend in Denver he remembered. A printer. That was a necessity. He loved it. "Bugger the Rothschilds," McFetridge would shout to the Colorado walls.

Tracy was the first to pass on information about the anti-Catholic group to Sister Susy. "That's good. This is a fine truth and all we can do for now. Continue to gather information. It will serve useful." She copied what she had to paper and kept a running account of the rumours. The Mollys were coming by stage, train and boat. They were coming by night and day. They talked in quiet sobriety through their nights.

Men laughed as they kicked the teeth out of the face of Jim Leary. They heard he was organizing a delegation to talk to the mine owner about the change in hours. "Go steal from someone else you Papist dog."

They dragged him further down an alley and pissed on him. He lay there, face down in the yellowed mud. He didn't remember why he was there and hoped they would keep laughing and go away. Their laughter grew fainter. After awhile he felt someone go through his pockets and then he was alone again. It felt better to be alone.

Dutch Honey picked up a tin. "Cannabis Powder One Pound $2.50" She held a bottle up to the light. "Eli Lilly, number ninety six, Cannabis Extract." There were tins, apothecary bottles and small envelopes all over the room. Their eyes were bloodshot. A bag of children's candy lay open on the floor. "Migraine Relief - One Ounce Tincture Of Cannabis. Cures Gonorrhea and Tetanus," she looked at the one dollar price tag, "Gonorrhea? You boys better not be holding out on me."

Black Thumb Bob, Neiderguy and Dutch Honey lay back, sunk in the couch and chairs. Their eyes drifted. Their jaws were slack. Occasionally their heads moved to look at one another. They lay deep back, embedded in the slow tidal weight of time. The room was twilight dark. There was a small table in the middle holding a few glasses. A candle burned.

"Which one of you is Baudelaire?" Said the cricket. "I must apologize for my late presence."

"If you died you certainly should apologize."

"You wouldn't have to write that drivel for the paper."

"I could tell the editor I have a loss of muscular sense and I couldn't find my pants and there were too many witches in the street..." Black Thumb Bob said. He left for the office.

"Writing with a fountain pen is like drawing a story," he later told the editor, "With your typewriter, it's like you have to draw two handed, cause you're not so sure of one. Typing will never catch on. You should concentrate by etching cursive writing into copper plate. You'd save a ton of lead type and machinery and time."

Editor pushed as much print as he could into the page as the reporter babbled. He tapped the leaden type into place with a wooden block.

"I have no money and bare hands and already I out number you," Black Thumb Bob said.

The editor looked up from the tray of wooden blocks. He slipped some letters into a space. He pushed another font into a space, "The alphabet, when fully loaded, has twenty six rounds. I can see you're mad and don't care if you get caught. Filthy stuff you use. Ought to be a law."

"Nothing but delusion. Dogs bark in hell and they all have your face," thought Black Thumb Bob.

He didn't have much hope and dreaded the typewriter. But the Rat Bastard Gazette paid his hotel room.

Four tabloid pages were laid out on a slanted table. The editor was sitting on a high stool in front of them. The pages were partially full of type and blocks. Wooden blocks held thin plates of etched reverse images. Editor was placing the type in long columns laboriously spelling out the sentences. He was following a hand written story given to him by one of his reporters.

Black Thumb Bob walked in. Star reporter.

The editor didn't look up and said, "Lay out your lines. Finish page four. Remember that squib for the tailor. You look like crap and you stink. I'm going in the back to make my supper. I'll bring you some coffee. Lay that type!"

He considered telling his boss that he was late because he was an opium addict but that would have lead to further complications.

He wrote his stories directly into the frames. Hand picked, letter by letter, he ran the narrow columns up and down, putting in empty slugs and double lines as dividers.

By two in the morning they were smearing ink and pulling the handle on the press. Perfect sheets came out each time. They stacked them to dry. In turn they slipped each sheet back under the press to imprint on the reverse. The impressions were deep enough to feel and the dampness of the paper and deep breaths of fragrant ink filled each with history. By five in the morning they had printed seven hundred copies. They drank to the two foot high pile. They passed out handfuls to the newspaper boys to distribute.

At seven in the morning a subscriber stopped by to ask, why page three was printed upside down.

Another issue of The Rat Bastard Gazette was out. He'd sell ads and subscriptions all week then print it on Thursday for a nickel. The masthead said, "Past Predicted Perfectly." There was a popular section called, "Rumours, Gossip & Lies" and the editorial column labeled, "Busted Teeth and Typewriters." He kept rooms upstairs and the business downstairs.

Later he'd print up some hand bills for the Comique. The theatre featured a talking dog, a comedy routine about Governor Pitkin and a headline tour of actors from England.

He left the newspaper office at eight in the morning. He stepped over a man sleeping on the boardwalk. Another was leaning against a hitching post with arms across his stomach as he vomited. He waited for a lull in the traffic of coaches, buckboards, wagons, steam cars, horses and braces of mules to scamper across the street to his apartment.

Dutch Honey was there. She was boiling some potatoes. "I'm making a stew." She took a hunting knife and sliced up some chunks of deer meat.

He put his hands on her behind. She rocked her bottom to his touch while dicing a turnip.

Geisel wasn't looking for a home. He was looking for a frontier. Buildings were going up everywhere. Two men were shoving one another and yelling in front of a saloon. They had stepped up to one another. They were shouting into each other's red face. Neither had yet reached for the long blades hanging at their sides.

"Giddy." He said to his horse as he angled into the traffic. He passed two men by the Dead Cat Saloon. He heard the words. "Wheel...axle...fourteen dollars."

The farmer was a businessman. Mack had acquired 160 acres. By using a plough with a decent tip and a strong horse or ox he could rip through an acre a day. The land was a quarter cleared of trees. The ground available for his farming was full of stumps, roots, rocks, gophers and woodchucks. Filthy and sweating he guided and pushed the plough, feeling the ox tug it through the big roots. The roots were matted like fish nets. Sometimes they would sweep up from the ground, snapping and throwing dirt clods at him. Gradually rough and ragged furrows were dragged into the ground. The stumps were often too big to even pull out with the ox. Not with one ox anyway. He'd find out about dynamite later. A creek ran to form a pool and the overflow carried on to join other creeks on the gentle slope. The pond saved him a hundred and fifty dollars as he wouldn't need to buy a windmill water pump. He worked when he was awake.

He kept half his money in the Leadville Bank and the other half under the hearth.

He had free title to the land and was considering a loan. He wasn't sure. Twelve percent was dear and would eat up a lot of income. He pondered it. The ox was making the return trip, dragging a new furrow in a jagged line towards the cabin. He looked back, noting all the birds that came to a feast of beetles, worms and roots. The sun was setting. He closed the door on the ox stall and took a turkey, hanging upside down, from a hook set into the outside wall. It had drained all day. Some flies were feasting on the blood. He plucked out most of the quills while sitting on the front porch. Once cleaned out he washed it and cut it up to fry while drinking some coffee. His hands hurt and he wondered about women. He'd have to get a cat soon. Otherwise he liked the peace and so far it was that. He looked for tomorrow and would sleep well that night. The scent of the fried meat and the warmth of the stove made the bare log cabin seem like a hundred years of success. Every moment was a powerful comfort and an inducement to live.

Mr. Flowers said, "My neighbour said he thought the cow was looking funny. Not right. I went towards it and it did appear to be wavering on its legs. Just as I got to it, it laid down on its side. I noticed some blood coming out its mouth. I thought maybe there was an obstruction so I reached down its throat. I had my arm in all the way to the shoulder and that's when I looked in her eyes and saw the lights go out. It was a nice cow. I could take her on a lead anywhere. If I said WHOA, she would stop. She was a good cow. So then I got the horse and dragged it back to bleed out. It was too much meat to waste to purification."

"Last winter the chicken coup got so cold that their combs got frost bite, turned black and fell off. Normally their body heat and their droppings give off enough heat," said Mr. Flowers. "The yellow beans were on the bottom close to the ground and the rain splashed mud up. So wash them well unless you feel like eating a peck of dirt." Mr. Flowers handed Mack a basket of yellow beans. "Like I said, I had to put my best cow down but after that, I'll tell you, the chickens were so scared that they were trying to give milk. I stopped in on Crippled Bill. Gave him some beets and sack of potatoes. I harvested six pounds for every half pound planted. Bill said he was doing OK but wished he had more visitors. I couldn't stay long, I still had deliveries to make and then Father Fontaine was walking in the door." He laughed.

The hay was stoaked. A wall of bush broke the wind. Chores, there were always chores. He pulled on the cow's teats. He would salve her udder later. The milk squirted into the bucket. The cow kicked up some straw. Mack picked some straw and dung out of the bucket and continued his motions.

"Give him a hundred dollars in pennies and let him swim the Arkansas. That's my vote," "Yeah. I vote. I feel the highroad is to choose between the ballot or the bullet. As it is, at every opportunity I haven't hesitated to draw my 'X' on the spot. I was motivated by profanity normally and made for the ballot place as fast as I could and brought mobs of guys with me and we voted like hell."

"Didn't blink an eye or feel a shred of remorse for any havoc or chaotic upset created by my mark. That's all my gang has. That and the right to bear arms. If there was no meaning at all at all to the vote because it was rigged like Dodge well..." He gave his head a twist and raised his eye brows. "That would be just a rotten day all around. No one would be pleased. No one would be happy. Here and there I know, folks in boot hill magically rise to vote and whisky bottles and dollar bills are passed around like handshakes in a whorehouse but overall it balances out better than some feather clad head taker telling us what to do cause his gang is meaner, I think."

Upstairs, Gentleman Joe talked with Sally.

"You will do. You will be. You will be a pleasure to yourself. If you want. I can be there. I'd like to be there. I mean, are you finished with this?" He gestured to the pile of her clothes. It can't be doing you much good unless you want to consider it a karma that you've worked through."

She looked at her ragged clothes and then him. She started to cry. Not heaving sobs but the tears ran down her face. "I don't know."

"It's OK to let go," he said, "a nice wind blows."

"Hey, Scampers. Here." Zeke tossed the dog a bone with some gristle on it. It landed with a thud disturbing some leaves. Scamper leapt up to receive it and then hurried over to give it a sniff. She fell to her haunches and started to gnaw, growling as she did so to keep away any phantom animals that might seize her delicacy.

She kept one eye out because that was all she had. She held the bone down with her one remaining front paw and pulled bits off with her teeth.

"Good for you," he called to her.

The prospector could see the snow coming. They even had some last week but it didn't stick. He wrapped a scarf around his throat and shut the door. The dog disappeared in a hole it had dug under the cabin. He brewed up some coffee and listened to her gnaw.

The Pinkerton's man received a telegram. It said. "Remain where you are. New client."

"Fine," he thought.

Tabor had been there since the beginning. He had claims all over the place and fingers reaching for more, it was explained to him. Buckskin Joe sat in a mahogany chair, upholstered in leather and carved by Spanish workmen. He crossed his legs and drank black coffee from a thick mug.

"So you see, basically what you would be doing is walking and riding around Mr. Tabor's land keeping trespassers, thieves and jumpers off."

"I understood it paid thirty dollars a week."

"Oh. No. It's twenty five dollars a week."

"I understood thirty. I had to meet three claim jumpers already. Leadville sure attracts them. Those particular three can't see above ground anymore so do appreciate Haws' needs and I will do the job but clearly it's thirty plus ammunition."

"Your price seems to increase with time, Mr. Hoyt. Mr. Edward Hoyt."

"That's true," Joe smiled, showing large teeth.

"Well, you seem a jolly fellow and able to settle our turf. You have your thirty, sir."

"And ammunition," Buckskin laughed.

"Yes," the functionary agreed. He stared at him, "What do you find so amusing?"

"That which confounds me, paints your face purple. A poem that just came to mind."

They settled the details and the functionary passed over a file of maps and coordinates with the location of various lay over shacks.

Buckskin Joe closed the door and continued to chuckle. He had a hundred and twenty dollars for his first month's pay in his pocket.

The functionary's next appointment burst out laughing. He discovered then, that his coffee had the contents of his inkwell spilled into it and his cheeks, nose and lips were well stained purple. "Dam, Joe," he thought, "If he wasn't already paid in advance." He stayed purple for two more days.

"His face was like an eggplant and every time he wiped his lips he smeared the ink across his cheeks." Everyone laughed. One Eyed Jacob pounded away on sixty-four keys enjoying the clink of tips landing in his jar.

Joe led his horse to a creek where they both drank. By the river bed, in the mud, were a series of foot prints. They looked like a man's only they were eighteen inches long and seven inches wide. He just stood and looked at it for awhile wondering what a giant that man must be and he resolved to keep his eye out and inquire about him. He fantasized about getting a circus together and going on tour with the Pawnee. He poked the coals of the fire and sorted out his bedroll. It was a luxury to have enough food and such pleasant camp conditions. He didn't mind setting up the old Union army pup tent in case of rain. It reminded him that he was still wanted as a deserter somewhere. He hadn't wanted to see the end of the war and had run back to his native home of Quebec. An army police detective had followed his trail for some months. He had engaged a confederate and planned to kidnap Joe on the Canadian side and bring him back across the border to New York or Vermont as he'd done with deserters a hundred times before and slaves before them. A Canadian soldier got one dollar a day, his American counterpart got three.

But that was almost fifteen years ago.

Meanwhile, back in Pittsburgh Pennsylvania ...

"They found McManus and O'Neil guilty," said Shea.

"What's the answer there?"

"Pack your best dress, I'd say."

"It was a set up. They were framed. They would have told us of their plans."

"No doubt they were. We can only pray for they had endurance on the scaffold."

"Whatever their mistakes were we can't have a noose on our own necks."

"A country is not created by cowards. At least this one had the sense to kick out the monarchy. Our Fenian cousins had less luck in Canada."

They were drinking tea that had long grown cold in the pot.

"We can't travel as a group. We'll have to split up and meet there. Cousin Susy has been generous enough. We'll start leaving tomorrow. Steve, you'll go first. Will should go on Thursday. Liam and Frank go on Sunday. I'll leave on Monday."

He passed envelopes to each of them, sliding the money across the table. One by one they left. Each thought of the work ahead, their commitments and items to pack.

None of them paid attention to the vegetable seller's cart on the corner. It was staffed by a Pinkerton's man. He had a copy of Sister Susy's telegram in his pocket. The word was out. He was to keep an eye on these bomb throwing barbarians.

They were murderous thieves as far as he was concerned and it would do fine if they were to hang here or there. Their guilt was evidence enough. If the court really needed some he could always make it up. "The fewer Irish, the better," he thought.

"They found another one. It was wrapped in newspaper."

Sister Susy shook her head, "Where?"

"Still Born Alley. Same as most others."

"It's shameful. A terrible sin," said Susy.

"The girls have no choice. They can't work long in that condition. They bring it along and then ditch it."

"Some of those girls are like slaves. It's white slavery," said Sister Lucy.

"They have no husbands. Sometimes they come all the way from Europe. By the time they get here they owe so much money it takes them years to pay the whore masters back. By that time they are so worn out and addicted to laudanum they are casualties themselves, maybe driven mad or to suicide."

"Who pays the undertaker?"

"Sometimes the house owner will. But more often than not a wagon will just pull up to the back door and the poor girl will be buried in the dead of night away from the town or, just as easy, the basement floor gets dug a little deeper."

"Their lives are a wreck and end up worse."

"Death is no mystery."

"This fight won't be fair," she said, "We don't stand a chance. We'll fight anyway."

Buckskin packed up his camp and rolled it up to put on his mount. He looked around at the ground and the rocks. It was a good spot to prospect in. The signs were there but it was Tabor's and one way or another, everyone knew the rules. If the situation was reversed the trespassers would do the same. For thirty bucks a week Buckskin would prevent that reversal of fortune from happening.

The wooden handles on the plough dug into Mack's chest. The pressure was constant and he was always bearing down with his body weight until his armpits ached on fire. Every time the blade hit a stone the plough would jolt and the thick wooden handles would crash into his chest and ribs. The skin on his hands was always ripping away to reveal pink moist flesh. The horse ate a bale of hay in the morning and another at night. Sixty bales a month maybe more. Really over seven hundred bales a year. Mack was working out how much land to grow hay for the work animals. How much greens for a hog, how much seed for chickens? Every time he added an animal he had to add acreage, supplies and seed. He was going to be ploughing for a long time.

The handle jarred catching him in the chest again and he thought of the elk steak waiting for him. The dog barked at the blackbirds. He kept his rifle mounted to the side of the plough.

Gentleman Joe poured coffee from a canister. "I'd like you to be with me. You don't appear to have any other alliances. I need someone to lay down with who's going to watch my back."

She had thick dark mascara around her eyes. Her hair was combed out and she was wearing a fresh dress he had bought for her, along with other necessities.

"Am I free to go? Can I leave anytime I want?"

He paused, "Sure. You're not a slave. Well..." He looked at the pipe they were using. "This for the both of us. Maybe we could find some good on the other side of it."

"And you thought I would bring you prestige and honour?"

"One is almost as good as another and if security and good feelings follow then it was right. Prestige and honour come by time and trial. This is a hand that's dealt to you. You look nice in that dress."

She thought about her fear and emptiness the night before. "Now this. A fancy hotel room, new clothes. What did he want?" He wanted her. If not for the reason he said then one she didn't know about. What could that be?

"Are you there, Sally?"

"Okay," she said. The bath, food and sleep were driving and refreshing her. She preferred a world that was clean.

She was, she had been after all Sweetwater Sally when all the men thought she was sweet. He must have spent thirty dollars on her. A year ago she might have laughed with the other girls about how much she had taken her John for. She looked at the approaching chill outside. "I don't really know what you expect. I don't know anything about cards really. You've been more than decent. I don't want to hurt you."

He looked at her. She had a sense of refinement and grace about her. The manner in which she held her wrist. The way she drank her wine using a linen napkin to press against her lips. The silent appreciation of the wine. Even with the limp from her bruised leg she carried herself with an early remembered deportment. She'd fell a pretty long way.

New York Louis was on the other side of Buckskin Gulch. He and his burro made their way along the rock face. There was no trail before them. Still the big flies attacked them. The brush snapped. The burro's ears twitched forward and they both heard water. There was a bend around some broken rock and then a fifty foot wide glen. A stream of water ran straight down the mountain side splashing the round rocks below and creating a creek. There were several small falls like this, creating a geological funnel of water about four feet wide and six inches deep. He could see, by the water line, that it was much greater during the spring run off. He tied the animal off and ran his hands over the cliff face. It was granite and he stood back noting the carboniferous ledges. There appeared to be some eruptive porphyry dikes as well. He would make note.

Louis was about fifteen miles from Leadville but a few thousand miles from home. This is what he came for. He walked over to the pack animal drinking from the creek. He gave it a salt biscuit and foraged in the leather panniers. He slid out a note book and made readings with his compass, drawing in the creek and the other peaks in view. He put it back in its oilskin case. "All that work and risk to carry these two things." He walked up the light incline, about ten feet from where the creek started, and set down his pan and shovel. He looked down at the clear water rushing over the round, smooth rocks. He pushed some of them away with the toe of his boot. He leaned over and cleared a two foot square patch moving all the bigger rocks and stones away. Then he took his shovel and scooped up a slice of the gravel and sand to put it into his swishing pan on the dry bed. The pan looked a bit like a coolie's hat but was stamped out of steel and had a series of upraised ridges running along its surface. He submerged the pan and its contents a few inches under the rushing water. He flicked off the bigger bits of gravel and small rocks with his fingers. Then using a circular swishing motion he kept undulating the pan with increasing vigor, just enough, so the next lightest layer of sand was swished out into the water. It didn't take much force and the lighter sand was gone. The ridges kept blocking and trapping the heavier elements. Once he got down to a bottom inch he placed the pan down in shallower water so that just the brim was being rushed over and passed a magnet into it. He worked the iron filings from sand back and forth freeing them of other debris. He swished the pan some more. Tiny yellow particles glinted up. Many tiny particles glinted up. The bigger ones he scooped up with his jackknife and tapped into a glass bottle. The remaining muck he dumped into a collection bucket.

He took another slice from the same spot going six inches deeper. He'd filled two collection buckets by nightfall. The creek was rich in pay dirt. It looked promising. Probably the source was way up there. He put his hand into a rivulet coming down the mountain's face. It was cold. He felt the trace of a millennium of drippings. He looked up. The water was cutting in a vein and washing the gold into the creek bed. It was accumulating as a fine, heavy sand. Once he removed the iron particles he was still left with a lot of black, heavy crap. He was tired as he sat back on his haunches. That had to be a mix of silver and lead carbonate. He turned his sodden boots towards the fire. He'd do some more testing in the morning.

The sun was just coming up as he turned the coals around and fed some kindling into it. He tossed some coffee grounds into a small pot to boil and quickly mixed up some pancakes to fry. He tossed two potatoes to the edge of the fire, wedged in by some flat rocks.

All night he kept seeing himself repeating the motion of gingerly picking up a small fleck or round pearl of gold with the tip of his knife edge and tapping it into his bottle. The pan swishing was the most time consuming. The further down the bed he went, the richer the sand. The last five pans had yielded over four ounces of fantastic wonderful gold.

Later that night he ate oatmeal and bacon. He smiled at the luxury and added a healthy dollop of brown sugar to the oatmeal. He had a good claim and proved it fast. He'd mark the territory and prepare to claim it tomorrow. He could scratch his name and date into the rocks and make pyramids of stone as markers. But he better take some out on the first pass. Claim jumpers and their complicated line crossing lawyers were more difficult than bob cats, grizzly bears and mountain lions.

For the next two weeks he dug and sliced into the creek and its bed, swishing and panning. His bottles, cans and bags quickly filled up with yellow silt.

By the end of another week there was no coffee, liquor was long gone, the bacon was too green and anything left was awful. He took down his camp. It was three days back to the main mountain road. He tied the tent pole to the burro's side and filled the canteens and bladders with water. The leather panniers carried a hundred and fifty pounds of gold. He'd left all but one of his buckets of sludge behind.

He wanted to return in time to build a cabin and process the black crap during the winter. Unless he sold the claim. He'd have to think about that. He led the pack animal back along the same path. He could see a vague imprint of his coming. A rotting log with the burro's shoe imprint on it. A broken green sapling. The trail behind was quite clear to anyone that cared to follow. As soon as he broke the brush onto the highway, people would take note.

If he returned with a registered claim and worked it, he'd need partners. If he went alone, after the news of what he'd taken out known, he wouldn't stand a chance. He didn't know of anyone in Leadville that loved him more than gold and began to lean towards selling the claim. The boring food with its absence of decent vegetables and the constant flatulence and uncomfortable toilet was part of the consideration. He pushed a pinch of tobacco in his pipe. It was the last pinch. It was a hard working burro he decided. He returned down the same steep incline and pushed aside pine boughs. Black fly jaws had locked onto his eye brows before dying. His ass hurt.

He saw three buckboards and some mule trains right away. More dust was being raised behind them. He fell in along side. Coaches came and went. Mainly it was wagons but there were plenty of men on horseback in groups of twos and threes.

One called down to him. "Any luck on the golden rainbow, sir?" He eyeballed the successful prospector like they were playing cards.

Louis shook his head. "Soon though," he said. He held up a three prong branch stripped of its bark. "It never fails. It's a twitching rod. I hold it out straight and when it vibrates I dig. You grub stake me on it and you'll see the elephant."

"I'll see a stick in my eye is what I'll see," he laughed and he rode ahead to join his group. "Idiots are coming here too," he said. His pals laughed.

That was another thing. Louis had signed for a grub stake and owed half the findings to the merchant. There was a lot to think about. He trudged into town. The boardwalk was still full. The first thing he did was register the claim. After, he went to the assayer's office with the bucket of sludge and a bag of samples. Then he went to see his merchant benefactor. He tied his animal off at the hitching post and walked into the store. He tromped down the center aisle. There was nothing clean about him and he sat in a half barrel cut away to substitute as a chair. He dropped into it. The Captain walked over. He handed him a five pound purse of gold dust and sat down heavy. "Another couple hundred pounds outside." He held up his claim. "It's a legal thing. Now how do you see it, exactly?" He told of what he'd done and seen.

The merchant didn't see a man who wanted to tough it out in the bush and dig a mine. It would depend on the assayer but in situations like this he often paid thirty five to fifty thousand dollars for the other half of the claim. The prospector thought that was something to think about. He walked up the stairs to Russian Betty.

He wasn't that fast with a gun and he knew where the slow gunslingers lived. Russian Betty was pouring another bucket of hot water into the wash tub. He smiled, wondering how many times Russian Betty would tug his pants off for thirty five thousand dollars. He eased into the tub. He hoped his burro was being well treated at the livery.

He was thinking about a mine shaft as she began washing his private parts with a soft cloth. She brought him a jigger of hot vodka with peppercorns in it. The best rumours about her appeared to be true. She toweled him off and walked him to the featherbed. The twenty dollar gold piece would carry him until lunch. She loosened the knots on the curtains and lowered the kerosene lanterns. He claimed his comfort. She brought him to tears. The pain was all different. He wasn't done. Betty lit a candle and poured some more vodka.

He was about the twentieth miner who showed up in town with a, hit it rich, claim that week. That meant more miners needed, more railroad ties cut, more whisky to drink, more ore to crush, more card games to play and black flies to swat. It just wouldn't stop.

"Why, that's New York Louis. He use to shovel out livery stables in New York. He showed up with twenty eight dollars left." That he'd made it this far and was willing to put all that he had left on a claim as opposed to drinking it away was enough for the Captain to stake him. "It was a five hundred dollar chance. Less really. Even sheepishly, men returned the worn tools, broken supplies and exhausted pack animals." Being dead was a fair excuse. All it took though was just one hit. One hit paid for blunders and empty holes. Meanwhile a bottle of wine was seven dollars and the carpet baggers were selling windmills for a hundred and fifty dollars a piece.

The men mainly stank. Families were showing up with kids all over the place. In the end he leaned towards selling out. Captain had the claim re-assessed, left some armed men to work it and offered Louis fifty thousand. He was lazy in the livery stable and lazy here. He negotiated for thirty five thousand and a one sixteenth ownership. It was agreed and the money changed hands. Now he didn't feel like risking his neck in the bush. He would think on that. In a month he would turn twenty. He decided on a better rooming house than an expensive hotel, maintaining his frugal nature. He pictured himself lying on a soft bed with his hands folded beneath his head while he pondered on what to do with his fortune. He had enough money to do anything in the world he wanted. He wanted to build wooden model ships. He would buy a house and build wooden ships. Then he would see. He never turned the roulette wheel once. He left himself the occasional soothings of Betty and a few sots of vodka. He just didn't know. New York Louis put cream in his coffee.

Dr. Adam Baulm, wondered if Geisel could reproduce photographs of his giant cannon ball for a presentation? Geisel listened to the man, set a price, and thought about renting some studio space for the winter. He could do some work and perhaps pick up a few local clients.

There was a portion of the second floor above a grocery store that he could have for twenty five dollars a month. The stove worked. The room had both indoor water and gas light. He saw how he could set up a darkroom and agreed.

His entrance was separate and he planned to place a studio portrait on the front door. Perhaps a notice in the paper. He made arrangements to board his horses and began moving his equipment out of the wagon and up the stairs. It took all day and by evening he was feeding the stove. He was eating some bread and cheese and a dried sausage made from local game. He drank beer out of a tin cup from a bucket full, purchased at a nearby saloon.

The knock at his door revealed a red eyed young man smoking a pipe. "Do you like gumdrops?" There was a smile on the other side of his beard. "I'm Leigh."

The studio behind his was rented by some artists. They were from Boston and Montreal. There was an easel with a partially done oil painting in front of each window. "I sketch the scene in by charcoal first. Then I wait for the colours." He poured a healthy dollop of scotch into two glasses and handed one to Geisel. "As an artist you understand the importance of light on a subject."

"Light is everything. It's exciting to move it around the glass and see it outlined forever. Just me and that image."

"Thank God there is another artist to talk to in town."

"Surely there are others."

"Bah. Posers. Weekend, aristocratic trash."

"These oils are marvellous. You have every line of the boot shop."

From his eyeballs to his lungs the searing burning of the pneumonia was tearing at him. The rain was cold and constant, almost white and frozen. His phlegm was rich and yellow. He nursed himself with the fire in the stove and the food he had left. Mainly he had beans. He needed everything and had the dust to pay for it. He just had to shake the bug and then move forward. He lay back on the bunk and pulled the blankets tighter. It was his fourth night of fever. He looked at his pocket watch. It was 8PM and long dark outside. Open sacks and buckets of sand and muck from his claim along the river bed were in various stages of having the high rich content of gold being removed. He would sit there all winter swishing and panning right on the cabin floor. It was there. He'd walked in four months ago.

"Yes. The 15th century Italians really had perspective down. I come forward with three hundred year old technique and ten year old scotch. You bring the cutting edge, technological replacement. A true spirit moved by the same clouds."

"I want you to take a special photograph for me."

They discussed the drama of a photograph, portraying his drawing of a street scene. Geisel felt he would have to be perched on a ladder to shoot down at the painter to capture both his sketch and the scene he was drawing.

"Those are fine lines. I'm not so sure. Perhaps if I was capturing some thicker, bold strokes. Let me set up in a few days."

"I'm in no hurry, Geisel. You must set yourself straight and take care of important matters first. A boiled egg, perhaps you would like a boiled egg?" He passed over a small pot with several hard boiled eggs rolling around the bottom. Rejected, he returned them to the top of his stove.

They were ready for a trial run. Leigh added a bit of kindling to the stove. "It's June. Still, up here, one looks for frost."

The street below was busy. Horses were tied off to hitching posts. Three Fingers Jake was entering the hotel across the street. He was carrying a small bag. He looked over his shoulder and then turned into the entrance way. He avoided the doorman's eyes.

The doorman held the door open for two women in beaver coats wearing large hats. They had just come in from Denver. They walked into the lobby. Three Fingers Jake was renting a room for two days. The clerk was gracious and offered him a key.

Geisel drilled a hole in the top step of the ladder. He'd mounted a post on the large wooden camera box and slid it into place. The challenge then would be to hold the camera still. They needed a cloudless day. "Or shoot at night."

"There's almost enough gas lamps out front of the hotel."

"Well, I'd have to use the flash anyway. It's worth it." He lined up the elements and checked the perspective. Geisel lifted the hood over his head. By sighting the camera during the day he could concentrate on the flash.

"Take off your hat. This isn't a formal shot. You don't wear your hat when you're alone."

Three Fingers Jake spread the kerosene around his room. He filled a bowl with more kerosene. He lit a candle. In about twenty minutes it would burn to a point, then it would ignite the kerosene in the bowl, setting the bed on fire, spreading quickly to a wet sheet of the stuff on the floor and then up the walls. Three Fingers left the room. He walked down the steps with his hat pulled low. He walked through the doors and out onto the busy boardwalk. He looked up and saw a bright flash from the second story window. He thought it odd that the gunshot had no sound. He turned quickly, making back for his camp out of town.

Geisel slid the wet plate holder out of the camera. "This I have to do right away." He walked back to his studio. Colloidal syrup dripped onto the hall floor in a trail to his dark room. Once safely inside he slid the glass plate into its waiting bath of developer. He set the timer and got the fix and wash ready.

He had caught the memory to perfection. He heard the artist start to shout. He came out to see and noticed the fire and smoke across the street. People were yelling. Guests were tossing their trunks and suitcases out the windows. The Tabor Hose and Harrison Hooks were ringing their bell. Horses were neighing. Men shouted to go here and there. Geisel and the artist stood by the window watching.

"It's at The Coliseum." A man shouted and pointed the way. That was the news in the late Extra, edition of the June 20th, 1879 Rat Bastard Gazette.

The stock promoter was showing his design to the mechanic. Copies of the *Scientific American* were scattered on his desk. Two slide rules lay on top of another drawing of a pump. "See this is flat bar that's been curved and joined. I had in mind an earth commode here and a ventilation window there. These wires will transmit the energy for the magnets."

"This would take two of my men at least a month to build. We never made a ship to Mars before," he looked at him.

"I can calculate a cost for you tomorrow. But I can't see less than a thousand dollars to get started. We'd be turning down other jobs to do this one." The mechanic picked up a slide ruler.

The Pinkerton's man, Lance had received the word. Some men were coming in from Pennsylvania. There were more than one. They were possibly cult members of the Ancient Order of Hibernia. They were dangerous to the social and moral order. They were a threat to any nation that enjoyed law and order. So now he had both the affairs of the heart and affairs of the state in mind.

The boardwalk was incredibly crowded. Crossing the street was quite a trick. Traffic was going both ways and horses, ox and wagon merged and meshed. A man on a horse cursed and pointed his gun at the driver of a steam car.

A man came running out of a saloon, his face covered in blood. He tripped into the street, almost getting run over by a wagon wheel. He fell face down and lay there for a minute. He pushed himself off the road and sat up. He slid a large knife out of a sheath, tied to his leg, and went back into the saloon.

There wasn't anything to hear. The wind whistled around the corner of the cabin. There was an ebb and flow to the wind. Sometimes it picked up. It sounded white and shearing. "It could skin a man alive."

He had cut no windows out from his walls. The one room cabin was light or dark depending if he had a fire going. Every week he washed himself with a hand cloth. He'd set a basin with water in it to heat. It was refreshing for awhile. He coughed for a long time.

He'd dug about ten feet into the mountain. He was following a vein of silver. He smashed and pried it out with pick, shovel and sledge hammer. Every four feet he cut timber to reinforce the ceiling and walls. Maybe he would hear them begin to crack before the shaft caved in on him. He crushed as much as he could with a sledge hammer. He pounded the richest stuff down to quarter inch gravel and scooped it into the iron pot. Every few days he'd cover the pot and surround it with fire wood. Silver melts at about 900 degrees F. In this way he accumulated crude refined silver. He shoveled the path from the tree line, where his cabin lay, to the two hundred feet to the mine entrance. The snow was shoulder high for most of the way.

Ned liked his room over looking Chestnut Street above the shoe shop. He could see several men in bowler hats and two ladies with big fancy hats pausing to look in Leiniger's bookstore window. A man walked by them. He carried everything he owned in a bundle on the end of a stick carried over his shoulder. He'd befriended another man on the road who carried everything he owned with a satchel in each hand. Several oxen lay down with their feet under them. The oxen looked blankly at the crowds going in and out of the hardware store.

A help wanted poster offered three dollars a day to cut rail ties. A pack of near feral dogs were ripping garbage apart. A covered wagon passed by every minute.

Millie was a sweetheart. Every week or two she received a parcel from San Francisco. Her clients considered it priceless. Word got out. At first people were upset as no Chinese were allowed in Leadville. Indeed, the last census held their noted population at zero. Once it was understood that it was just being handled by local business people, it was merely frowned upon. Cloud City was the capital of a nation of free will. There was some destiny. It was a land of those that did have the courage of their convictions. Anyone got to do anything they wanted and they got to do it all the time. Alex de Tocqueville worried about the future of America and democracy because America desired leaders. People wanted masters but not here.

It was just too clear. The President could read. The Governor could read. Over two or three years Leadville, all by herself, was paying off the entire Nation's debt. America was being serviced by a staff of thirty five thousand haulers, hewers, whores and roughage that were paying off a gross national debt that had taken millions of Americans a hundred years to accumulate. The citizens of Leadville were the angels dancing on the head of a pin and nothing must interfere with the flow of the silver from west to east.

There is always a secret service. This one understood that great fortune had to be protected from thieves. Pinkerton was an agency staffed by those loyal to some higher calling than themselves. While under-cover, Lance had heard both Marx and Engles speak in New York to some working men's committees. Marx's writings, in The New York World, drew some attention as well as thirty years of publishing his *Manifesto of The Communist Party*. It couldn't escape the ears of The Mollys. He saw both groups as enemies of the State. Economically and in reality the Mollys didn't want to take over the means of production for themselves. They didn't seek to occupy their boss's mansion and send him to work in the mines. They merely sought more cash for their labour. Although, on that note, they did so on short thin patience.

The Mollys were aware of Marx and his writing but they didn't see it. Certainly they identified with one another based on class and social origin but they knew they didn't run the show. They were workers. They weren't merchant princes with Ivy League school diplomas.

They weren't patent holders of marvellous invention and they weren't born from the right sort of families. There were other necessities of what it did take to run a modern nation in competition with absolutism with stern demagogues and Kings. The Mollys represented the guy on the end of the shovel. The guy on the end of the shovel didn't necessarily vote for this or approve of it. Some got in its way. It must have been the charisma of the stinking of over a hundred miners that made the shadows dark enough for the Mollys to take shelter in. Because they did arrive, one by two. No one saw them. They walked up the steps of Charity Hospital. They sat in the drawing room at the Provisional Nuns Freedom house. They gathered and then dispersed to wait.

He survived the fever, went to town and traded gold for life. He prepared some pan bread. He mixed in some yeast, water, sugar, oil and salt. He beat the flour into the mix. He smoked his pipe while punching the dough. Once the dough readily sprang back from his finger he tossed it in an iron skillet. He pulled his watch from his pocket and noted the time. He'd let it rise for an hour. He lit a pair of hurricane lamps and set them on the table. He set down a thick earthen mug in preparation for a tea. The water would be hot enough soon.

He placed both feet up on a stool and picked up the book he was reading. It made him feel warm to read of coral islands and volcanic rock.

The Voyage of The Beagle by Charles Darwin. He'd picked up a used 1847 edition at the bookstore. He'd had to pay ninety eight cents for it and resolved to read it before the winter was out. The corners of the pages were being stained one by one as he ate his buttered bread and drank his hot tea. He'd read two or three pages and then lean back in the chair and close his eyes. He pushed against the rails of the ship to stare at the naked black women waving and laughing on shore. He wished he'd been young and alive in the 1830's when the world was still exciting. He would have enjoyed going on a shooting expedition with Darwin.

Chapter Seven – Queen Victoria

The mine paid in gold coin. The shop keeper paid his accounts in gold and silver coin. Wise old maids nursed their jars and cans of small change.

"Eagles and double eagles, that's gold. The French called money 'argent'. That's silver. The Constitution, that old thing it says, "...only gold and silver shall be a medium of exchange." Well that's pretty clear. All debts get paid on one or the other. Everyone wants it. Now we got all this cash showing up. As if we didn't learn enough from the Confederate dollar folly or the inflation of the British pound. This damn gold and silver is the only thing you can't create out of nothing. That's why they call it precious metal. Now I know you're saying it's whatever people want to give value to has value, as if everyone could wake up tomorrow and declare that mercury or granite would be a medium of exchange. There it is.

As far as I can tell banks have been around for a long time. I read about groups making loans for collateral in ancient Rome at 22% interest. The crazy British bankrupted their country by trading gold for tea and silk. The Chinese must have thought them insane. Queen Victoria was as beautiful and brilliant as Europe could design. She really was a Queen and well on her way to be Emperor. Does the sun set on the British empire?

The British retaliated by selecting just a few ports of entry along coastal China.

So at these three or four ports and by way of traditional criminal gangs and friendly landlords the opium poured in. The inexperienced, the unread, the innocent, the farmers, the simple, the forest creatures that make up a country, you see, are totally unprepared for that brand of carpet bagger. They are absolute targets. I think part of what we've learned about the war against the Indians is that superior technology wins. You can chain an adversary by disease or drug addiction. Drug warfare or germ warfare is cheaper than cannonballs. We gave the red man deliberately infected blankets covered in small pox, measles and mumps. Since the Chinese had invented inoculation and pasteurization a good thousand years before her island was even being dry humped by Vikings she tried the white dragon. She tried to weaken and, more importantly, corrupt their officials.

"Victoria was a student of history. She understood that it was corruption that brought down empires as much as bad war planning. The corrupt officials would get use to and be involved with the secret, foreign, agents necessary to procure the drug and by that very act, their allegiance is thrown into question. Opium doesn't grow in Cloud City. Opium doesn't grow here except on a pretty perennial in grand dad's garden. So no, Vickie has got the Chinks by the short and curly. All that gold her grand dad exchanged for tea and silk. That threat of a few hundred million people with access to modern ocean power. She read Adam Smith. The wealth of nations lies in the minds of people. Destroy the minds, destroy the nation. Terrific if you don't like nationalism."

"Between the eunuchs and the opium related officials she had them balls or no balls. So I'd be real concerned about any drug or drug money that doesn't come from our own land. Alcohol, hemp, corn liquor, peyote and tobacco see, that comes from right here. Silk, tea, coffee, coco, chocolate – this all comes from somewhere else. Every penny spent on coffee is a penny exported out of our nation. Every penny spent on silk or chocolate is a penny that goes against our balance of trade, so that's why there should be high duties on them. Free trade by definition would destroy any nation that took part in it and only benefit some international company floating around the world like a fixed dice game. The trader, the company, becomes the house. Given a finite amount of hands being played out, win or lose, the house takes a steady percentage. Eventually it would have a majority and then all of it or almost all of it. Look at Medici or Rothschild, when they show up you got trouble. The blood is about to run in the streets. They knew this stuff. Abraham Lincoln knew this stuff. Lincoln was not stupid. He knew the Bank of Rothschild was financing both the North and the South. Southern tobacco. Southern cotton. Cotton processing technology. Gunpowder technology. Iron clad ship technology. Scientific acumen. But none of that can produce gold or silver out of thin air. The printing press could bankrupt us. Cash is phony money. And who are these people who order the production of cash? Gold is perfect. You don't have to put your trust in anything else. A little bit of it goes a long way. It reflects the way of things. Everything else is a gamble."

Gambling, Dan knew, was for losers and there was little point in losing. If he leaned forward just so, the hem on his jacket moved near his hand and he could switch dice from a clever hidden pocket. Tonight he would make a well timed bet on box cars. These dice only rolled fours. It was incredible the way he could switch them. He examined his profile in front of the full length mirror. He practiced switching dice for an hour. He shaved. After breakfast he returned to his room to work on his cards. He brought out a screw punch and slid each of the four aces into it. Carefully he turned the threaded bolt and created the slightest depression on the edge of the coloured border. He made similar impressions on the other face cards. It wasn't visible. But he could feel it as it flew under his finger tips. He practiced dealing and smiling and telling a joke about a general store clerk in Denver while studying himself in the mirror.

He liked the people he played cards with. Most of them were fine people. He liked their company. Some were serious assholes. Most of these cowboys had only played cards in the bunkhouse with other illiterate range hands. Maybe some of the players he would be up against had three or four hundred hours of playing time a year.

He opened his satchel. There were twenty card decks on the bottom from a variety of manufacturers. Some new, some well worn. He took the full length mirror off the wall and leaned it against the table. He figured he'd practiced almost two thousand hours that year in solitary dealing. He was a regular at three different games in Denver. In his last two days there he burnt each game and didn't leave a penny on the table.

He cheated them all and smiled and left. He was better than God. He practiced winking in a particular way to formulate another fake tell for others to pick up on.

This evening he planned to be drawn into a game with a grocer and a boot store owner. They liked to see new faces and were a jovial lot with their other friends. He had four thousand dollars in cash and gold for tonight. He planned to scare the pants off them with wild betting and high stakes and then lose eight hundred dollars. They would invite him back. He would tell some funny jokes. They wouldn't mind eventually losing ten or fifteen thousand dollars to him. He kept a Derringer in his vest pocket and another under his belt just in case anyone did mind. Everyone knew the Ute Indians could attack anytime as they had before. It wasn't right to not carry a gun. Besides which, tough guys like to carry guns. If he had to reach for his holstered pistol it would probably be too late. The Derringer might help him make it to his horse. He looked in the mirror and practiced shaking his head and pretending to laugh at someone else's joke while he moved the Queens up the deck. He had a shaving mirror propped against the long mirror to study a side view. He laughed and winked at himself. "I am naked beneath my coat of scars."

He found out early as a kid. People don't expect to be cheated right away. They're paying attention to their own cards. They're figuring the odds of pairs, straights, flushes and if they're going to start coming. He knew what the odds were. They were a hundred percent in his favour. He loved advantage playing.

He was seeing the country. He decided against going out that night and continued to practice. He left only for super. He laughed and drank shots in front of the mirror all night while dealing out hands for imaginary friends. He cut the cards so many wonderful ways. He switched packs from secret pockets. He was very smooth.

Black Bart was renting The Dead Scorpion. It was a forty by a hundred foot saloon. It was a beautiful operation. Faro and dice games were fixed and ideal for all the fresh arrivals. Two ladies were boarding on the second floor. Men were singing, "We are a Fenian brotherhood, skilled in the arts of war. And we're going to fight for Ireland, the land that we adore. Many battles have we won, along with the boys in blue. And we'll go and capture Canada, for we've nothing else to do."

As predicted, the population of wagons thinned. The snow was clearly going to stick. Sleighs would be sliding through next, driving up the price of goods with the higher transportation costs.

Geisel was hammering. "Hand me that plank."

"Sure. So this will be the darkroom now."

"Yes. The front windows provide a marvellous sun. I can do studio work there."

Chapter Eight - Hibernia

Susy knew she was going to be a nun at her first communion. She wouldn't only be a bride of Christ, but a soldier too.

"The city only pays us seven dollars a week," she looked down at the man in the bed. He needed more sulphide drugs. They would be provided. He may or may not live but the trauma would be reduced.

"Make sure the doctor pays attention to him."

She walked down the floor. She stopped to examine a chart at the foot of a bed. O'Sullivan had his ribs wrapped in bandages. Both his eyes were swollen and red. His jaw and face were in a cast. He had a job and would again. He would pay his debt to the hospital.

This dormitory had fifteen beds on either side. The floors were long plank that had been washed and waxed a hundred times to a dark yellow brown shine. Its hard waxed surface revealed every speck of dust. Beside every bed was a narrow side stand. Gunshot wounds, broken bones, alcoholism, knife wounds, pneumonia kept rotating through out the ward. There was a similar ward for women down the hall.

"What are you in for?" She asked a patient.

"Not drawing fast enough." He looked her over. "What are you in for?"

She moved on to the night log book and a younger Sister held it open for her. Susy's inspection was complete. She returned to her office and prepared to meet Danny. He was the last of the group, having stopped in Denver for a week to chase down his printer friend.

There was a light rapping on the glass of her door.

"Yes," she said.

The door opened. Sister Heather put her head in, "A Mr. O'Sullivan is here to see you."

"Yes. Have him come in."

"It's good to see you, cousin." Once the door was closed behind him he embraced her. He grasped her shoulders and stood back. "As beautiful as your mother," said Danny.

"You're not supposed to grab nuns." Her cheeks glowed red. "Have you seen any of Leadville yet?"

"It's incredible, like a big fair."

"You have a room. I wrote the address down. You can start from there. I guess you have your ways. The others are staying at these addresses.

He looked down at the paper. "You look very much in charge here. The hospital is spotless and looks so efficient." The windows behind her were bright. "Yeah. I'll find the boys. We'll have to slip away. The boy with the broken face... Leary. Will he live?"

She nodded, "He'll live. Lord knows what he will have to do to win a girl's hand. But he will be able to work and feed himself. He'll get out of that bed."

She pushed a small pouch of gold coins over the desk to him. "There's two hundred dollars there. We're tired of seeing good boys being wasted by these heathen bullies. These anti-Catholic guilds are insults and two of our girls were raped last week while we waited for you."

"Two of the Sisters?"

"No. One was a wife of an outspoken miner. The other his sister. It's gone beyond simple intimidation tactics. We may as well have the old landlords of Ireland telling us how and where to live. It's totally unacceptable."

"We're here like ghosts, Susy. You'll see our works soon enough. This file is most prudent. I'll burn it shortly. Your face is so beautiful. Every baby would struggle to grab your nose."

She smiled and kept smiling.

Tom O'Grady shoveled ore into a cart. It was Friday. He liked to pretend he was shoveling gravel over his supervisor's spontaneous grave.

His shift was over at seven. At least it was supposed to be over at seven. Last week they had lengthened the end of the shift until nine. They didn't give any notice or extra pay. The men were mad. Their backs hurt. Their eyes were dirty. Their lungs ached. A third of them walked with a limp. More than one toe had been banged from rocks and heavy tools falling. The men looked at one another. Six thirty and no mention of a change in time. Someone whistled.

"Will I see you at The Bloody Unicorn, Tom, or The Black Rose tonight?"

"No. Tonight I'm seeing my cousin."

The men left the mining shack window. All walked a little straighter. This mine paid eighteen dollars a shift for five eleven hour days. Take it or not. They took it and some prospected on the weekends. Others nursed their wounds. Some fermented and boiled in the saloons. All took it as adventure.

He felt the coins in his pocket. "Can't wait to change clothes, Tom."

"A bath. I've got to have a bath, Sullivan."

"Did that evil eye devil search you for nuggets?"

"Yeah. He told me if I stole anything it was a hanging offense. I was going to tell him he was stealing my labour but I didn't. I need this and next week's pay too."

"Still saving for your wife?"

"And three kids in Cork. Ten more months of this. I miss those kids looking at me. My wife and her eyes watching me and giving me a good plate."

"A man's family. Maybe someday for me too if my purse were big enough."

"Oh, the women they like a big purse." He hitched up his belt and laughed.

Geisel was taking stock of his chemicals. He made a note and thought to check at the drugstore for refills before he sent away by mail.

People liked Neville's Saloon and Hotel. Montreal Murdock took a pipe from his vest pocket and held a match to it. He leaned his guitar up against a yellow door. He took a few draws and set it down. He picked the guitar up slowly. "Here. Fifth fret on the G string, then open."

"Okay. How about this?" Jacob worked over a three bar melody on the piano, then repeated it in a lower chord. Bruce picked away, following up on the melody.

A covered wagon painted with signs, colourful stars and displaying a huge, American flag was stationed near Tiger Alley. "Folks, I just want to tell you. I just want you to know. It would be a big favour to me if you would help me help others. Let me set aside my own self interests." He held up a small box with a bold, red label on it. "Dr. McNeil's Healer and Tonic pills have been absolutely proven to reverse and completely cure the modern diseases of modern man. Only through years of European research and by spending his vast fortune has Dr. McNeil succeeded in producing the most modern nineteenth century scientific curative for less than. I'm telling you now, for less than one dollar a box. Included, at no additional charge, there has been provided top grade, clinical instructions for each application. These patent pending wonders will not only cure drowsiness, they will prevent migraines. These curative wonders, a marvellous invention of a God fearing medical man, will actually cure syphilis. In only thirty days your symptoms will disappear. No one can do better than that. That's science for only ninety-five cents a box. That is incredible or double your money back. The company address is on each and every box. They hide from no one. God is on our side."

The pills were excellent. People called them, horse pills. They were half cocaine and half opium. Untreated, the symptoms of syphilis would have retreated on their own in thirty days anyway, only to return full blown in twenty years. Henry liked to take them with beer. It really smoothed out his day. A day like any other.

People crowded around the wagon, rolling dollars and coins into the salesman's hand. He was loved.

Captain Gifford's store smelt of leather, lye, candy, coffee, tea, mink oil, perfume and apples. The city needed everything so he bought everything hardware, notion and sundry that he could. He had a two month turnover on goods - capitalist's dream. He checked the lid on a barrel of smoked herring and another of salted cod. He had a fine display of both long and short arms and a wider variety of ammunition. Several bolts of cloth were being looked at by some ladies of the silver set. "Do you still have that tea service, Captain?"

She ordered two jars of pickled sausage, wine, ammunition, licorice whips, coffee, kerosene and a seed catalog. "I'll go by the distillers and pick up a barrel or two for the cellar. Just in case the rats aren't drunk enough."

"We need more cats."

"A boy's first rifle. Is there a sweeter day? That's wonderful, Tom."

"Short stock and everything. He'll need extra ammo."

"Compass. Copper wire. Generator."

"If there was a way to be wrong you have achieved it in the purest fashion. Perhaps you could receive redemption through the ingestion of sherry. Pungent yet somehow vile to the taste. It shows no mercy to the palette."

He stood there staring at him while eating through an apple in a continuous dripping bite. The juices ran down his beard. "Things working out well for you, boy?"

"Why, The Rat Bastard Gazette is the finest newspaper west of the Mississippi. If we say shootings are growing in numbers then that's it. Be damned if the city wants to be capital. Killings are up." He drank from the bottle. He carried his pistol high up on the inside of his right arm. He was a south paw.

A prince from Luxembourg wished to place an advertisement. He sought some guides for an expedition. He and his companions with a few cases of champagne and guns and tents. The editor just stared at him.

"We'll be staying at The Grand."

"Oh, they carry pistols everywhere; down their boots, in their skirts, on their hips. But anywhere they are they got to reach for them. Look for the reach."

"As of Feb. 16th we're pulling real money out of the ground. Silver is legal tender. All the ounce is missing is an imprint. People just don't get it. It's cash in the ground, on the ground or the ground itself. It's hilarious, dirt is money. Of course another thousand or two will come in this month. What can I sell them? What do they need?" He said.

"The land all around here is free. You get your deposit money back after a year. Well maybe you get it back. Either way whatever isn't owned by prospectors you can claim for your own. Farm it somehow. Any live stock that can deal with thirty foot drifts and thirty below zero will do just fine." Gifford said.

Pinkerton Detectives, they're just the best. They wear nice suits and such fine pants. They didn't go for any nonsense. With them there is a tomorrow. They lean towards justice but not at all times or at all costs. Not in the dark. They were here now. He knew that. They were all supposed to be long gone and dead swinging in the breeze during the summer solstice of 1877 with Campbell, Kehoe, Doyle and Kelly. That was justice. Certainly enough to suit a mob. Calling anything justice just about always made it so. If it wasn't justice at least it was movement. "If you shoot first there's no need to ask questions."

"Yes?" she said, "I think you need a peppermint stick." She took a stick of candy out from a jar and gave it to the little girl. The bell rang above the door and another customer walked in. "Good afternoon, Shelia. I just received those two bolts from San Francisco today. Real silk. Kept it special for you first." She pulled two bolts of cloth out and laid them on top of a counter full of Levis.

Shelia ran her hands over the material. "Oh, it shimmers. Such a lovely pattern. Oh, this is beautiful silk. The black, red and silver threads are so fine."

"Mommy, you said to get yeast," the little girl put the stick of candy back in her mouth.

"I better have a half pound of yeast. I just can't get the sourdough down right. Two bags of flour..."

Sister Susy thought of Tracy and how she might be. If her daughter had straightened out any. It had been awhile and she resolved to see when she brought the claim papers over.

"This is the best idea I ever had." The promoter had impressed himself. He ran his hands over the smoothness of the ball. It was the size of a room.

He put the book down. "I must be an old soul. Humility is apparently our last life lesson," said the book store clerk.

She added a handful of oats and a tea spoon of celery seeds to the dough. On reflection, she opened a jar and added two cups of raisins. "You could live off of my bread," she thought. After another ten minutes she stopped kneading the bread and sliced off hunks of it to roll out and then roll up into loaves for the second rise. At ten thousand feet she would have to wait an hour and a half for the second rise. By then it would be time for the men to get about their morning routines. The bread only needed twenty eight minutes in the oven after that.

She heated up a pan full of pork drippings and molasses to spread on the bread. They might hit the table groggy but her boarding house breakfast for the working man was gunpowder.

They left laughing and chatting fueled on caffeine, sugar and a thick coating of flour and lard. It would serve them well. Flour, grease and coffee had built the west as much as anything else.

Mrs. Bindlepost was always full. She listened to what they talked about. She had come to understand a lot about prospecting, at least, in theory. She was taking in laundry from others. "If I don't learn to nickel and dime I'll go broke." She was thinking about the capital outlay for a still out back. She could flavour the stuff with vanilla or almond perhaps and call it a liquor like the French did. Flavour it up and sell it. Almost all the men who boarded with her had been gold seekers. One was a teacher and another a book keeper. But most of the other few dozen had the gold fever.

Dutch Honey passed him the hose.

Black Thumb Bob inhaled.

He passed the hose back and put a board on his lap. This was his portable lap top. He picked up a steel pen and continued etching shadow lines onto a copper plate. He was making an etching for *Leslie's Illustrated News*. It had hundreds of figures, buildings and wagons. He had the details of hats, beards and tacking. He competed with the photograph and in some senses picked up finer details.

Chestnut Street was busy like any other US city. It would be published in two months. He carefully carved into the softer metal sixteen hours a day.

The table beside him was covered in paste and liquids for burning into and creating his pictures. His finger tips were black and green. He focused on a wagon. He made a small partial loop for a horse hoof. He completed a page every two weeks. He sent a package to Europe once a month selling to the major magazines and papers. *Le Parisian, The Strand, Leslies' Illustrated, The London Advertiser*. His room mates were insane writers and artists. The Breckenridge rooming house had lately given itself over to the flow of actors and writers. He and his confederates had pooled together and rented a floor. Life was grand. All boundaries were loose and artistic boundaries were only self inspired. "Dogma is not my birth right."

"Take a walk down outlaw road," he thought.

Maybe he could forget the pain here. He looked around and decided to grow a beard to fit in. He saw a newspaper being sold and he was glad. There had to be an intellectual center somewhere. He thought to buy a new hat and a pair of boots.

"Well, hell." The manager opened the door of the Little Pittsburgh office. The rear window was forced and broken open. Of course the richest mine in the area didn't keep any bullion there and so had no need of a safe. But it was a nerve center of hiring, transportation and other infrastructure duties.

"They took the telephone." He immediately wondered who was responsible for paying for it.

They just got the five dollar a month phone system installed. It hooked up various mines and mine floors to the head office. He went to the wall from where it had been ripped. The receiver was on the floor. It was useless without a receiver. More bits of the phone were scattered here and there. "Vandalism. Maybe an unhappy worker or mine owner...Mollys?" He wondered.

Harry sat on a chair in his room at Nevilles. He had the mine's phone upside down on his table and was unbolting the hand crank generator. The rest of it he would crush and toss in an alley.

He removed it and examined its output leads. He slid out his contraption from beneath the bed. He placed a block of slate beneath the magnetic hand crank and bolted it to the board. He wound the well patinated copper wire around the enclosure. The balanced quartz motor mounted in the middle turned on its axis. He lowered the magnetic ring and found everything centered.

He eyeballed the components against the compass point and radiating degrees down on its base. Carefully he slid thick glass plates into grooves along the board and lowered another thick glass plate on top of that. When the sides were glued together he'd created a transparent hermetically sealed box. He fixed this with zinc oxide fumes and turned the crank. The vapor began to glow.

He watched the quartz piece spin. He drew designs on the glass plate in the static with his finger. He stopped and timed how long the glow continued. He watched his name fade. Henry considered modulating the frequency by moving the ceramic dial of blue stones.

He looked around and heard the dog shifting itself in the closet. The dog was no fan of such scientific sorcery. He took another pull of the pipe and thought about a thicker gasket around the hand crank handle.

He spent all his time either working to produce food or improving his shelter. He knew a wife followed by children would make life easier and give meaning to him.

"If you were a guy..." she says to him.

"It was the most remarkable thing I'd ever seen. We'd crossed into Yuma a few days earlier and had made camp on the edge of the Mojave desert. He'd been through before and always tried to camp near the out croppings. Weirdest stuff I ever saw. One place we came upon was all these mounds of boulders. All round like balls and as big as houses. There were piles of them like handfuls in a bunch. Huge, perfectly round and nothing but flat desert all around. I had no idea where they could have come from. One night we were at the foot of this small mountain. We had a fire going and had built it up pretty good. The wind started to blow. He says, "Watch this."

"These tumbleweeds start rolling. These things were huge. When they get the size of wagons and come racing at you. You better be out of the way. I see how it could kill a man on a horse." Wolf said.

"I just don't know. The question is, are you full of it to here or here?" He held the edge of his palm to Wolf's throat and then to the top of his head.

Dutch Honey and Sweetwater Sally came in together on the same wagon. Dutch Honey had married the editor of The Rat Bastard Gazette. Sweetwater Sally had stayed too long, marrying the street, and her last kiss at twilight was interrupted by Gentlemen Joe's sense of righteousness and perhaps, boredom.

Joe looked at her. She was sitting at a desk by the window. Her hair shone. There was a stillness about her. She was in the moment, dwelling on what was the case about her. She knew a lot about men, he felt. He could be open around her.

"Let's say, there's enough for the pipe and enough for day to day living. What then could we become? What would we lean towards doing?" He said.

"Given our life lessons already taken? Each unique?"

"Yes. I suppose so."

"Men always want me to do things. That's my lesson so far. They want me to do things, make any promise. I'm still here. No one took me along."

He reached for his hat. "Let's go for a walk."

She touched her eye. There was a light yellow bruise showing. She reached for her hat and posed in front of the mirror primping up while he slicked back his hair.

"Men are always after me to do things too. Sometimes they want my money. Sometimes they want to give me their money. They want me to turn out to be a cheat. They want a piece of me." Joe looked out the window.

"I met one man who wanted you to stab him in the head just a little while ago," she said.

"See, just like that. He was an idiot. Everyone wants something. That's why we have legs to walk towards it." He fixed his hat.

The board walk was thick with people. The road was congested with wagons and livestock. The noise of a steam car startled some horses. It was a glorious Saturday morning. The shop keepers had polished their glass. The influx of paint had splashed all the store fronts with brilliant colours.

"Look at those people. They look like they just walked in. It was the only way."

"How can they allow cars on the road? Cars don't belong on the road. It doesn't make any sense."

They brushed against many people along their way. They paused at Leinger's bookstore and went in.

"*The Strand*?" He asked.

The clerk handed him the latest issue. "You must be following Sherlock Holmes, are you sir?"

"I just have to. His logic, conceit and just bang up story is marvellous. And I must have the latest by Jules Verne please. English or French it doesn't matter."

He noticed her pausing to examine some book titles. He was excited she could read French.

The, would be, seed salesman watched the poker opponent across from him go white. He could feel the man's cold sweat. Acid was burning in the mark's throat as his bile rose. Classic signs of betting too much was physical rebellion. They had both laid down their cards. Dan had a full house and the big loser three queens. Another man would nearly faint at the sheer stupidity of his play. The hammer of foresight gracing the path of a fool was always present. The other players whistled. He'd lost the last six hands but took this one. Eight hundred dollars plus a gold claim. It was everything the man had spent his two years working on. Dan took it in five minutes with a pair of Kings stacked and flipped into his hand. The other three were left with half their stakes. They would play again. In a week or two he would take a little more off their table.

"I didn't know just what way that was gonna turn out. Jed, I thought you had a straight when you folded to his raise I was surprised. I'll tell you what, another two hundred and I'd a folded thinking you had four of a kind. Let me buy everyone a shot." Dan said.

"Thanks, Dan."

"To decent Dan and his long whiskered jokes."

Dan left the bottle on the table and made his way up the street towards his hotel. A light rain was falling, so only the desperate and the busy were taking an evening path.

He kept one hand resting on the bone hilt of his holstered gun. His way was soon blocked by two women leaning on one another. They were clearly drunk or drugged or something. One dropped her purse while they continued on in their oblivious way. He stooped to pick it up with the intent of being rewarded with a free blow job when he realized his stupidity and received a smashing knock to his head and a kick to the stomach.

The two women raced back and bent over the knocked silly Big Dan. The two Sullivan cousins, in dresses, went through his pockets while the assailant went through his jacket and below the belt. In thirty seconds he was fleeced of two thousand dollars, two handguns, several Derringers and a half pint of rum.

"Stolen liquor always tastes best," said Danny O'Sullivan to Lorne O'Shea." He removed his bonnet

"It will be fun to tap that fat barrel again," said Lorne pulling off his corset.

"There must be over a thousand dollars in cash, more in gold. This gives us a proper start. Our Lord is a good one." He pulled the dress over his head.

He opened a dresser drawer to put the disguise away and noticed a half dozen dynamite sticks. "I see you were shopping for more than just lipstick."

"May as well get right to it. Fast. Hard. Unfair. Hide. Do it again."

"Hey. I didn't get a swallow of rum."

"Hear's an eagle, go buy us all some, young runt."

Big Dan woke up yelling, scarring away a pair of human relics in worse shape then he was. He'd been left in Tiger Alley and about to lose his boots. For some reason he still had his watch and the gold claim. He pushed himself up from the stinking mud. He felt small pebbles sink into his hand. He still had his holster but it was empty. He patted himself down. His wallet was empty on the ground. He had only a Bowie knife left on his belt but at least that. He knew he had more money back at the hotel and resolved to continue on his way. It gave him time to think about the attack.

He knew there would be no more after her. He didn't care. Then he was angry. Angry at her and angry at himself for spoiling him for other women. He could never get that close again.

They took turns punching him in the face. The O'Sullivans, Shea and Donnley punched Denver Slim across the cheeks and jaw. They held back. They didn't want to break his jaw or ruin his capacity for communication.

He was part of the group who burnt down Danny's shack, surely part of the gang that messed up the kid in the hospital. His arms were tied behind his back. There was plenty of blood dripping from his face. There was hunger in their eyes. A final lust for blood. They would find out what he had to say.

They put a table in sight beside him.

On the table were two hammers, a tong, a saw and a hatchet. His eyes were sad, hot and fear. He began to cry. But he wasn't ready yet. He needed to be beaten some more. He held his breath while they removed his boots.

"Yes," he said, "Really. Yes."

They worked on him, each learning something new about his own heartlessness and man's attempt at loyalty. He thought it might be related to pride. It looked awful. Pride could just turn a man into a puddle. A shuddering mess. It was easy to kill him off and call it an end. They knew who he had worked with anyway. He would disappear. They wanted retribution and to put a stop to enough before word got out. They would pick a few near by trees for them. "Gone to Protestant Hell," would read one sign. "Catholic Defense League," read another. The meaning and drift was clear. Up the ante. The stakes were raised.

"It all counts. Every bit of it. Every action. Every statement got recorded somewhere in someone's mind." Neiderguy passed the hose. The cannabis smoke stretched into tomorrow.

The Parker Davis one pound tins were his current favorite. He was guaranteed to have no migraines or asthma. He didn't move much from his chair for several months. Some bodily functions but not much more. Dutch Honey came and went depending on the deadlines of her publishing husband. He didn't mind where she was. He knew she had to be someplace. Artists immobilized by East Indian tea did not make him jealous. When he asked her to fulfill something she did. She loved him completely. She asked him for everything he had. He always wished he had more to give. There was no harsh truth between them. He put out a paper, drank and worshiped her.

They met a year earlier. He was coming out of the theatre and she was standing near, close enough. Her price was agreeable and her demeanor charming. He thought, why not? And asked her to marry him and she said yes. She wasn't the first woman of Leadville to move from being a fallen dove to wife. Choices, it's all about choices. She said yes.

He made notes for the Thursday edition. "Two men found hanged with signs on them. James Gang observed passing through town, enjoying the theatre, back no doubt when the train is running. Taxes, to pay for grading and leveling of roads. Steam cars, a nuisance scaring horses and the public at large. Every idiot mechanic with time on his hands is making his own James Watt mobile. They are dangerous and stupid. Cars have no place on the roads."

He heard some noises in the kitchen. He walked in and saw a full bottle of whisky on the table. Dutch Honey was stirring a stew and wearing only an apron and a feather hat. "My life is the best life," he thought.

As soon as he heard about it, Henry knew he had to know more. The stock promoter, Adam Baulm, was easy to find. His share certificates looked legitimate and the cannonball capsule of the highest quality. He just needed to be sold on the propulsion.

"The electric generator simply creates a magnetic field just ahead of the ship and pulls it along," Adam sorted through some stock certificates.

"It's what works. There's less gravity up here in Cloud City. At 10,200 feet altitude an extra two miles from the earth's core makes a difference. I've thought of everything."

"I have to have a seat."

"An investor is born," said Adam. He adjusted his glasses.

They worked out the details.

"Everyone says you're going to Mars."

Henry said, "It's a guarantee. We shook on it and I paid cash."

"Well that's it then. What about your dog?"

"Obviously the dog goes along," he looked down. "Good, Shep."

"Telegraphs, telephones, steam cars, photographs, typewriters, repeating rifles. Now you say a ship to Mars. Makes sense to me. The big question is cash. Do you figure there is cash in it?"

"Just think of the possible fur trade if no one has been hunting or trapping all this time. Look how much that bastard Hudson made up in Canada."

"It'd be crazy to not go to Mars. It only took me a moment to think about it."

"Is it a ship or a bullet shape or wagon or sled?"

"It's a cannonball."

"A cannonball? I'd of used balloons."

"Yeah. He said he thought of that but they're harder to aim and slower. Besides it's already mostly made. It's the Cannonball Express," he said and lit his pipe. "We're scientific now. It's going to be a real expedition. Lasalle would be proud."

The promoter was delighted. He'd found the perfect investor in Henry. He had the money.

The vehicle was almost ready. A similar one was being started for livestock and another for hardware.

The smell of the fresh horse dung in the streets was pleasant on such a fine day. There were buckboards loading in front of most of the stores.

Two men were fighting with Bowie knives behind The Dead Scorpion. They danced and jabbed at one another slashing for an arm or searching for an eye. Captain Gifford received a barrel of coffee and another of nails.

At ten in the morning about a hundred and twenty saloons were full. Geisel had prepared a back pack to commemorate the out lying landscape. Dutch Honey rolled against her husband committed to baking breakfast at noon.

"It's a habit," said Gentleman Joe. He was washing his hands for the tenth time that morning. "I have a game coming up. I have to focus. This appears to be part of it." He shrugged. "And how about The Anthenaeum afterwards or The Carbonite? Let's take in some theatres tonight. Balcony seats would be the way to go. Buckskin can arrange that I do believe. Have you appropriate attire?"

The three legged dog was going crazy, running up and down the outside of the cabin. It was searching for Bernie, the ground hog it had seen earlier. Soon Scampers rolled on its back and began to twist in the dust against temporary relief from fleas. The groundhog scrambled out the other side of the cabin. The dog was slow but efficient in its one paw scooping of the soil to make a hole under the cabin while her master read of far away birds, lizards and parasitic plants. It wagged its tail knowing it was doing the proper thing. Dogs are happiest when they are doing the proper thing or up to bad boy mischief. It toiled away, one scoop at a time.

Sweetwater Sally ran her hands up and down the bark of one of the pine trees growing in the Carbonite Concert Hall. She and Joe had been shown to their balcony. He had reserved it for the two of them. Champagne was sitting in a bucket of ice. The curtains were still down. An orchestra was warming up in the pit. Lime light scoops were being filled. He admired the pearl necklace against her throat. A waiter brought in smoked salmon canapés and miniature quiche tarts. The table and chairs below were mainly facing the stage. Men were playing cards. Waiters circulated with trays of beer and shot glasses.

They heard a scream.

"You stole from my poke the last time." The man speaking was digging a broken bottle into the eye of the man screaming.

"Shut up. Shut up. I can't hear the piano." Four waiters tossed the pair of them out into the street.

Twenty one armed bandits were absorbing one and five cent coins.

Oyster stuffed quail was brought to their table.

The winner of the first dog fight escaped from it's cage back stage and tore the hoop jumping poodle into high pitched shreds. All the miners laughed and shouted. Two men from the audience started shooting the poodle corpse. The crowd roared. Next a man recited Moliere. Jessie James eyeballed a dancing girl and fingered his hotel key.

Two men took to the stage and began telling jokes about President Hayes and his electoral contest with Tilden. A rear curtain was dropped and scenery shifted into position. The lime light revealed an apple orchard. The orchestra began the William Tell overture while a woman was bound to a pole. An upended playing card was fixed to the top of her head. For openers Buckskin Joe came racing out of stage left towards the woman. A costumed Indian charged at him throwing himself at his feet. Joe summer-salted in the air, easily clearing the Indian. He landed in a crouch on the ground and drew his knife to throw it and slice the playing card in two. The woman smiled and clapped her hands.

"He sure is a fancy thrower."

"That's one of his daughters, Ella."

One eyed Jacob was in the orchestra pit admiring the show. His wife, Rose, had taken their baby to visit her mother for the evening. He had been assured of several solid months of pay to come. He listened while a speaker recounted what it was like to man air balloons during the war. That was followed by a very moving opera which lasted nearly an hour, spell biding the audience. Six men yelled, "No," When the star stabbed her self in the heart. The curtain fell. Men shot guns in the floor and ceiling.

Julia Kay walked on the stage like she was made there. She held her face up and sang. Her waist length brunette hair shimmered and moved against her honey hips. The crowd became an audience and stared. They imagined that the beauty she expressed was theirs.

Julia Kay carried them. Flowers were found and thrown to her feet. Her teachers were proud. When Julia took her basset hound for walks men took off their hats and smoothed back their hair.

"I bet they don't have theatre of this quality in Luxemburg," said a Lilly Lurue sitting in a European Count's lap.

"'I thought that bitch was barking in hell.'" Was the last thing he said to me in Denver. Then I find out later that the cash box is missing and the Sheriff shows up with papers from three different wives. So now we're all here. I'm going by the name of Bert Laiscell," Buckskin Joe said. "Mabel has it down that I'll be managing the New Antheneum Theatre for awhile so we will be having some astounding acts. By God this is 1880, man. The handbills must be bold. Our Professor Of Magic and the black arts can pull a goat out of a hat. We will be presenting the finest troupe of Shakespearian actors that England ever had. The borders must be thick. At least three different typefaces," Joe explained to the printer. "I've got competition. J.S. Langrishe is playing at Tabor's Opera House at least until the end of February."

The Rat Bastard Gazette reported on May 29th, 1880 that 1,324 actors, musicians and bands started a parade on Fryer Hill and continued down Jefferson Avenue. Candy, peanut, apple and other sidewalk vendors benefited from the impromptu parade lead by Langrishe. "Typical of our lively town," was the sub-headline.

"You should have seen it on Wednesday night. I paid a dollar and there was Bert. He gets blindfolded and someone puts a bag over his head, then he climbs twenty feet to a tightrope and runs and dances in the middle. Get this, two guys come up on a step ladder and hand him a chair. He balances the chair on the rope, sits in it, holds a two hundred pound boulder in his hand while one of the guys on the step ladder cracks the rock open with a sledge hammer. That was Buckskin theatre of the finest quality."

Buckskin was proud of the billing and refreshment sales. His end was fifteen percent of liquor sales and a piece of the gate. "We need some tomahawk throwing, that's what we need. Some rabid dogs fighting a bear and the opening of Henry the Eighth Part Two." He thought about next week's spectacular handbills and posters.

He said to the printer, "I've had some good nights here, Bill. Miss Mabel Rivers so honoured me with management of the New Anthenaum Theatre on State Street. One night Jessie James and his gang rented a private booth and left two hundred dollars in tips. I gave them a deal on some grub when I was running a grocery store back in Kansas and maybe, they were on the run."

"Pass me that file on him," said the Pinkerton Man, "He stands out too much."

He read, "…'Buckskin Joe, born Oct. 4, 1840, Lake Magog Quebec. He took a stage coach to Boston, shipped around Cape Horn to California. He was a lumberjack, trapper, circus acrobat, soldier at Bull Run, high wire walker."

"He played 16 musical instruments, Scout, grass hopper fighter, miner. He found 22 mines, prospector. He fought claim jumpers, the 1879 Ute uprising. He was a wagon train guide, leader of an orchestra called the Arkansas Border Brass Band and another called the Cow Horn Band. He has several daughters.'" He said, "Seems ordinary enough but I'll watch him. I'm waiting for a telegram."

Joe would also later prospect for gold in Nova Scotia in 1884. He would become a Deputy in Oklahoma in 1890. He was a circus owner of the Pawnee Wild West Show. He'd get chased out of the Honduras during a revolution in 1901 while mining. He was free.

"Alright, lets say you're black. You probably got here during the last exodus out of the South. What with the Union army finally pulling out and tension and memory being what it was that year and the year before, a lot of use-to-be slaves, moved north and west. Them Klans men ghosting about. Is that about it?"

"Well. I'd say no. Except for me actually being black. That parts right. I didn't know my mother. My father escaped from a slave plantation in Brazil and walked to California. He got there about two years after the big rush in fifty one. I was just three years old then. But California stayed a slave free state. I worked steady and grew up with the freedom to live second class. As far as these hip hugging six guns go I'm just saying maybe I'm not the fastest shootist but I ain't apologizing for stepping on your shadow. I can run cattle, play guitar, read and write and cipher. I can bend horseshoes, speak Spanish, French and English and sometimes roll a lot of sevens."

"I could use a man like you."

"What if I don't want to be used?"

"Well, what do you want?"

"Lately, I like a fair share."

"That's a lot to ask for."

"True enough it is."

"The pay is fifteen dollars a week."

Black Charlie laughed. "It's two hundred dollars a month to do a job of this nature. Certainly it was in Lincoln County."

"You were there?"

"Everyone was there, dead or alive. Then one leaves, dead or alive. I left after about nine hundred dollars worth of troubles. Now you tell me you got troubles. You got troubles in trouble city. Leadville is the capital of trouble, Dodge is nothing. I don't know how that happened – I just know about the two hundred dollars part. That and this place invented trouble."

He was hunched down in the cold creek water. Every wrinkle on his well creased face was dark with grit. His skin was tanned from the sun. A straw hat gave him some shade as he panned in the shallows.

Geisel noticed him after walking up a rise. He took off his pack. The horse was grateful.

He waved to the prospector and began to set up his equipment. He extended the tripod. The prospector wondered if he was making a survey or what.

Geisel walked over to the man and explained that he was taking photos to document the frontier and not doing any fancy claim jumping. In fact. If he was so interested he could set his box camera and horse right there and take sun paintings.

The prospector swished while Geisel set up his mini-darkroom. He made mental notes to improve his portable set up.

The prospector was as old as Geisel's uncle and was taking out a few ounces a day.

"There's still some easy stuff to pick up off the ground yonder but I'm tired and this is my last summer here. A few more months of a couple ounces a day with the occasional nugget and I'm headed back east and getting a farm in Vermont. Just one big enough to die on. But I want to be close enough to town that I can get a haircut and something to hear about over a glass of beer. It's difficult to not hear a human voice for so many months at a time. The insects are so loud it drives me crazy. I can't wait really. Sell this claim and cabin for a thousand dollars and I'm gone. Can't believe the Utes didn't cut my throat at Mill Creek. September 29th 1879, that's when you could have got a nice sun picture. Guess they're chased back to the other side of the mountain now."

"Yep, Leadville then the stage to Denver then a sorrowful goodbye in the cat houses there. All this talk makes me want to leave sooner. In Vermont I'll get my gold from maple trees. The syrup is a powerful nectar." He wasn't going to stop talking for a while.

"This is bad business. Not too many are going to stand for it," he looked at the dead man. It's face and eyes were wet with flies. A paper was pinned to the corpse's chest. "Gone to Protestant Hell," it read.

The hanging site was just South of town, in a grove of trees left standing near a telegraph pole. It wasn't so secluded as to remain hidden for long.

"Who do you think did that, Sheriff?"

"Well we'll find out who this is first. I've an idea who it might be."

"You can tell from that gold tooth it's Denver Slim."

"Denver Slim Identified." Scribbled the journalist from The Rat Bastard Gazette.

"Anti-Protestant Mob Debuts." Wrote the Republican Weekly.

The Pinkerton's man frowned and scanned the faces of the slowly assembling crowd. Would he find one of his Mollys in the scene? He walked over to the Sheriff. They lifted the body slack and then cut the rope to lay the body on a blanket.

The Sheriff draped the wrapped corpse over the back of his horse. The Pinkerton's man walked around the immediate area. The ground was hard and dry. He found no strips of cloth or lost horse shoes. A well used road was twenty feet away. He stood at different points sighting the hanging tree.

The Sheriff rode back to town with a few others beside him.

The Pinkerton's man rode up alongside and said to him. "I think that took at least three people to do."

"There wasn't much wrestling around there anyway."

"Maybe he was already dead."

"A dead two hundred and ten pound message? Will there be others? Will they stink as bad? I prefer winter murders with fresh tracks."

"So you say you didn't recognize anyone of the men who beat you?"

"I didn't actually see any faces. I saw boots. I felt boots. I heard laughter. I was curled up on the ground. I couldn't really tell you if I was being beaten for ten seconds or ten minutes. After awhile, I think I passed out."

Was anyone mad that you took this beating?"

"Everyone." He fell asleep.

Sheriff Kirkham nodded. The boy was a mess. He was leaking pus. His eyes were filled with blood and red like a devil. The doctor said the cornea was actually stronger than the eye sack and it was the eyeball sac behind the cornea that had been punctured. There were going to be complications.

He had sent a policeman to check on another body that had been found. It too had a sign attached. Likely they would be connected. "Pal of Denver Slims." There was a clover leaf with skull and cross bones drawn through it.

"That's enough for me," he said to the Pinkerton man, "It's your Mollys. They the only ones to be more clever than to be caught red handed. They've started hitting back."

His wife would have his dinner ready soon. Her dumplings and chicken gravy tasted better than not solving murders. If no one talked, he had no case. If no one saw it and came forward, there was no evidence. There were no clues.

"If there's anymore bodies tonight, it's your problem. Tonight I get a fantastic dinner. Earn your hundred dollars a month. Start drinking now. See if the taste of whisky makes you feel smart. Don't let any dead bodies run away. See what the doc might say tomorrow. He's usually more sober by noon. We sent for him earlier but there's no moving him."

He said to a policeman in his office. "How about you, Pinkerton? You a man with a sense of humour? You don't look like you'd laugh if the Pope fell down a flight of stairs. You don't look like a laughing type guy to me. You ever smiled? See a hanging you favoured?"

"I like the ones best that aren't mine, Kirkham."

"You are a laugh riot."

Mrs. Bindlepost made eight pies. Four were raisin and four were turkey pot pies. One pot held the boiling raisin mix, the other frying butter and flour for a white sauce. Once the last pies were in the oven she started punching the bread dough. While the bread was rising she went to the laundry room and began stirring the tub full of pants and shirts. She agitated them up and down plunging them into a froth. She could do four tubs today. There were four clothes lines strung out back. She laid a towel down on the table and turned a dozen mason jars upside down. A large pot of eggs boiled on the stove. She searched for a jug of apple vinegar for the pickling. Her cat was scratching at the back door. Soon it would leap to the kitchen window sill. She would notice it and pour some cream off the milk jug for it. When she let the cat in she automatically checked the near by cords. She noted that it was time to order more ash. There was lots of maple. She pumped some water up for the morning coffee. The pies cooled.

She tore off sheets of paper.

The pies would be cut and divided for her boarder's lunches. All of them paid the extra fee for surrogate mother packed lunches. She swept the floor. The cat ran under the stove. She opened a trap door set in the kitchen floor. It led to the root cellar. She was suspicious and wanted the cat to explore the area. "Bold mice can make for fat cats," she thought. "You get to work," she shook a finger at the cat, "go protect my cheese and apples."

Two school teachers and a lawyer were drinking brandy. Being civilized men they kept their hands on the table. "Don't give me any of that Ukrainian Gogol crap. I'm telling you Goethe could only touch Shakespeare on his death bed."

"That's where he made his last deal, anyway." He slammed his stein down on the table and laughed.

"The trick was of course to insulate the Faraday cages and then find the correct proportional distance to one another within the rarefied field. Adjusting the distance accelerates and decelerates the vehicle." He anticipated the next question. "A two day trip."

"Two days. Where's the commode?" He laughed. "That's going to be an uncomfortable trip."

The Promoter said. "The commode is over there." He pointed.

Chapter Nine - Amusement

"**Why** that grocer is a dirty scoundrel. When Frank Spears and I ran the Athletic Grocery we didn't need to resort to that sort of behaviour."

"Yes. I saw penny weights glued to the bottom of his scale one day. On another he actually scooped the marrow out of the bone just before he wrapped it up."

"They'd shoot him anywhere else."

"Here's an idea." Buckskin leaned over to their ears.

They entered the store about five minutes apart. Jessica wore her shawl and carried a parasol. Buckskin had changed into a regular suit with a starched collar and One Eyed Jacob was looking over a counter full of coffee pots. Jacob went to the cash register first, to pay for a coffee pot.

"Like that wrapped, Mister?" The grocer pointed to the roll of paper and cone of string.

"Thanks no. I'll be using it in a minute. He moved away from the counter while Buckskin's wife twirled her parasol and said. "Oh wouldn't you be so wonderful and have some sewing thread that matched the colour of my lips?"

The grocer took the opportunity to lean forward for a closer inspection of her lips and perhaps a quick or not so quick downward glance at her exciting cleavage.

It was during this primal moment that Buckskin tied the end of the twine to the belt loop of his companion's pants and then circled back to the rear of the store. He took his time positioning himself behind a stack of kerosene railroad lanterns so he could see the huge cone of string gradually shrink. Two other customers had walked in the store attracted by the twine stretching down the boardwalk.

An amused customer pointed to a trail of string, "That's a good attention getter, Harvey. But how will you wrap parcels without twine?"

"What?" He said. He turned, "Hey," he ran outside, pulling and following the string. He saw Jacob and gave a yank on the twine succeeding only in breaking it off in his hands. Some young boys noticed the fun and went chasing after the loose end snaking up the block. The grocer returned cursing.

The grocer and his wife kept a fine house on the end of State Street. There was a long porch in front and a fenced in backyard holding a wood shed, some turkey pens and a chopping block.

"Ned went around to the back and tossed a few good sized rocks to get the gobblers going. So while the grocer is at the back door shouting into the dark, Allie ties a string to the door knocker and jumps down into the bush."

"Buckskin crept up the steps taking his pet skunk and carefully sets it down by the front door with a saucer of cream. He tied a butterfly reefer knot from the joint of its tail to the door knob and quickly left."

"Everything was quiet. The parlor room and kitchen lights were on. The skunk was drinking the cream. We hid across the street and watched while Allie starts yanking hard on the string attached to the door knocker. The grocer flung the door open which catapulted the surprised skunk into the house. The grocer slammed the door shut, shocked by some blur. The knot unraveled, freeing the skunk now terrorized by the shrieking wife chasing what she thought was a raccoon with a broom. The frightened animal ran clawing up the walls, scampering and spraying all over in a panic for its life. They were both yelling and coughing by the time the skunk flew out an opened window," said Jessica. The bushes across the street were flattened by the group rolling on the ground laughing.

"You could see through the window. The picture frames were sideways, the curtains were torn, the chairs were pushed to the center of the room. She was yelling at him, "Oh, oh," she was touching her hair and smelling her hands. They ran to the front yard. He'd kicked the dish of cream and that was all over his boots. He was waving his arms and tearing off his shirt. Neighbours had long been drawn out by the commotion. He'd caught a full squirt on the first launch of the skunk when it shot off the porch. After that they were both immersed in a fog," Allie said.

No merchant, cleaner, or dealer would touch the stuff. They were forced to burn the rug, couch, pillows and two stuffed chairs. The walls had to be stripped and re-papered. It was hilarious. He wasn't even sure who did it since he'd cheated everyone.

They spent a week airing out the house.

Buckskin said, "That was a nice skunk. It used to come right up and eat cheese out of my hand. I'd trained it to fetch a ten dollar piece and bring it back. Poor thing probably still is running. But holy smokes that sure was a great gag." They laughed all night. It was three days of bathing before anyone would admit the grocer's entrance.

At seven thirty, at Captain Gifford's house, there was a séance. At eight o'clock in room 337 at The Clarendon Hotel there was a $2.00 admission for a series of Edison Recordings. An enterprising carpet bagger was making a Western tour with a phonograph and a variety of rolls. At a quarter to nine Sweetwater Sally would guard Joe's back. By midnight three men would have killed each other in gun fights.

Sister Susy was ordering coffee for the doctor. He was mildly drunk and had two knife wounds to attend to. One woman was brought in already dead from an apparent suicide with laudanum. Sister Lucy closed the woman's eyes and crossed herself.

Big Dan shook his head in surprise.

"By George, your three Kings, ten high, take the pot, Dan."

"Who would have thought a pair in the hole?"

"I was going for that flush and when I didn't get it I went for bluff."

"I guessed I might a done the same."

Big Dan left three hundred dollars richer. He went to The Silver Dollar.

At three thirty in the morning, Gaiten withdrew his rusty knife from in between Charlie's ribs. He didn't know the man's name. He dragged the body behind a pair of broken barrels and went through his pockets. He found a pouch of chewing tobacco and three dollars in his hat. 'Three dollars will buy enough beer for tonight," he thought.

The editor dreamt of lead slugs filling galleys. He would wake once and awhile during the night – forget his imagined headlines and pull his wife close, to touch her in a familiar way.

Bad Bart was handing fifty dollars over to Mattie for an opium addicted woman to replace one that had recently stopped renting a room.

At five in the morning Henry put his rifle down and crawled across the floor. He pulled himself up to the bed. It was a cloud with a dog on it. He held on, gripping the sheets tight. He wished he had his rifle. The sun began to break. Wagon trains rolled in with their morning loads. Henry passed out.

Deiter began his opening routine and swept out last night's sawdust before throwing another bag full on the floor. He wiped down the counter. He served the first beer and shot at seven fifteen. "Morning, Pete. How's the trap line? See any Utes?"

The miner swung his legs off the bed and scratched the one eyed dog's ear. "Ready for another day?" Scamper's tail flopped up and down. It wanted to curl up in the available warm spot. The prospector lit some kindling in the stove and set a coffee pot on it. He opened the door and stepped outside. The pine was strong. He heard the echo of someone chopping wood. He took a pair of long johns off his clothes line. The dog came out to pee. The man spit on the ground. He looked forward to some panning.

The Pinkerton's man put the telegram in his wallet.

"The cone strainer, then continue sifting," Chef said.

Erin pulled the foot long conical strainer off the wall and rushed it to the chef's side. He returned to the pastry counter. He was anxious to show he could do good work. He wasn't trusted to mix the ingredients but he was sometimes allowed to weigh and measure them out.

"I've been all the way to grade seven, sir."

"I don't need a scholar. I need a dish pig."

Erin had been in Leadville for two months with his father. In digging his first mine it had collapsed and killed him. The thirteen year old boy returned to the streets from their camp.

A policeman had heard he hated mining and was asking shopkeepers for employment and tipped him off to the Interlaken Hot Springs Hotel.

"You get a room, food and eight dollars. Monday off.

Erin had to get a hair cut, wear a white shirt and tie.

"To wash dishes?" He said.

"And pots too. And taking out the garbage. Enough to fill a twelve hour day. You will be clean and sharp. The doctors in this town aren't clean enough to take out my garbage. Don't be late, sick or take a day off."

Erin's room was a cabin near the hotel. He didn't know what to do. He was still in shock over his father's death. Lots of work seemed to be a good idea. "That would keep you out of trouble and away from all this sin," said the copper.

The eight dollars a week allowed him to buy blankets, kerosene and candles. He had picked up some dime novels to read. He didn't often go to town and the glorious characters of books inhabited the lonely pine trees that surrounded his cabin.

"I'm out," said Henry. "That's it for me." He pushed his certificates over to the stock broker. "I understand the Little Pittsburgh is up again today. Sell across the board. I want to be out of everything by Friday this week. Give it all up to the bucket shops."

The broker knew Henry to be shrewd. "Something up? Something I can help with?" He looked at the chalk boards.

"I'm taking a trip and I'm not totally sure when I'm back. This should all clear out for a bit over two hundred thousand or so."

Devlin didn't know it would be Sullivan but that's who it was when he answered his hotel door.

The bottle came out quick enough.

Barney Devlin was ill. He'd hoped the Denver climate would help. He wouldn't make it to next spring. The journey from Montreal had been a long one. He'd held his constitution as best he could on the trail but he saw the end coming. He was glad that for the moment he could escape the rumours and innuendos of being involved in the assignation of Darcy McGee. The Queen lost one of her Members of Parliament and John A. Macdonald was still mad. So he ransacked the man's office, so he employed James Patrick Whelan, the man that killed him. That was ten years ago, April 7, 1868. People should forget. But he remembered Kate Scanlan's tavern in Montreal. Enright and Kinsella were there.

"Shoot that bugger like a dog," they agreed. "Sparks Street in Bytown. That was the only way. See how the Orange Order liked that? The Orange are using the same methods in Leadville. Marginalize, isolate, polarize. The Lt. Governor operates under blind law." Devlin showed his clenched fist to Sulivan.

Sullivan took a folded broadsheet from his jacket pocket and showed it to Devlin. "McGuireism is Alive in Leadville."

"You're in it. You can't win and you have to fight. The Governor will turn a blind eye to Tabor. He's the grand silver General now. They love him back east."

Sullivan said, "No. They can't do that. It's against the Posse Commitus Act. The army can't attack civilians."

Devlin raised an eyebrow. "They don't think that way. They think, 'better to protect the silver and later suffer the editorial umbrage.' You'll see. But you will need to last in battle. That job printer, McFetridge. He'll print up any paper you need. Put it on my tick." Half way through the bottle, he said, "Don't get me started on John A. Macdonald and rail roads. That bastard. Well he'll have his hands full with Riel and Dumont shortly." A St. Patrick Society newsletter discussed his views on the building of a school on St. Urbain and Dorchester street in Montreal. "What kind of horsemen may be derived from this?" was a small headline. It questioned the need to provide education for a modest fee.

"Maybe there ought to be a way to be able to win a Leadville strike. If you haven't met you will need to meet Michael Mooney. He's big on the Knights of Labour and swinging pick handles."

Sullivan noticed the big open windows and felt the coolness of the open room. Copies of *Hansard* and *The Kingston Whig Standard* lay on the bed. A stack of *Montreal Gazettes* filled two chairs. Devlin was editing, *The Freeman's Journal*.

If there was ever to be an Irish shadow government, favour would be found here. "I hope we're all disciplined enough for this."

Devlin said, "I want you to meet someone. Louis. Let me tell you about him. You decide. You should take him with you, I'd say."

Sullivan listened. Later that night he went to the provided address. Introductions were made. A candle burned.

"Was that just anger and bravado, that stuff I heard about you in Pennsylvania? You lead a street full of strikers against Pinkertons?" Sullivan asked.

Louis looked into him, "No. It's like you know... You're beyond sure. You walk into a panic stricken crowd. They're running everywhere. They're running away, afraid. The bullets are flying. There's smoke and fumes everywhere. People are yelling and falling. You walk into that, ramrod straight as calm as snow and in seven minutes the crowd turns into a self controlled mob on the attack. And it grips you and life is cheap. Faces burn with rage, passion lives. The righteous walk into bullets, explosions, fire, smoke, the screams of satisfaction. It's fantastic," he said. "You never felt so alive, when you throw yourself at cannons and fight the point of bayonets."

"We need you in Leadville," said Sullivan. "You must come to our fantastic, loud and near-decent, Leadville."

"Discipline is the Achilles heel of the poor and uneducated," Louis would lament.

Devlin's obituary would come out. Long later, on February 8th 1880, he'd have a grand funeral in Montreal.

Black Charlie looked over the mine. He'd taken the job. He was part of a group that guarded the mine's bounty and payroll. Ugly piles of tailings were everywhere. Cyanide and mercury leached into everything. Drinking water was brought in by wagon. Strong winds were constantly blowing the sharp dust. Walking and riding in the winter storms of sleet was to face a hurricane of nails.

Captain Gifford said, "The table rose up and I swear I just about needed a change of pants."

"Said it was an angry Ute Indian spirit and that I should bury a hundred gold pieces." He was sweating.

"Let me come to the next one. I've been to these before," said Buckskin.

"Well we're meeting at my place again tonight."

"I'd like to come early and make some preparations."

Buckskin arrived. After a few shots he examined the table that they were to sit at. He picked it up and checked its feet and legs and looked at the edges beneath it. "This will be amusing," he said. He rode away and came back with a heavy box. "Here. Give me a hand. We'll see what kind of spook we can catch."

"This is a portable battery, some cable and clips. In seventy-eight I was with the Occidental Traveling Show. Professor Wiggins was our magician," Buckskin said.

He ran the wire along the edge of the table and then to a battery hidden behind the curtain. "The insulation is very thin but will stand casual pressure from someone's hands. If I think what's happening is happening then you should see some spiritual ether glowing. Here, run this wire beneath the rug there. We used them all the time in the circus," he laughed. "When the metal hooks under the faker's shirt sleeves come into contact with the electrified wire he will jump with blue static pouring out of his ears."

Any alley was home. He wore three shirts, two pairs of pants and long underwear. What a stench though. No laundry or bath for six months. Mainly doing a lot of laying around in the mud and dust. Peed himself again. He was waiting. He wasn't sure what for. The vibrations of heavy wagons trembled the hard ground. He rolled his head to the left and shifted his back.

He had neither hat nor gun. He was free from the want of justice. Desire remained swollen to strength by magically delicious little bottles of laudanum. A cold ditch was as good as a warm bath. He'd given up working for it. Begging or finding more unconscious prey had just enough occasional pay offs to keep him stumbling for awhile more. Not a long time more.

His kidneys were barely operating and his liver swollen over his belt, "You could lend me thirty cents. Thirty cents?"

His stench was offensive, far beyond simple filth and accumulated body sweat. People turned before they heard him. "Thirty cents?" He held out his hand. It was half clenched and shaking. The bouncer pushed him outside. "Don't come back."

"I hope we fit in his dream," said a pedestrian. If you didn't have a dream there was no point in being there. All he had was dreams. Probably the most successful of the lot.

They were shadows. They passed him by. They moved fast and strong like upright horses. He checked his hand for money. He clenched nothing. He slept outside. The jail would no longer accept him. "He can't come in. It doesn't help him for a minute."

The best part of his day was coming up. He slumped over and passed out. It was like winning a prize. Life was good. He went to the toilet in his pants. Loony Leo forgot. No one else knew or remembered. His past reputation was safe. His current reputation was fair. He was just there one day like a broken board. He was crawling with opium addicted lice. Sometimes he blinked. He'd made it to Leadville while others just dreamed about it.

Chapter Ten – Nobel Exercise

Sullivan cut the twine he had tied around the dynamite sticks and pushed it into a sack. They had practiced for a couple nights. Sullivan waited by the tree on the west side of a tailing pile. John signaled that the guard had left the shack for his rounds. Sullivan had a thirty second window to walk quickly to the mine entrance then wait five minutes to just as quickly pace back. Before leaving he would of course light the fuse. It was a powerful feeling. He could hear his heart pounding in his throat. Being exposed on his way across the frontage was a very naked feeling. All the while he listened for a double whistle, meaning to run for it. He kept an eye on the time flipping the lid on his watch. He tried not to think when he scratched the match. He was alarmed by the brilliance of its light. He held the flame to the end of the fuse and quickly eyeballed the detonator caps. Everything was in place. Once he got to the trees he picked up speed. He heard a short whistle and found his cousin holding his horse. They were away for another half a minute before they heard the explosion. It brought down fifty feet of roof, wall and posts. Production would stop for three days and some of the mining cart rails would have to be replaced. The peace of mind of some mine owners would be replaced by fear. The owner and shareholders of the Sweet Pine Silver Mine would be furious and vengeful.

A crude note was nailed to the door of the guard shack with a dagger. "To blow the wax out of yur ears. Increase the pay. Fix the hours."

The sheriff looked at the mayor and Lance. "That's enough," said Tabor. "This now goes to Governor Pitkin." He looked at the sheriff. " By my book, when things start blowing up, they are out of control. It's out of control. On top of which my shares in this mine dropped by a third."

"How do you know it wasn't one of the New York Working Man Associations? They've been starting troubles here and there," Tabor asked.

Lance said, "No. I don't think so. Those are guys who listen to Karl Marx. They wouldn't demand an increase in pay. They would demand the whole mine and kick out the owner."

"They sound like claim jumpers," Tabor stared at him.

"They want it all. No. This bunch, they want more and not all and they will bomb and spread terror before they will have a dialog. That's part of their viciousness. You don't just quite know where or when they will strike. Just that they will," said Lance.

They tethered their horses in front of The Silver Dollar and went in for whisky and cigars. They each leaned against the counter in silence. People moved around them, searching for card players and drinking companions. They sipped at the shot glasses.

There was a mirror behind the counter shelves that highlighted the saloon's bottles and glasses. Sullivan saw his reflection and that of his partner.

"To doing." He raised his glass.

"To doing." His cousin raised his glass.

They shot them back and ordered beer.

"What doing, boys?" Russian Betty placed her hands over each of their buttocks.

"Oh, Betty. You pull my heart right out. I know we need your guidance tonight. Have you met my cousin?"

"Your cousin is strong and he smiles like a tiger," she lifted his hat and put it on her head. Her heavy perfume cut through the atmosphere and made their nostrils twitch.

There was a roar on the other side of the room. People were crowded around a hand full of card players. Gentleman Joe had just pushed another eight thousand dollars on the table. Four players were left. Sally was beside him. Fast Eddy was deciding what to do. He had two pair. Henry had dropped out. He was looking at the players and the piles of gold eagles and notes. Captain Gifford was looking forward to taking the pot home. He called, secure with his full house and pushed his chips forward. That left Big Dan who for all his tells and manners looked like he was trying to decide if he should keep bluffing. Big Dan called and raised five hundred more, "I might as well call this my final hand for the evening, I suspect."

Sally stood away from Joe. She had felt him stiffen. Gentleman Joe could see that his Jack of spades was not nicked in the upper corner. It was nicked in the prior round of play. But the nicked Jack wasn't in the deck Big Dan was dealing. Not, that deck because he had switched decks. Dan's suitcases were packed and waiting by his hotel door. Dan knew his straight flush would beat Joe's full house.

Gentleman Joe knew the proper thing to do was to plunge a knife through the man's hand into the deck of cards.

He had to have the other deck on him still. That was the thing. Joe played with some chips considering the raise. The deck had to be on his left side. Swapping a complete deck was quite an art. Anyone that could do that shouldn't be underestimated.

He said to Russian Betty, "Can you wiggle your hips and smile?" The cousins were smiling.

"I have a four poster upstairs. It has the great power. It can bring you to your knees." She grabbed the front of Sullivan's pants and gave it a tug. "All of you to your knees," Betty said.

"I'd say I was delighted."

"Then we are delighted."

Russian Betty turned to lead them to the staircase. "A four poster."

The invisible pocket sewn between the seams of his pant leg contained the swapped deck of cards. Big Dan took another nervous look at his cards. He scratched his head like the last time he got caught at bluffing.

"You can fight for free. You don't have to walk all the way into the saloon and spend two bits on a beer. You can walk right over to that guy there leaning against the hitching post. He already doesn't like you. You can give him a shove and see if he's ready to go. Maybe stick a knife in his eye." A filthy drunk was cat calling to a nervous couple on the boardwalk.

"Fight for free," he shouted at the man. He spit.

"You wanna get lucky, Mister? You want to get your self shot? You want to lose it all at the faro table? You want to get drunk, beat up and arrested? Just how do you want to get lucky today?" The drunk pointed to a nervous thin man in a suit who looked disgusted and reached for his Derringer.

Two men were standing away from the bar counter. In a second they were pushing their chests against one another. Their throats were thick and their faces were red. Two friends of each man crowded the scene. They were shouting at each other. They squared off. The banjo player nudged the guitar player with his foot. They continued playing. "We play through saloon and free for alls any time. It's what we do," said the band leader.

Another man joined the growing melee. Two bartenders were serving drinks at the counter.

"Oh. Rick just caught one in the eye. Guess I'm in it." Another man got in it.

"Why are you going in on it?"

"Well, when there's twenty guys fighting, why wouldn't you?" He punched a stranger in the cheek.

Woodpeckers hammered at the trees. The wind moved everything with a constant swishing sound. Mrs. Jane Kirkham had heard that woman's speech. The one at Billy Nye's Saloon a few years back. The woman that wanted the vote. She shivered in the morning dew. She was hiding at a bend in the pass. A stage would be by in a half hour or so. She had prepared a tree to fall across the road and block it's team of horses. At that point she usually leapt forward and confronted the driver by shotgun while screaming at the occupants to come out, line up, cough it up. She found the quicker and firmer she worked the more comfortable her victims were. She took their gold and sent them on their way. It was her third stage. She felt the weight of the gold in her pouches and rode over then down a ridge to a logging trail. She would arrive home in time to wake her husband up with coffee and griddle cakes.

She heard him rise and walk out the back door to the outhouse. A basin of warm soapy water and a fresh towel was waiting his return. He put on his vest with the sheriff badge.

"More coffee, sweetie?" She kissed the top of his head and slid another cake into his plate.

"You're good to me," he said.

"I'm glad that you think so," Jane shook her long red hair.

The little saloon was crowded. "They've got us so divided. It's hard to find enlightenment with everyman hiding in his own wardrobe. Scared of the light and hiding in the dark. Shall we shout our message under beds and behind wood piles?" said the Molly.

"It's not like they have to do more. They would have to do less. The less they do, the more put out the mine owner will be. He wants his gold. He'll give up a few more pennies for it. He doesn't want to do the digging."

"If the army costs ten cents less they will bring them in," shouted a miner.

Another Molly spoke up, "They can't. It's unconstitutional since Reconstruction. It'll just be the workers and the goons. We can't much lose by head count anyway."

"What about the railway workers? The army shot hundreds of them in seventy seven during their strike."

Michael Mooney said, "this country ain't built by cowards. Overturn their beds."

They passed the deck around, playing five card stud for matches. They drank coffee all night.

Geisel had never had so much space to himself before. He didn't need to worry about clients. His card stock was showing up in saloons all around town and being mailed out in packets and pouches. Last week he was paid twenty five dollars plus materials to go to a camp where the owners hit it rich. They were all interested in his gear and the process. The three of them posed stiffly beside a small hole in the mountain. The hole was square and framed by logs with the bark still on and notched at the ends. The men wore frock coats and bowler hats. They held pick axes and shovels in their hand. One held a rifle almost as long as he was tall. At their feet was a large brown bear. Each had a gun on his hip. They were shaggy hairy men. It was a photo of raw natural energy. Men in bowler hats digging into rock, fighting bears and cave ins. If they lived to tell the tale back east, they would tell a spell bound audience about hauling out two thousand ounces a day. Meanwhile, Geisel made reproductions. The men were delighted and measured out some dust for him. His wagon and portable set up proved to be part of his advantage in making a livelihood.

Sister Susy checked the bull whip against her saddle horn. There were three men working the claim she leased from Henry. It was a weekly inspect for her now. Henry was selling everything off. She would have to make a decision soon. She may have taken a vow of poverty but her hospital didn't. The growing community didn't.

A long string marked off the claim. The men were shoveling gravel into a rocker panel and gathering the residue into buckets.

There wasn't much vegetation left. The whole area was being gradually strip mined. Rock and flattened shrubs lay at the edge.

"Short on mercury," one of the men shouted up at her.

She dismounted. She unloaded a mule loaded with supplies. Everyone was working for shares. The dust piled up.

"Henry wants out," she said.

"Way out. From what I hear."

"Your share is waiting." The men helped unload, fueled by a modest search for whisky.

"That pouch," Susy pointed.

The remains of a campfire was stoked. The men put a coffee pot on a grill. "Water is ice. But it's bringing down lots of new flake. We're cutting into a new vein too."

"That's stamping, crushing, separating and filtering."

"Expansion. Probably worth it, but..." she said. She passed out some soft biscuits and bit into one.

"But that's a whole new procedure."

"Plenty there. Lots of heavy rock. Look at that yellow," he held a stamped out metal mug of coffee to his lips. He filled it one third with whisky. His throat warmed. His fingers were always cold. He cupped the mug with both hands.

"That was my niece's husband you shot. I thought it was a good thing. Piece of work he was," he said to Sister Susy.

The fighting got closer to Gentleman Joe's table. The table was knocked and all the chips moved around. Dan stood up and punched some clod in the head. "Buffoon." It was his only out. He didn't like the way Gentleman Joe was eyeballing him. The buffoon struck back and sent Dan crashing into the poker table. Chips, cash, drinks and cards were scattered.

"Better to sacrifice the count," Dan thought. He pantomimed fury.

Buckskin Joe and the other players stepped back with hands on the hilt of their pistols. The game was over and Big Dan still had his neck. The fighting pulsed to the other side of the bar and they watched a dozen or so men get pushed out.

The whores applauded the remaining winners and the band played louder. People danced and drank.

"Ploughed over and hung over."

"I'd tell him to go fuck himself but I don't give free advice," said a bloody nosed winner.

"See how things pan out?"

"Well," the gamblers said, looking at the mess on the floor.

"Can't believe no one pulled a gun. That a record broken," said Gentleman Joe.

"I know I only had forty dollars left. You guys cleaned me out," said Goggles Jake.

The bet money was returned to satisfaction. "I think, the hotel for a quieter drink," said Dan.

"That's how I see it," said Gentleman Joe. He was up on the evening, recovered his eight grand but not happy. "I might not be back here." His face was red.

"A few thousand more came in this week. The newcomers, you can spot them cause they clean up a bit and want to look their best for whatever awaits them. The fabulous, filthy, shit-covered, hairy, stinking, miners are the greeting committee. And they're looking their best." Laughter. They paused to watch. A half dozen people stopped and stared down the alley.

A cart stopped in the mud. A man came out of the alley. He was dragging a lifeless body. Loony Leo would beg no more. He grunted while tossing it. Another man covered the body with a dirty blanket. "He weighs a lot for a drunk. He really stinks too." Leo was dead weight and offered no favour.

Adam Baulm adjusted the amplitude of the magnets. It had a capacity to move the capsule about twenty million miles an hour. He was quite proud of it and looked forward to closing both the door and circuit.

Buckskin sat down on the padded chair. He lit his pipe. Next he strapped the seat belts across his chest and lap.

"Dog is quiet," he said to Henry.

"That's cause this is going to for sure blow up. Listen to it howl in a few more minutes, singing her dog song of death to come," Henry struggled with his seat belt.

"Yes that's it. Keep a fresh outlook. Maybe a giant Martian ground hog will eat both of you. I'd bet two dollars cash on that," Geisel tucked a spare field camera under his armchair.

"No. I'll feed him, you first for distraction, then shoot it with tears falling from my eyes," said Joe.

Henry settled down in his seat and scratched Shep's head. He checked the padded case containing his static box.

They heard a great whooshing noise and then the cannonball interior was black.

"Better light a kerosene lantern."

"Look at the stars."

Buckskin lit a match, raised the glass cover and held it to the wick. Grey shadows flickered, showing gaping mouths.

"I suppose if your calculations are off then we just keep going."

"As long as I'm within a quarter of a degree we'll be captured by the planet's gravity," Baulm said.

"If you're going to smoke that pipe, open a window for God's sake. The dog has fouled itself as well."

Within a few hours the red planet was growing in view.

"Bang on I'd say."

"Put on the brakes pretty soon."

"Strap in and prepare. Let's avoid the dangerous rocks and rolling."

"We're headed for those green edges. See the green circling the fringes of the ice caps?"

They began to notice the shimmering of rusty red water in the canals. They could see the system of canals feeding the water from the ice caps all across the land mass. He cut off the cannon ball's magnetic generator and allowed it to free fall. The direction was favourable. The dog howled in its bolted down cage. Adam Baulm flung open the door and stepped out. The dog came running out after him. Both peed in the sand. They all noticed the mast and sail of a boat about then. Everyone was going to surprise everyone else. People brushed their hair and put on their hats.

Buckskin warned, "Stay close. We'll need to head back soon enough. Oh. I'm easy to beat. I get out drawn all the time." He smiled.

Buckskin Joe followed. He drew his pistol after they kicked the door open. He looked at the approaching men.

He looked back behind him. Other passengers and crew were leaving the vessel. "I hope we are welcome. Mars looked big enough for everyone."

He shielded his eyes and looked up at the blue sky. He could see the sails of a ship coming down a nearby canal.

Three cannon balls flew over the horizon and landed rolling to a stop in the desert. The balls were weighted like loaded dice and so rolled upright. "That way no passengers would hang upside down. I told you I thought of everything," said Dr. Adam Baulm, turned space engineer.

They stood there with their hats off, taking in the landscape.

"There's some soft topped mountain ranges that way."

"Lots of desert. There's some ridges over there."

"Then there's the two things coming our way." Geisel looked up from under the hood of the camera. He replaced the lens cap and hurried away with the dripping frame.

Buckskin alternately placed his hands around his pistol grips then let his hands fall to his side. Finally he hooked his thumbs into his belt.

As the individuals got closer, the dog barked. The strangers raised a hand up, showing an open palm. They got closer. They were Martian men. The Leadville travelers looked at one another.

He approached the face. "Hey Geisel. Get a load of this." He waved his hat and pointed at the nose.

Geisel would set up and take a photo of all of them standing in front of the monument.

Geisel, Henry, Adam and the dog followed the Martians and got into a spare boat there along the bank. They followed the other sail boat and continued up the canal. A crimson red man held the arm of the rudder.

The canal walls were brightly inscribed with colourful symbols and signs. Beautiful murals of abstract colours merged into shapes were painted here and there.

They came to an entrance. A few feet above the waterline was a large tunnel. They got out and walked through the tunnel. It was lit by bright phosphorescent light in the ceiling. They came to an exit opening into a large inner city. Red fauna, foliage, red trees as far as the eye could see. Huts and long houses were built along grid patterns with a large stepped pyramid structure in the center. Iron was everywhere. Iron statues towered. They met some priests in red robes.

Buckskin looked at the Martian things and thought he could take one to the Pawnee's Circus. "Would it eat through a wooden cage?" He wondered. It's two eyeball tentacles twisted around. Its red fur looked like it might make a nice coat if a bunch of them were sewn together. "The thing lives on water. We all do of course."

Henry took out his box. He was proud. He wound up the static machine and drew a picture of the chief's face. He knew it was the proper thing to do.

That did it. The Headman watched, horrified, as Henry stole his life and face.

Suspicion was everywhere. Everyone was nervous. Martians begin to shout. The gang felt uncomfortable and worried. They looked at one another. They ran for the hills via their little sail boat, shooting, shouting and took off. Everyone was flustered and upset. More sail boats came up the canal to pursue them.

"The future can't last, the past is forever." Adam Baulm puffed.

"I've been here and I've been there as well. I don't know how much I care about the differences so much as I care about being alive," said Henry. The dog barked. The Martian thing bumped around pulling on its rope.

"I thought we'd be there for more than two minutes. Holy smokes! What did you do, Henry? You're going to get us all killed," said Buckskin.

They ran like hell, floating and desperate. Buckskin and Henry fired their guns into the bunch of angry things behind them. Shep ran ahead, barking, with Dr. Adam Baulm and Geisel right behind. They made it out of the tunnel and into a boat with the current going their way.

The Martian men pursued in several other craft.

The human party sailed briskly down the blood red canal. They found their previous steps in the mud and jumped to shore. All got soakers. They were afraid. Geisel gripped his case with white knuckles and his breath came in and out in rapid gasps. Dr. Adam Balum regretted his weight and felt ill to the stomach. His legs were pumping air and giving out. They weren't going to make it.

Buckskin shouted, "More of the bastards!" They saw a half dozen of the Martian men around their craft trying at the door and portholes.

The humans started shooting and yelling until the Martians were either dead or run off.

They got back into the ship. Shep growled at the Martian thing that Buckskin had stuffed into a makeshift cage. "Throw that switch!" Buckskin bashed at and stabbed at the hands interfering with the closing of the hatch.

Geisel yanked on the handle. The Martians screamed and Shep barked.

"Sit down, everyone," Adam threw the switch and the Cannonball Express returned to the sky. All the share holders were intact.

The link on Dan's cuff lifted the Jack of diamonds off the discard pile.

He would order a salmon soufflé and Champaign when he was done fleecing the boys at the Rat's Ass Saloon. There was a glass jar sitting in a place of honour. A rat had been cut in half, painted gold and stuck, tail end up, in a jar. The Ginger Kid and Butcher Knife Joe were considering what to do with the two pairs and a three of a kind they got on the first draw. Ginger Kid got three sevens, king high and opened with the $150 he received that afternoon for a good mule. Butcher got back an empty Ace but no four of a kind and raised another fifty. Dan drew the pair of eights left on top, to bump the pot another $75 he thought might be left in their pockets. It was a close one but he had them all the same. They were done and dealt with. He bought a round of drinks, told an impure story concerning a hotel cook in Kansas City and slid out of the saloon towards The Grand.

Limpy had a decent camp. He ran it by himself. Himself and a mule. He didn't abuse the mule and he talked to it a lot. He had abandoned his job as a teamster after buying the claim for a hundred and fifty dollars. After a month of exploratory holes and then digging into the face of a wall of rock he hit some good yellow. The further he dug his pick into the rock, the wider the yellow streak got. He was moving a door into the mountain about a foot a day.

At twilight he stirred up the ashes and walked around the woods for some old timber. He liked this part of the day. He'd put together a table made from the knotted and forked limbs of fallen tree branches and used a stump for a chair. It was sturdy enough for him to lean his elbow and rest his chin while he watched the stew pot.

Elk, water, potatoes, pepper, salt and local greens. He tossed in some old bacon fat and flour. Limpy knew what he was doing. Good gold ore was showing up regular. That morning he had dug his pick into a sedimentary layer and broke loose a big chunk of stone. He saw the glint of gold immediately and bent down to pick it up. It was a string of gold. He worked at it with his knife and pried it free of the granite. He narrowed his eyes and scratched his head after pulling free a perfect gold chain. It was a simple gold chain made of a few dozen links. It looked like it could have been part of a necklace or bracelet. "I'll take it anyway I can get it," he thought. He fingered the chain and drank black coffee from a cup. He spit the grounds onto hot stones by the campfire and watched them sizzle. He pushed it into his pocket.

At thirty three, Limpy knew he'd hit it pretty good. When he was twenty eight he was trapped. At one point he mustered out of the Union army and walked away from Reconstruction as a Private, a winner, with two legs and two arms. After that, a memory of hopeless horror. He laid in his St. Louis hotel room. He looked out the window. Death would come to them all. The world would stand by.

He sent a letter to his cousin. "Nothing matters. I have no hope."

He laid in bed watching his back pay shrink. He performed basic body functions. He didn't even bother with the plenty of whores downstairs.

He laid there thinking about what could have been, what might turn out and how difficult it was and stupid it was when at best some cursing underpaid grave digger would finish the story with a hurried shovel full of dirt. He could barely move.

Two months later he got a letter from his cousin in Ohio. "I use to have hope. I even had dreams. I thought I was working towards them. Time moved on. The clock ticked. Some nights I lay awake planning and wondering. I had these hopes. Then I hurt my back from an angry horse. After that, I hoped I wouldn't be tossed out of my room and hoped for a job making crates. I had this hope I would make good, set everything right and overturn my regrets. Then I lost hope. I abandoned hope. I left hope behind, cut out as excess, spurious, distraction. Now that I'm hopeless, I do what I want and feel as a great burden lifted. I have what I'm doing and seeing right now. That's all that's left. I just watch the show. I've earned it; that right to watch the spectacle unfold. When I judge less, care less and hope less I can hear the voice of the stars. Abandon all hope and fly." That was his last line.

Limpy took a job hauling freight. He found jobs easy to get and left them often. He found himself heading westward and on to the gold fields of the Colorado territory. Then he just bought a claim. He had no hope. He had gold though. He was glad he waited for gold and stirred the ashes.

"There won't be one grand final fight. You won't scream and club your way through an awe inspiring old testament victory where good triumphs evil and we dance as one in the street. What you will have is five hundred battles. A hundred fights and five hundred more battles. Because you realize it's not a war if only one side is shooting." The crowd had given its tacit support to hand their destiny over to the hot heads and other players in the crowd. Mooney shouted to the growing gathering of angry, short-changed miners, "Live not on your knees but as one blood, filled with hatred begging for death."

"To throw yourself against the wall, in anger, may demonstrate bravery, you might take out a few flies but really it's most often a waste. Better to show up 500 times and act for the most appropriate moments. Throw the first punch and move on. Circulate and throw another punch. You're gonna lose. Everyone is doomed to die. I don't know why I fight with and for a stranger that I would normally ignore or be disgusted with but it makes the most sense. So we've shown up having lived another day. We bring gold," Sullivan held up his fist.

Chris was surprised by the frankness of Sullivan. He'd pretty much admitted to being a Mollie and who some of the others were. This week, news like that got one lynched or shot. Chris wasn't in on it. He wasn't a Mollie. Sullivan caught him earlier about to set a fire outside a mine manager's house.

He'd met Sullivan before but just over some beer. It occurred to him if he partnered up maybe he could set a lot more fires.

Sullivan said to Chris, "You getting caught doesn't help defeat anything. They just justify their budget for rope."

"People don't want to fall in behind guys who get caught and hung other than singing a song like, 'John Browns' body lies a moldering in the grave...' Brown was as good a field General as you could want though," Sullivan said.

Things weren't going well. They were tied to their seats but the Martian thing had gotten loose. It vomited. They were rolling faster. They were spinning backwards pinned to their seats filled with fear and regretting breakfast. The April 1880 newspapers would record their thunder.

* They were coming down west of the city breaking through the clouds. A long swath of tree tops gradually working down to the stumps were applying the breaks to the cannon ball's descent. It careened off a canyon wall and began to splinter ejecting Buckskin still bound to his seat. He rolled until he hit some rocks and passed out. He didn't hear the other passengers yell as the ball continued to roll, bounce off some rocks in the rapids to be smashed to pieces at the bottom of a waterfall. Henry, Geisel, the glass negatives, the men, Shep, the Martian thing, the vehicle and all its components lay in pieces below fast water in the Arkansas River.

* The cannon ball returned to earth rolling off a cliff and crashing into the Arkansas River. The crash shattered and destroyed all of Geisel's work. He drowned in the wreckage. Buckskin dragged himself to the river bank. No dog in sight. He could see smoke rising from the forest. The cannon ball was carried into the rapids to be pounded by floating logs and current gradually disintegrating. The promoter's body swirled and turned caught in an eddy. Buckskin tied a bandanna around an open cut on his forehead.

* Buckskin moved in his seat and felt his bloody head. He cut free of the belts and sat up. He shook his head still half drunk in unconsciousness wondering if he had any broken bones. He looked around hearing nothing and seeing trees. He tracked back for a bit, saw some wreckage, a tripod leg lodged upright. The rapids and finally the impossibility of the situation defeated him. He staggered down the falls to find some clothing and valueless flotsam along the shore line.

He was miles from anywhere and surrounded by a Rocky Mountain spring chill. He sat down with his back against a tree. Everyone was dead. Shep too. He looked at the sky and thought how he had nothing to show for the adventure. He stared at nothing.

He limped backed up the gulch to the tree line. He missed his wife. He wanted to hear his daughters play again. The beginning of a new moon was coming up. He gathered together some kindling. He put together a small set up of dried bark chips, dead grass and dried pine needles on a flat rock.

He pushed a bullet out of his ammunition belt. He worried and worked it loose and poured gunpowder onto the material. He knocked some rocks together with a spark that sent the powder flashing. He spent the night half sleeping and feeding the fire. Heavy shouldered timber wolves moved around his site quietly looking sideways. In the morning he would head east. Blurry, he picked himself up at dawn.

Buckskin walked into an armed camp. It was Palmer's men shooting at track layers and surveyors from a rival railroad. He came up behind them but offered no threat and seemed oblivious to their situation.

He turned the offer down of hired gun and continued his tramp to Leadville. Horses and coaches passed him by as he homed in. He had enough in a box at Tabor's bank to get him out. He just wanted out.

After two weeks a mob of angry investors burnt down Dr. Baulm's cabin. He was denounced. His notes dust.

After Buckskin told the story an investor said, "You guys landed in the next county. You wanted money for a circus and wanted to divide the spoils. Henry didn't agree, so you killed him. Adam Baulm is probably in New Orleans by now. And Geisel's photos are gone too and you, the biggest teller of tall tales in camp."

Buckskin had nothing to show, except that he had returned.

On June 1st 1880 Mrs. Thomas Kittie Kelly whose husband died two months earlier of gunshot wounds in Murrays Saloon on 2nd street, spent all of her time in despair at his bedside. She couldn't find out her murdered her husband. She was dragged off her husbands' grave. She was later found with a noose and had drank a 50 cent bottle of Laudanum. June 28, 1880 Texas Jack died. He got a job as a guard in the Tabor Light Calvary, got pneumonia and died. He left his wife penniless. He'd married Josephine Morcacchi who performed in 'The Black Crook' and had opened a dance studio. Hundreds of actors and actress's lined the street for the funeral procession. In August 1880 Buffalo Bill and family help to return Josephine to Lowell, Mass.

He left town at about that point. It was a welcome ride. He'd heard Costa Rica mentioned and resolved to find it in an atlas. He'd look up at the sky ten thousand more times but he'd never tell that story once more again.

Leigh was saddened by the news of his new found friend's death. He remembered their last dinner together. Him, Geisel and Her. There was so much wine. They laughed so much. The roast chicken fell to the floor and they soon joined it. They were mature artists alone on the frontier. Their peers were competition and inspiration. He drank some more. He pushed the paint some more.

It was a loud city. It never stopped shooting, yelling, fighting, dealing and pushing to exist. Her sister was growing up on a pig farm and she nursing in a gold fever town.

The Sisters began clearing beds. The doctors began sobering up. Troops were pouring into the city. They didn't come for nothing or out of nowhere. Clean and folded stretchers were lined up against the hallway walls. Some local matrons were ripping cloth for bandages. Chloroform masks were lined up. Saws were inspected. There was a nervous, chilled, hyper-reality in the air. A command prohibiting the assembly of crowds was being prepared. Editorials denouncing the violation of the Posse Commitus act were being shaped in columns. Miners were readying themselves.

"A belly full of babies and a man down the mine," some little girls sang as they danced around a mud puddle with daises in their hair. People checked their stomachs. Soldiers followed orders. Handbills circulated, rumours were confirmed. Everyone stopped buying goods and products. The weakest stores and merchants closed first. The miners had stopped working. Business, property and goods were sold by massive auction.

It wouldn't be the first time. It wasn't the last time but it was the time people remembered. "Give me a minute to gather my strength."

"No. No. You don't get time to gather your strength. Now is when everyone's strength is used up. Now strength gets taxed. There will be a loser. Strength will be diminished. Men will be sucked dry and wasted."

"Is that what you wanted?" Sister Susy looked at the line of soldiers. Their bayonets glinted in the sun.

"They aren't supposed to be here. This is against the Posse Commotis Act. It's against the Constitution itself."

Sullivan said, "Is it what you wanted?"

"Pitkin is a bastard. He's washing his hands with the Constitution," Mooney said, "It's his turn to take point."

"We ran off the Ute, now Tabor wants to run us off. It's the gold. Why do they have to try and get it for free? Well today everyone will pay a price for it. Jesus and everyone else, Sister." He looked at her. "We'll need Jesus in our fists today because we sure don't have justice in sight." He walked down the steps

"This fight won't be fair," she said.

The Mollys had taken delivery of explosives for non-existent mines and gave blank stares when informed of certain dead men hanging as fruit in trees. They were rarely seen in each other's company. They didn't talk in public.

"Haven't you lived long enough yet? Come out from that alley. The numbers are here. We'll stand and then stand forward. Fighting is a good thing. We'll do the good thing and do it best. What's best for us," Sullivan was quoted on June 28th, 1879 in The Rat Bastard Gazette. He would say it again to larger crowds. "Don't die hiding."

Troopers and angry mobs began to approach and press against one another.

"What are you looking at? Are you looking at me because you're some kind of poofter? No cattle on the range, ran all the sheep off and now you feel romantic? I'm going to shove that rifle up your arse," a striker yelled at a young trooper standing three feet away.

Another yelled, "Are you telling me to shut up or calling me a liar."

The recruit tried not to look nervous. He wasn't supposed to be in the front. He was supposed to be counting rotten cans of meat shipped from Chicago with the quartermaster. Men were getting closer and taunting him and his fellows. He hadn't been given any order to fire.

They looked at him with strange eyes. They seemed so convinced and full of hate. A roar ran down the line as a frustrated woman unloaded a chamber pot onto troopers from a second floor window.

Men moved around. Their officers watched, for the moment was near enough. Some good killing was needed. Some needed murder.

The trooper looked the men over. They were dirty. Their clothes were dirty. Their faces were all worked up. They weren't right. They should stand down and quit the strike.

Towards the end there was no single view. Bottles, rocks, lumber flew through the air towards lines and clumps of uniformed soldiers.

They returned fire right away and threw smoke grenades into mobs. There were groups of ten and twenty being led by experienced Knights of Labour and Mollys. The crowd numbering thousands turned to hundreds within the hour. Heads were washed with rifle butts and shovels.

It went far when pushed too far. Several mine entrances exploded on que. Soldiers shot. People screamed on the ground holding a bloody face or leg.

Three troopers walked over to an inert man in the middle of the road and began to kick him. Four boys had pulled a barrel of rocks on top of Leos Grocery and were blindly throwing them down to the road where they guessed troopers might be.

Gangs chased each other. Mooney was caught quick and handcuffed by the police. The Pinkerton's man pointed out the Sullivan cousins and three of them had their eyes kicked out and then they were stomped to death.

Those that returned to work did so at the same wage. Covert hand bills rotted in the mud.

The smoke never cleared.

The city had tipped the scales in drawing attention to itself. "The camp had turned to settlement and must settle," the Governor thought to himself as he cast a fly.

His aide would know what to do.

When he returned he could publicly criticize Tabor's actions, for the sake of form. Maybe launch a well paid investigation committee. But Cloud City was going to behave. Grant would want it to behave.

In the end, Dan took one suitcase and left. Dan thought he would be out of Leadville as did the hundred odd teams, wagons and coaches going in opposing directions.

They were stuck in a narrow one way canyon. Two men helped him pull his leg out of the mud. His stomach grumbled. There had been no movement forward all night. Dawn came with a buffet of wind. Leadville was a memory but the pass was truly blocked.

Dan left the coach and jumped knee deep into the snow. He stepped through a drift into a trench formed by other frustrated men who wanted to see what was the problem. The pass through the canyon narrowed to allow passage for one wagon only. The trails on either side weren't much better at the best of times and in the winter, filled with snow and mud. Coaches and wagons were on each other's tail, filling the passage on both sides. The snow kept falling and the wagon wheels were kneading the ground into a mush of mud, manure and urine from all the horse teams.

It was wild at night. So cold. Men packed into the coaches hoping body heat would pull them all through.

By the second day there was nothing else to do. Passengers and hired drivers took the horses one by one on a foot pass near the canyon rim followed by the luggage and piece by piece the wagons. It took three days of back breaking work to move everything this way. Wagons loaded with ore and other bulky or heavy materials remained fixed where they were. There were no latrines along the way.

"Move your ass!"

"I'll kill you both."

"Let that guy with the wheel pass."

A family slowly trudged by, carrying bags on their backs. They dragged a narrow sled of planks behind them flattening out the dirty snow. Their wagon would be rebuilt on the other side of the pass by nightfall.

Dan was rolling a wagon wheel up the foot pass. He pushed it up a narrow trench one arm at a time. His wet gloves pushing on the spokes and grasping the iron rim. He'd made the trip twice. The spokes and rim were covered in two inches of muck. Everyone's clothes were wet with old sweat and filthy snow. Rocky mountain air blew back and forth. Wearing three pairs of long johns helped. Pretty much no one could feel their toes. In this way about a hundred wagons and eight hundred people experienced western travel in a mode skipped by the *Baedecker's Guide*.

"There's the last wheel," Dan said.

"We will be loaded in an hour now. Look, that whole way is clear. Guess you got your ticket's worth," said the coachman.

Dan climbed into the coach. There were six of them sitting on seats made of hardened wood covered in busted leather, bursting with straw. Three more men were riding on top with the luggage and driver. Everyone was covered in frozen grass bits, mud, snot and fresh ice. Everyone's clothes were smeared with stinking mud. Most had bleeding hands. Beards were filled with snot, tobacco juice and mud. Hats were bent, twisted and covered in mud. Horses were starved and covered in mud. The passenger seats were covered in mud. The air was so frozen they couldn't smell each other which was very good. They were too tired to complain and rode in silence covered in crap and mud.

Dan felt he had what he needed and dreamed of owning a saloon in San Francisco. He knew the odds were in favour of the house and he'd have no problem keeping the cheaters out. He wouldn't need to cheat if he had a house of his own.

He felt bad about walking in the hotel lobby so filthy and awful. But he wasn't alone. Several of them in like condition were staring at the crystal chandeliers, gilded ceilings, formal dressed staff and petticoats by the yard. The marbled floor was so grand. The oriental carpets were new and the counters so dark and rich. The hotel clerk was use to shit covered clients.

"Rough passage, sir? The canyon..." The manager held his palms out in a sincere apology for nature.

"A bath and a bed," replied Dan. He pushed two twenty five dollar pieces over to the clerk. "I'll stay a few days."

"You're welcome. Suite 325." He placed the key down. He rang a bell on the counter with a clang. "Boy," he said, "Get a grip."

Dan went to his suite.

Gentleman Joe saw Sally moving in the light of their room.

"It's not hard to find the vein. They just keep moving around. Oh. Oh," Sweetwater Sally said. She was boiling hot. Her clothes were damp with sweat and rain. Her body cringed and recoiled when he touched her. She turned to him, the needle now being held high in her mouth by the plunger. The business end of the thing stared at him. "Don't try and cuddle me OK? Not that."

It wasn't working. Earlier she poured white powder into a spoon. She added water from a tin cup. She mixed it back and forth with a match stick. She liked playing with it. It swished back and forth. She imagined what it would be like. She took a small folded piece of cloth from her tin box. The same cloth she'd been using all along. She drew the liquid through the filter into the needle.

"Ouch," she said. "I had it and then I don't know. The side of my hand is numb and my thumb hurts." She continued to wiggle the needle under her loose rubbery skin but the vein was too illusive. She drew the plunger back to at least fill the needle with warm blood and keep everything in solution.

She pulled the needle out. A trickle of blood squirted out. She dried it with her sleeve.

"Come to bed, Sally," Joe said. He loved her.

Inkslinger Charlie thought how far he'd come. He remembered the tent would leak during rains. The winds were crazy. He had a tent, a typewriter and he charged that dollar a page for typed or hand written letters. Between the still existing timber and the hearts and souls of illiterate man, he caused a newspaper building to be hacked together. Before winter, teamsters brought his precious crates from his old ink buddy, Joe in St. Louis. A rolling flat bed press with lead type gave birth to the Rat Bastard Gazette, a place where truth could come along for the ride. Side walk vendors hawked his broadsheets along with baked apples and shots of whisky. Entrepreneurs of all stripes sought out his advertising rates. Within six months he'd expanded to ten pages complete with a staff of two writers and a pressman. A dozen kids took it in and out of bar tents and street corners looking for a nickel. It bought feathered hats from Paris for Dutch Honey.

"News is about a nickel," the editor said. "And if we have a knuckle full of nickels we can punch a hole in the wind. We can tell people which way the wind blew. We won't get all of it but we'll get some of it, some of the time. That sound brave?"

They listened to some gun shots.

"I don't walk towards gun shots anymore," said Black Thumb Bob.

"Not even noon yet," the editor said.

"There are some new actors in from Chicago staying at the hotel. I'd like to inscribe their current emotions and favours into an article. We can place it beside the ad taken by The Coliseum," said Black Thumb Bob.

"Yes, get some of that. See if they brought a talking dog with them. I don't want to be the only paper in the district that doesn't have an interview with a talking dog. It's about reputation for God's sake. Let's show some class." The editor pushed some ink across his forehead. He needed that talking dog story.

With-drawing prospectors would follow rumours to Dawson, Nova Scotia and the Central Americas. The Cape of Good Hope with its ferocious Zulus, would sound promising for many more. It's best when there is a mountain.

Leadville would create a nation of men and women in advance of any named State. A place known only, and first, by its most extreme conditions of peril, spirit, weather and action. It's stories and breath would pile up in near exhausted slides of desire, always desire to the most extreme for the sole and greatest reward of pure gold – the element which can fulfill any human wish of destiny. No matter bought with which trial.

It was open. For a few more charismatic years, Leadville was open for business. Until the graph line that only goes up finally broke to down in 1893 with a collapse of the silver market and another depression.

A stage coach brought Susan B. Anthony. A train would bring Ulysses S. Grant. Many bottles would bring Oscar Wilde and vast outrageous applause to Lilly Langtree as the freedom party continued. The churches, the schools, the growing presence of law and the culling of the herd would bring settlement and reserve. It would go on to further legendary strikes, leading to the United Mine Workers of America and found the most advanced mining technology institute in the world. Potentates would continue to send their emissaries. The rush would funnel to something, mainly rewarded by big deep mines. The stuff that lay in rivers and scarred across cliff faces was spied upon, taken and sold.

The cold, clouds, bitter winds, chill and dust blew through a landscape of emotions and dreams drawn from the jungle and empire. Tunnels driven and pushed and extended into the silver veins rained a continuous and never ending supply of money. Money for all and everyone and forever towed in thousands more. If you weren't there. If you missed it, then you didn't know the dream, driven by reality, thrust to ground.

-end-

Appendix

1859-1860 Slater party takes $8 million in gold up California Gulch. By 1865 there is no gold left. Everyone tosses out the black gravel sand stuff.

1860 Oro City gold camp. Augusta Tabor about the first woman to show up in 1860.

1877 Sept. Susan B. Anthony makes a speech.

Healy House 1878 Two story wooden clapboard house. Harrison Ave and Main St.

Tabor House 1877. Two story wood. Horace Tabor Mayor 1878. Owns Matchless Silver mind.

Tabor Opera House November 20, 1879. Tabor grubstaked some miners to about $37.00 worth of supplies. Got rich over night with the Little Pittsberg mine.

Leadville Herald Democrat newspaper 1879.

In December 1879 there were 136 telephones. Telephone exchange on Main Street. U.S.Grant visited Leadville in 1880 August on Private D & RG train.

Eighteen Irish hanged during Molly Maguire hysteria 1870's Pennsylvania coal mines. "Molly Maguireism in Leadville."

1880 Michael Mooney leads strike. Governor declares martial law in Leadville. Mollys and secret society of Cloud City. Strike broken by militia.

Anti Catholic Vigilance Committee murder, beat and commit arson on Irish.

St. George Episcopal Church 1880

1880 Six newspapers. A miner got $3.00 a day.

300 inches of snow in an average winter. One hundred to two hundred mile per hour winds.

Manville & McCarthy Hardware Store 1881

Clipper Saloon 1883

1883 Oscar Wilde packed Tabor Opera House.

Tabor Grand Hotel Four story brick. 1883-1885

Annunciation Church 1880 Bell installed 1885. Unsinkable Molly Brown married there Sept. 1, 1886.

Delaware Hotel 1886 Three story brick. $60 thousand dollars to build. Harrison Avenue. Frequented by Doc Holiday and Butch Cassidy.

Silver Market Collapse 1893 Millionaires go broke.

Leadville High school 1900

Irish community from Beara Peninsula West County Cork. Previous copper miners. Sullivan. Murphy. Walsh. McDonald. Lynch. Ryan. Harrington.

Average age of death is 33.

Evergreen Cemetery

Cloud City is at 10,200 feet elevation.

'Please don't shoot the piano player he is doing his best.' a common sign.

Rancho Escondido

Bat Masterson and the Earps also stay and pass through Leadville.

Alvinus Wood and William Stevens buy out played out gold mines from 1875 to 1878. In 1879-1880 there is a 'Boom.'

December 1877 Several hundred people in the Leadville area realize what lead carbonate means.

1879 35 thousand people flood into Leadville. Home of all the advances in technology of mining. 1880 July Denver and Rio Grande Railroad comes to town after fighting it out with Sante Fe Company.

1881, March 25. Leadville Electric Light Company issues two thousand shares at $50.00 each. By Davis, Dill and Bartow. DC, Edison?

Telluride was AC by Ames in 1891. Ames Power Plant. Biggest lit city in the west.

1880 Thirty producing mines. Ten smelters, six banks.

Sulphuric acid is used as a wash to produce silver sulphide.

1893 The U.S. Is on the gold standard. Sherman Act.

Ice Palace Jan. 3, 1896

The Silver Sunbeam by John Towler, Pub. 1864, bible of photography.

Andrew Meyer 'Groceries Meat' store

Photographer O'Keefe & Stockdorf

Chicken Hill on west slope of Carbonate Hill

Leadville Weekly Herald

Lots of log houses by 1878, hundreds.

Mattie Silks held a big brothel franchise

In 1879 the brothers went to Interlaken Hotel at foot of Mt. Elbert 23 miles south west on Glacier Lake.

Colorado women physicians spoke in big saloon election day Sept. 1877. Tobacco smoking and rough looking crowd. Question of Woman Suffrage Oct 2nd, 1877. Susan B. Anthony speaks in Billy Nye's' saloon. He says. "I'm not a communist."

Leadville Visitors: Jesse James, Susan B. Anthony, Oscar Wild Buffalo Bill, Grant, Lillie Langtree.

Leadville & Buena Vista March 7th, 1879. Sheriff Kirkham shot his own 38 year old wife, Jane Kirkham, while she was holding up a stage.

Wagon Wheelgap to Lake City to Oro City with Gov. Routt to Leadville to Denver.

Sept 29, 1879 – troops ambushed at Mill Creek by Ute Indians.

Charles Dow later to be Dow and Jones went to Leadville in 1879 as a reporter for Providence Rhode Island Journal. He goes to New York in 1880 and meets Edward Jones.

Carbonite Weekly Chronicle 1879-1923

Leadville Weekly Herald 1879-1880

June 28, 1879 Point in time. Mine violence blamed on Molly Maguires. Supreme court said Peter McManus and John O'Neil found guilty of murder. Leadville has 19 beer halls, 120 saloons and 118 gambling houses, 35 brothels and a variety of opium clubs. Many women commit suicide. Two main Madams are Mattie Silks and Mollie Mae, Sallie Purple. Sill Born Alley is a nickname for a place where babies are tossed out and girls are found dead.

Local Wildlife

Bobcat, chipmunk, coyote, monarch butterfly, elk, mule, deer, red tail hawk, turkey, vulture, raccoon, otter. Desert to snow climate. Great blue wind flower. Milkweed, crocus, hyacinth, mule's ear, vetch, wild rose, daisies, violets, clemantis, hop, flax, blue bells, clover. Earthworms introduced a few hundred years earlier by Europeans.

<u>Time line</u>

Sept 1877 Susan B. Anthony comes in to Leadville via stage coach and makes a speech about suffragette cause in Billy Nyes' saloon. Dec 1877 hundreds find out about lead carbonate. 1878 Tabor hits it with the Matchless Silver Mine. There's a forest fire in May 1879. In June there is a fire at a major hotel. Buckskin Joe shows up in July 1879. 35 thousand people flood in to Leadville. In Sept there is a fire in another major hotel. In the fall there is the Ute Indian uprising. Nov 1879 the Tabor Opera house is completed. April 7 1880 Buckskin Joe leaves. In July 1880 Grant comes in on the rail road. There is a miners' strike in 1880.

April 4, 1878 George Hook and August Rische hit silver ore on Fryer Hill.

Absinthe was available.

$350 in 1879 is about $6,700 today.

Leonhard Summer said that he was riding his horse into Leadville and along the way met a man who had walked from Kansas City to Leadville in ten days to win a $350 bet.

Ben Guggenheim bought some flooded mines called the A.Y. And the Minnie Mine.

Claims to 1872. Lode claims 100 feet long by 50 feet wide. Creek Placer 100 feet up and down gulch, wall to wall.

George Sand. Mark Twain pubs The Adventures of Tom Sawyer 1875 Ibsen pubs The Pillars of society. 1877 Henry James pubs The American. Zola. How Gamblers Win – The Secrets of Advantage Playing Exposed by Gerritt Evans pub. 1865 Bat Masterson born Nov 26, 1853 at St. George Parish Quebec.

1873 Remington the gunsmith produces a typewriter.

1876 Colorado gets Statehood.

1877 Giovanni Schiaparelli observes canals on Mars.

By 1879 The Clarendon Hotel and The Grand Hotel were present.

Thomas Agnew had an office Agnew Mines & Real Estate on Chestnut Street.

The stage coach fair to Denver was $7.00.

The Tisdale sawmill was located in Iowa Gulch. There were posters up advertising for 300 tie cutters.

The telegraph was present. Sending a telegram from Leadville to St. Louis was 60 cents for the first 10 words and then 4 cents a word after that. The Leadville Weekly Herald and later the Leadville Daily Herald were owned by Mr. W. R. Phelps. E.G. Dill was managing editor. In the fall of 1879 snow locked the city in. Freight wagons worked for the Kansas Pacific Railroad. The Olympic Theatre has orchestra for performers and normally includes dog fights. A piano costs $500.00 Frank Smith is the Leadville detective. He is a private detective who works for the Mayor James. There is also a Marshal Duggan. The Marshall received $180 a month. The Captain $150 a month. There were thirteen officers who received $100 a month. School is taught in rented rooms. People are robbed at gun point. Men get stabbed in the face. Attempted rape and rapes of drunk women. A hundred drunk men shoot at a fraud con artist they are chasing out of town and they all miss.

Miner Boy Mining Company on eastern slope of Breece Hill above Evans Gulch. March 27, 1879 Owned by Peter Conlay, M.C. Kennedy, James Dahoney, J. Buchanon, H. Leaser, Dennis Sullivan, sold to A. McLeod June 17, 1879 for $75,000. Assayed at 1029 ounces of silver per ton and 945 ounces of gold per ton. Extracting 20 tons a day. Employed 35 miners.

In spring 1879 there is a general cleaning up of reeking filth. Roads are graded with eight inches of slag covered with gravel.

In late May 1879 forest fires cut through pine forests. Smoke and ash bother everyone.

The fire came to the edge of town and the wind blew in the other way. Housing was cabin, shanty. There were shaft housed above the mines. In June 1879 the Coliseum Theatre across from Grand Hotel caught fire. On Sept 10th a fire consumed the block across from the Clarendon Hotel on Harrison Ave. People who have no money go to The Sisters Hospital. The city pays $7.00 a week per patient. Crowds will stake out some ones claim. John Lieninger had a book and stationary store. Frank Gay had a foundry and machine works. J.S. Langrishe plays at the Tabor Opera House until Feb. 27, 1880. Between 1879 and 1880 real estate went up 10 to 40 times. By 1880 there were seven schools with 450 students. Any china men who showed up were kicked and stomped to death. A black man could live with a white woman but without social approval. Point is no one got lynched for it. Barrels of salt were transported. In 1878 the Clarendon Hotel is on the corner of Harrison Ave and Main St. considered the largest and best hotel. The Bank of Leadville is owned by Tabor and has $50 grand on deposit. On Jan. 14, 1878 Gilberts Little Wagon Shop is on the corner of Pine and Chestnut. 18 citizens meet there to name Leadville for incorporation. There are about 70 houses, shanties and tents. Population about 300 people. Gov. Routt calls for the election of a mayor Feb. 2., 1878. Tabor is elected. Marshall Campbell is the police magistrate. George Geegge who was a pioneer and a druggist was made treasurer. There was a 2nd election in April 1878 a few months later. Tabor was reelected to Mayor. George O'Conner was made town Marshall. On April 25 Marshall and O'Conner were murdered by James Bloudsworth. Mart Duggan was appointed Marshall the next day for $125 a month. By spring 1878 indoor water and a water works from Chestnut to Spruce St. Much better by Oct. The Coliseum and Comique were two of the bigger theatres. A Feb. 5 census of 1879 held that the population of Leadville was 5,040. Of that 4,954 were white, 86 were coloured. Chinese were zero. Pitkin was the Gov. of the State. Leadville election April 1st 1879 William James was elected Mayor. John Zollars was treasurer.

In 1840 Cannabis was used to ease the pain of tetanus. Lloyd Brothers Cannabis was 74% alcohol and 26% Cannabis. Sold in one ounce bottles for migraine relief. Marrel was located in Cincinnati and sold 'Indian Cannabis fluid extract made from the tops of the flowering plant...stimulating action is followed by anesthesia and loss of muscular sense and is an excellent remedy for gonorrhea...'

Eli Lilly started up in Indianapolis in 1876 on Pearl St. Their catalog featured 'Poison Fluid Extract No. 96 Cannabis 80% alcohol 20% Cannabis. Parker Davis also sold Cannabis Powder by the tin at $2.50 a pound. Squibbs sold 'Cannabis Indica. Cannabis or Indian Hemp. The dried flowering tops of female plants of Cannabis Sativia (Fam Moraceoe) grown in the East Indies, gathered while the fruit is yet underdeveloped and while it is carrying the whole of its natural resin. We use select tops only, no stems. Info from www.antiquecannabisbook.com

Leadville Strike Details June 19, 1880 to Sept 27th?

Michael Mooney is an organizer. He worked for the Little Pittsburg mine. He was a Knight of Labour.

They demand a wage increase, an 8 hour day. Gov. Pitkin allows now Lt. Gov. Tabor to issue orders while he is in Cheyenne. May 26 in the Chrysolite mine.. Dec 1879 200 men meet on Carbonite Hill to discuss an 8 hour day. Jan 1879 Knights of Labour organize in Leadville. They are considered the richest mines in the world. May 26, 1880 a rule is passed about no smoking or talking while working. There are rumours of a wage cut. Some supervisors feel bad and just quit rather then enforce the rules. May 27 there is a march. They want a $4.00 minimum daily wage and an eight hour day. San Strousse closes his dry goods store and moved the contents to Georgetown. He was a republican man. May 24th, 1880 huge delinquent tax sale. Leadville Weekly Herald - May 29, 1880 Thursday morning parade starting on Fryer Hill crossing to Jefferson Avenue, pick up band. By summer 1880 there were candy, peanut and apple stands all over the place. There were sidewalk peddlers of all kinds.

The Coliseum Theatre Fire is June 20, 1879 at 130 West Chestnut Strec at 1:44PM. The Tabor Hose & Harrison Hooks arrive on the scene. The fire started in the apartment next door at 132 West Chestnut above the Miners Arms Saloon Building on the second floor. Three buildings burnt down. Brahms Clothing, Miners Build and Coliseum.

Jacob Schloss was a major liquor wholesaler at 34 State St. in 1879. In 1880 he moved to 116 West Second St. Pioneer Bar.

Doc Holliday is safe in Colorado from extradition on a murder charge in Tombstone Arizona. He is an opium addict and has pneumonia. Works as a card dealer. Arrives in Leadville in 1882. Doc Holliday has his final shoot out with Billy Allen July 21, 1884? Jury finds Doc Holiday not guilty March 28, 1885.

News Time line

1877: President Hayes elected March 2nd. He beats Tilden by one vote. Tilden won the popular vote. June 21 Ten Molly Maguires hung at Schuykill Country and Carbon County Penn Prisons. Alexander Campbell, John 'Black Jack' Kehoe, Michael Doyle, Edward Kelly. July 14 General Strike US railroads. July 20 Army shoots workers.

1878: Feb 16 Silver dollar becomes US legal tender Feb 18 John Tunstall killed, starting Lincoln Country war. July 1 Canada joins Universal Postal Union. July 26 A stage coach robber like to rob coaches in Calif and leave poetic notes behind. Oct 15 the Edison Electric Light Co. starts. Dec 12 Joseph Pulitzer buys the St. Louis Dispatch for $2,500.00 Dec 18 John Kehoe executed in Penn. 'Last of the Molly Maguires

1879: Jan 11 Zulu war. Feb 28 Southern blacks leave south exodus. July 19 Doc Holliday makes first kill in New Mexico Saloon. Sherlock Holmes being published.

June 24 First performance of O Canada

Photography

4 x 5 glass negatives

Daguerreotype 1839-1870 $5.00 silver clad copper plate

Calotype 1845-1855 Badly washed photo on paper

Ambrotype 1854-1865 Thin negative on glass

Tintype 1856-1945

Brown Period 1855-1870

Wet Plate Print 1853-1902 11 x 14 & 20 x 24 sheets of sensitized glass. Wet collodion plates. Ether and cyanide part of the process.

Step 1. Outside or inside coat glass plate with collodion. This is a premix of cotton, acid bormide iodine, syrup type of liquid. 2. In the dark room dip wet glass plate into silver nitrate solution for 4 minutes. It creates a silver halide coating. Place in light sealed box. 3. Insert box holding wet plate into camera while wet. It drips. 4. Remove the slide covering the wet plate. It is now ready for exposure.

5. Remove lens cap for 20 seconds to five minutes. Re-insert slide covering glass plate.

6. Remove holder and bring to dark room. Remove exposed wet plate. Pour developer over plate, a mix of iron sulphate and acetic acid. Rinse glass plate with water. Take plate out of darkroom.

7. The image is fixed by washing the glass plate in a tray of sodium thiosulphate which removes the unexposed silver halide.8. Wash plate with water. 9. Varnish plate with heated varnish. Pre-heat the glass before doing so. 10. To make a print in dark room:. Albumen print (egg white) from collodion negative. Flat paper in albumen dry. Float paper in silver nitrate then dry. Place paper against glass negative and leave in sun. Hold down flat with glass.

Mawsons Original Standard Collodion For The Studio or Field, Mawsons was a popular brand name.

American Optical Field View Camera

From *The Silver Sunbeam* **by John Towler, published in 1864.**

Instantaneous Process of Lieutenant- Colonel Stuart Wortley. Collodion.

Ether 1 ounce.
Alcohol, spec. gray., .802, . . 2 1/4 ounces.
Iodide of lithium, 15 grains.
Bromide of lithium, 6 1/2 grains.

The pyroxyline is first steeped in the iodo-bromized alcohol, and the ether then added.

Silver Bath.

Re-crystallized nitrate of silver, 35 grains.
Distilled water 1 ounce.

Iodized by leaving a couple of coated plates in the bath for several hours ; acidified at the rate of from two to three drops of nitric acid to the ounce of bath. Leave the plate in the bath longer than you would if the collodion contained only iodine.

Developer.

Sulphate of iron 2 ounces.
Distilled water 12 ounces.
Dissolve.

Acetate of lead 24 grains.
Water 2 1/2 ounces.
Dissolve.

Mix the above solutions, and when the precipitate has all settled, decant off very carefully, and then add:

Formic acid, (pure,) 2 1/2 ounces.
Acetic ether, 6 drachms.
Nitric ether, 6 drachms.

From this stock-developing solution take as much as is required, and add acetic acid, according to the temperature, generally iii about the same quantity as the formic acid. The developer is kept on the plate until the necessary detail is brought out; after which the plate is well washed and fixed with a weak solution of cyanide of potassium.

Intensifier.

Pour on a saturated solution of bichloride of mercury; as soon as the proper color is attained, flue plate is thoroughly washed, and a five-grain solution of iodide of ammonium in water is poured on and off until the desired depth has been attained. (The reader will comprehend the rationale of this proceeding by carefully perusing my remarks on this subject in a preceding chapter.) After this the following solutions are used:

No. 1.
Pyrogallic acid 12 grains.
Water 1 ounce.

No. 2.
Citric acid 50 grains.
Nitrate of silver 10 grains.
Water 1 ounce.

Pour a few drops of No. 2 into No. 1, and pour on and off until the negative has assumed the required density. After which wash the plate thoroughly in several waters, dry and varnish.

Valentine Blanchard prefers a bromo-iodized collodion, although under certain conditions he admits that a simply iodized collodion is more rapid, but at the same time there is less contrast. The silver bath is composed of re-crystallized nitrate of silver, forty grains to the ounce of distilled water, and saturated with iodide and bromide of silver. It is always *supposed to be acid,* to which is added a small quantity of moist oxide of silver; after the solution has beers sufficiently agitated, it is filtered, and then acidified by a weak solution of nitric acid, containing three or four drops of acid to one hundred of water. This acid solution is added very cautiously, until the picture is quite clear and free from fogging. A bath so prepared is very sensitive whilst new, and it is only whilst new that any bath is likely to produce instantaneous results.

The developer consists of the sulphate of the protoxide of iron, generally thirty, and frequently fifty grains to the ounce of distilled water, acidulated with glacial acetic acid, because the ordinary acid contains impurities.

The negatives, when they require it, are intensified with a saturated solution of bichloride of mercury in cold water, until the film is of a uniform gray color; they are then washed and treated with a solution of iodide of potassium, (one grain to the ounce of water,) by pouring it on and off until the film assumes a greenish-slate color. There should be no greenish line on the wrong side of the plate, for this is an indication that the strengthening has been carried too far.

Hockins uses simply iodized collodion; his bath contains thirty grains of nitrate of silver to the ounce of distilled water, and is iodized by throwing in a proper quantity of iodized collodion; it is then filtered. Two minims of pure nitric acid are added to each eight ounces of the bath, which is prepared twenty-four hours before using.

The developer consists of Formic acid, (strong,) . . . 2 drachms.
Pyrogallic acid 20 grains.
Distilled water, 9 1/4 ounces.
Alcohol 1/2 ounce.

This is kept on the plate until the operation is complete.

Claudet's Developer.

Pryrogallic acid 20 grams.
Distilled water 7 1/2 ounces.
Formic acid 1 ounce.
Alcohol 6 drachms.

Publishing my first book, ***2012 Rabbits and the Happy Apocalypse on Shortwave Radio***, was a tremendous experience and experiment. How much of an eye opener it may have been and how it fits the tradition of tall tales remains to be seen. It's available on Amazon.com where fine electronic and printed books are sold. The title says it all, it's a pleasant end of the world novel. I wanted to take my turn at the genre. I used the idea of an apocalypse within a Canadian context, free of zombies and sporting a grin. The idea was to tell a whopper around the camp fire while stepping on the tail of the tiger.

This, my second novel, is also available through Amazon.com, ***Cloud City Colorado in 1880 – Too Far West***, was practically a laugh riot of historical fiction. I played within the restrictions carved in stone but found room for a story that I bet Buckskin would have enjoyed. I hope you got a kick out of it. Research could have gone on forever and with joy. It doesn't take long to realize, that when looking for the primary root of the old wild American west, that Leadville provided many primary source anecdotes and stories for films and books but perhaps under different names. I understand now. In reality, all those far fetched stories were probably toned down from even more extreme facts. A trilogy, plus one, of Leadville novels written by Ann Parker is a must read if you enjoy the place and period. The magical shelves of the Denver Public Library held many micro-fiche time capsules, otherwise lost to memory. The astonishingly well preserved Ted Kierscey photo collection of glass plates was a valuable archive as was, of course, *Buckskin Joe, a Memoir* by Edward Jonathan Hoyt, edited by Glenn Shirley. The Colorado Historic Newspapers Collection, as maintained by the Colorado State Library and the Colorado Historical Society was absolutely invaluable and I say everyone should enjoy the search. Don't touch our libraries. The rest is history.

Sincerely, Roy Berger